The Cane, The Puzzle, and Magic

by

Vicky Burkholder

The Cane, The Puzzle, and Magic

Cover Art by *Kristian Norris*

The Wild Rose Press, Inc.
PO Box 708
Adams Basin, NY 14410-0708
Visit us at www.thewildrosepress.com

Publishing History
First Edition, 2023
Trade Paperback ISBN 978-1-5092-5103-2
Digital ISBN 978-1-5092-5104-9

Published in the United States of America

Kaeden studied the damage, then stared into Liz's eyes. "That's a gunshot wound. Fresh."

He closed down his emotions and dealt with her wound. So, she had finally returned. After two months without a word. They didn't know where she'd been, when she would be back, or even if she had survived her latest job. Kaeden had never met anyone like Elizabeth St. John. She made him madder than anyone he'd ever known. But he also couldn't get her out of his mind. She was a drink of water in a dry desert.

"She was shot?" Charly grabbed Liz's arm to look more closely.

Liz stared at Kaeden, and he stared right back.

"Yeah. Fortunately, he had bad aim."

Kaeden kept his gaze on Liz for a long moment, then pulled out the antiseptic wipes. He grasped her arm and cleaned the gouge up. Kae bit back a grin when Liz gritted her teeth against the pain that he knew she had to be feeling, as he cleaned, salved, and bandaged her.

"You enjoyed that," she accused.

"Maybe." He cleaned up the wipes and bloody wraps.

She shrugged. "I probably deserved that and more."

"You think?" Kaeden knew he wanted too much from her. He wanted what she couldn't give him, and she'd told him so. She didn't stay in one place long enough to do a relationship. Unfortunately, his heart refused to get the message.

Praise for Vicky Burkholder

Winner of the 2022 Hooked on a Book Contest

~*~

[*Lost Among the Stars*] "A unique story set in space with realistic characters and an entertaining romance subplot. The world building is well-done. This satisfied my love for science fiction, romance, and suspense all in one. A must read folks." 5 Stars.

~Michelle Godard-Richer

~*~

[*Searching Among the Stars*] "The attention to detail was impressive and I applaud Vicky Burkholder for creating a realistic yet imaginative world. The romance subplot was heartfelt and angsty. The emotions ebb and flow which made for an unforgettable reading experience. If you love science fiction romance, pick up *Searching Among the Stars*. If you're looking for a futuristic romance, you'll fall in love with *Searching Among the Stars*. Highly recommend!" 5 Stars.

~N.N. Light

~*~

[*The Gingerbread Lodge*] "After reading *The Gingerbread Lodge*, I felt as if I had somehow fallen into a Hallmark Movie! The characters inside Ms. Burkholder's book have you laughing, shedding a few tears, and wanting to do a fist bump with your BGFF, and do a happy dance all at the same time." 4.5 Stars.

~Mistress of Book Reviews

Dedication

To my family, my Bootsquad, and my amazing editor. You all know who you are and how much you mean to me.

Chapter One

It's never easy to fight a friend. It's even harder to kill one.

"You bastard! That was my favorite pair of boots!" Liz kicked at the piece of black, tarry sludge sprawled across the sandy lane then yanked off her melting boots before the slime could eat through to her feet. The blob, in a horrific caricature of a human mouth, managed to spit out an acidic spray toward her. Fortunately, the spit only hit her boots, allowing Liz to get in a final shot. Smoke rolled off the carcass. The stench—a mixture of sulfur, skunk, and ammonia—had her gagging. Liz mouth-breathed, advice from a morgue attendant, but that didn't help much.

At least the residents of the housing development on the outskirts of Orlando would now be safe. Or safer. After all, Orlando was a huge city with people—and nonhumans—from all over. Liz hobbled back to her car where she retrieved a pair of non-organic sandals and a special notice tag from the back. She stuck the sandals on her feet and returned to stick the tag on the blob that had recently been camouflaged as a gator—a gator that proved unkillable to the local cops, but not to her type of weaponry and why they'd called her in. Liz glanced at the cloudless sky.

"Hey, bosses, I'm done here. This mess is all

yours," she said out loud. Even though the beast she'd killed had looked the part, what she killed had not been a gator, or anything else known in this world. But dead beasts weren't her problem. The Powers-That-Be had someone else who did cleanup. Like other special agents for O.W.L.—Occult World Logistics—she took care of the nasties. Someone else took care of cleaning up.

When Liz got back to her car, she had a surprise waiting. An envelope stuck to her steering wheel. A plain, white, business-sized one with only her name, Elizabeth St. John, on the outside in fancy black calligraphy. In her locked car. Sitting in a sandy spot with no tracks around other than hers. Before she looked at the letter, she turned on the car and the AC, hoping to cool off a little. Then she took a bottle from a cooler in the back seat and took a long drink of water before she pulled a snack bar from her bag. Anything to avoid looking at the contents of that envelope.

Every time Liz got one of the letters, something horrible had either happened or was going to happen. Something that went beyond the norm. Something that belonged only to those realms where human logic had no hold. And she'd be the one to go out and take care of the problem. This wasn't the first time she'd gotten one of the letters. Over the last ten years, Liz had received dozens of them. They always meant bad news. Always. But she'd never gotten one while already on a job.

"What the hell? Seriously? I just got done here!" Liz touched the envelope and reeled as the visions struck her. Earthquakes, volcanoes, cataclysmic storms, cities laid to waste, and millions of people dead. Liz swallowed hard against the sour taste rising in her throat. She had to take care of this and fast. If she didn't, the darkness would grow. The coming evil would be unleashed against decent people who didn't deserve the horror they would face. The letter dropped from her suddenly nerveless hands, and Liz leaned back against her seat, trying to breathe.

"Okay. Okay. I get it. Massive destruction on a cosmic level. Back off the visions unless you want to pay for cleaning my car."

The sweat on her hands had little to do with the Florida temperature as Liz once again picked up the envelope. She took her knife out and slit the top open. Inside, she found a wad of money—ten one-hundred-dollar bills. A thousand dollars? Usually, they just deposited her pay in her account, which amused her. Angels—or whatever the bosses were—had bank accounts? The bosses never sent her real cash. Never. "I'd say thanks, but I'm certain I'm not going to like what's coming."

She opened the note that came with the cash. *Buy new boots. Bannig is back.*

Liz let the paper go as her body went numb. Her lungs refused to work, and the scar that ran across her ribs, a remnant from her last encounter with Bannig, burned. She'd barely survived that time, and now the Powers-That-Be wanted her to face him again? Joshua Bannig. Her recruiter. Her trainer. Her friend. Taken over by a demon bent on generalized destruction. The last time Liz had looked him in the face, she'd hesitated, and he had almost killed her. Though Liz hadn't finished him off, he'd disappeared, and she figured she'd hurt him enough he knew not to come back.

The string of choice vocabulary she uttered would have scorched even his demon's ears.

"I'm supposed to be on vacation!" Liz bellowed at the roof of her car. The air conditioning blew the sheet of paper in front of her. "You promised me after I took care of the blob, I could have a vacation. A real one. With sun and sand and palm trees and cabana boys. This was not a vacation, and facing Bannig is not my idea of a cabana boy or a good time."

She banged her head against the steering wheel, trying to deny what she knew she'd have to do. Liz had seen enough evil in her life, and bringing a little good to the world by fighting off beasts, like the blob, was the least she could do. She considered her job a way to help level the field. Evil made her life a living hell, and she liked getting back at the bad guys. But Bannig?

Liz lifted her head and saw the paper that now floated above her. The knowledge of what might happen pounded into her brain. The psychic vibes coming from the sheet were stronger than before. Bannig was coming. And soon. She laid her head back down. "I really do not need this. You hear me? I don't want to do this anymore. Can't you find someone else? I'm sure you have other agents who can take care of him."

The paper hung there, like a stern teacher frowning at a recalcitrant student. She'd seen the look often enough to recognize the expression even from a sheet of paper. Silent and uncompromising. The letter floated down to hang in front of her again, and she resisted the urge to stick her tongue out. Barely.

"Fine. All right. I'll take care of him. Where do I need to go?" She looked inside the envelope for directions. Empty. There were always directions, but not this time. No notes, no map, nothing.

"You planning to tell me where I need to go?"

The paper didn't move.

"All right. Fine. Be that way." She pricked her thumb with her blade and smeared the drop of blood over the pad of her thumb then pressed the bloodied digit against the bottom of the paper. The crimson print disappeared, as always, and the paper dropped into her lap. Then she saw a new line of writing at the bottom of the page. A line that hadn't been there before and consisted of only two words, but those two words turned her blood to ice.

Go home.

Chapter Two

Liz spun out of the animal reserve in a shower of sand and pebbles and headed north. She didn't even stop at the local cop shop to tell them their problem had been taken care of. The bosses could handle the niceties.

She'd lived in a lot of foster homes over the years, but her first time in Clear Water had been the absolute worst. Fortunately, her stay had been short. The home parents she'd been assigned to weren't the first to dislike her—that had happened too often to count—but they were the most hateful. They'd locked Liz in her attic room, letting her out only for bathroom breaks, so she became an expert at escaping, even spaces with barred windows, no trees close by, and no nearby roofs. That had been ten years ago, and she'd left there with little more than the clothes on her back and a beat-up motorbike that barely got her to the next town. Liz didn't understand back then, but the practice she'd gained as a kid helped her in her job now. Made her wonder sometimes…

When Liz went back to Clear Water five years ago, on another assignment, she'd found the place greatly changed, enough that she'd decided to settle there, not something she'd ever done before. Up until then, she'd lived out of her car and cheap hotels. But now, she had an apartment. She had a part-time job at a local diner, one where the boss accepted her sudden disappearances. And she had acquaintances…and friends. She'd be a minion in Hell before she let Bannig screw that up.

Liz sped back to the little motel where she'd been staying, threw her meager wardrobe into a backpack, and stowed her crystals, each one in a separate compartment in a special box she'd constructed for them. She left her key and enough money on the dresser to cover her stay, trusting that the owner—who was also the maid—would understand, and tore out. In less than a minute, Liz jumped in her car and headed out on a narrow back road, aiming for the interstate, glad for the lack of traffic.

As she drove, she thought back to the first night she'd returned to Clear Water and met her boss-to-be from the diner—Charlotte Maria Theresa Fogelsanger—Charly. Liz didn't care much for most of humanity, but she did have her soft spots, and Charly occupied one of them. When they met, Liz had been on assignment and had pulled up to an eatery in the center of town. A single waitress tried to wait tables, bus them, and tend the register in the packed joint. An older woman behind the counter looked ready to drop, and an aproned hunk stood behind the window, cooking. They barely kept up, but nobody seemed put out by the wait except the waitress. Liz had assessed the situation in less than a minute, hung up her coat, and went to work. Though the waitress, Charly, had protested, her arguments were half-hearted as she saw Liz knew what she was doing. She'd offered Liz a job on the spot, which she'd taken. After all, her assignment paper told her to come here, though Liz wasn't quite sure why.

Usually, she went in to take care of bad situations like the Florida blob, but not this time. Working at the diner with Charly seemed to be the job.

Liz found out later Charly had inherited the establishment from her parents. They'd taken a rundown, almost dead dive and turned the diner into the place to go. After their deaths, Charly took the eatery up several notches by adding better menu items than run-of-the-mill bar food and made the place more family friendly. And her changes worked. That was Charly. Never half-tries. When she set her mind on a project, she did so all the way.

Over the past five years, Liz and Charly had gotten to be good friends, although Liz kept the details of her real job from Charly. She explained all her trips out of town were due to her job in security but never specified what type. Which was the truth or as much as she could explain. Charly accepted Liz's explanation, and Liz. And no way would Liz let some demon screw that up. Then, or now. Or ever.

Less than a mile into her drive through Florida, Liz ran into a detour and ended up on a road that dead-ended in a swamp.

"What the hell?" Liz stared through the windshield at the moss-draped trees and wet track that went straight into the black water. "Since when does a detour go into this kind of mess?"

She'd thought the situation odd enough that a bypass from a public road devolved into a one-lane sandy track, but that happened sometimes. One misplaced sign, and a driver would be trailblazing, especially in the middle of nowhere, no matter which state. If Liz hadn't been driving carefully, she'd have ended up mired in the brackish mess.

With no place to turn around, she threw the shift into reverse and backed out. Though certain she imagined what she saw, the trees seemed to have moved inward since she'd entered the trail. The sides of her car scraped branches and not because of her driving ability. The closer she got to the main road, the thicker the growth got and the more obscure the track until she ended up making her own path.

"I know this is no damned detour. And I know for sure this track was a road when I turned onto it," Liz yelled at the forest. Then her senses tingled—a phenomenon that happened when trouble was coming—and she hit the gas and got out of there as fast as she could. She finally got to a paved road and turned around. The sun lay low in the sky, which was weird since she'd killed the blob around noon and hadn't been gone more than an hour—or so she thought. Plus, the detour sign she'd seen earlier had disappeared. Why that surprised her, she didn't know. "Blasted detours that aren't detours anyway."

She had barely turned onto the second detour when the trees got too close for comfort. Liz really did do some creative driving, then, rapidly backtracking to the main road. She ignored the following deviations unless other traffic also took them. She crossed the Florida border around midnight in a downpour that got worse as she drove. The storm chaos led to a major tie-up in traffic. She'd spent nearly ten hours to go a hundred and eighty miles—the distance to the northern Florida border, normally a three- or four-hour drive, less if a driver pushed the speed limits and knew where the cops sat—which she did. Between detours, traffic accidents, and the weather, someone was trying to keep her from heading north. And Liz refused to pay attention to them.

Shortly after midnight, Liz pulled off at a little mom-and-pop station still open. After gassing up her SUV, she went inside to get food and beverages for her trip. She loaded up on bottled water, caffeinated drinks, and energy bars. Next thing she knew, a dripping slob of humanity ran into her, knocked Liz's basket into a shelf, and glared at her as if she was in the wrong.

"Excuse me." Her sarcasm went over his head. Fine. She moved away, shaking off the water he'd dripped on her, and headed for the checkout.

"Hi, miss. You got in just 'fore we close. How can I help you?" A middle-aged woman wearing jeans and a Jacksonville Jaguars T-shirt stood behind the counter, smiling as she rang up Liz's purchases and the gas she'd pumped.

"Can you tell me what the weather's supposed to be like for the next couple of days along the east coast?" Liz kept an eye on Drippy in the mirror above the counter. He hadn't bought any groceries. He simply stood there, glaring at her. Alarms went off in her brain, but no tingles. He registered as no more than a regular human sleazeball and not an abnormal. Though the term human was iffy at best, she figured. He fit more in the Cro Magnon category.

The cashier, her forehead wrinkled in a frown, handed over Liz's change. "That's what's so strange. We're supposed to have perfect weather this week. Nobody seems to know where this here storm came from." She bagged Liz's purchases and handed the bags to her.

Uh-huh. Nobody knew, but Liz could guess. The storm was meant to delay her if not stop her outright. But she would not be stopped. "Thanks." Liz leaned over the counter to get a little closer to the cashier. "You might want to watch that guy back there."

The woman nodded and glanced at an open door behind her, and Liz caught sight of a shadowy form and the glint of metal. "I've got coverage. But thank you, miss. Y'all drive safe now, you hear?"

Liz pulled up the collar on her windbreaker and dashed for her car. A big motorcycle had parked on one side, a little closer than necessary for pumping gas. Though she sympathized with any riders in bad weather, if that belonged to the impolite hulk inside, he deserved what he got. She pulled away from the pumps but waited a few moments in the shadows of a billboard to watch for the biker. Though the cashier may have had coverage, Liz wanted to make sure. She didn't usually deal with normal human beings, but this cretin didn't exactly rate high on either the human or the normal scale. He came out less than a minute later and jumped on his bike, and the Open sign in the door flipped to Closed. More comfortable about the clerk and her coverage, Liz left, going a different direction than the biker to get to the interstate.

Then the heavy rain turned to a serious downpour. Liz drove barely above crawling speed and passed several cars pulled off to the side of the road to wait out the storm. She glanced at the leaden sky. "You might as well drop the waterworks. The detours didn't work, and neither will this. I am coming."

Liz smirked when the rain stopped. She might have won this skirmish, but the war was just beginning.

She got as far as Virginia before stopping for some real sleep. She'd taken a cat nap at a rest stop after the storms stopped but needed a few uninterrupted hours. A dull headache throbbed, and she felt as though the entire sand reserves of Florida had taken up residence in her eyes. She could have continued on and finished the trip, but she'd learned never to go into an unknown situation exhausted. Another seven hours of driving to get to Clear Water would have her more than bleary eyed. She pulled off at a decent full-service truck stop over the border in Virginia. Dark trucks filled the lot, but there were only a few cars at that time of night.

"What can I get you, hon?" a middle-aged, bottle-blonde asked when Liz sat down at the counter. Though the dinner hour had passed long ago, and she saw less than a handful of people in the place, Liz preferred her surroundings that way.

With the bulging envelope in her pack, Liz decided she could splurge a little. "I'll have the baked ham special and a decaf coffee."

Liz glanced at the nametag on the woman's uniform. "Millie? Can you do me a favor and give me about thirty minutes? I want to grab a shower first." She hadn't had time to wash the rest of the slime off from the non-gator in Florida and wanted to be clean. Living out of her car did have its disadvantages at times, but she preferred her car over some of the cheap hotels she'd been in. At least her car didn't have any bugs or vermin. Ugh. Liz simply could not stand bugs. Go figure. She handled what she did but got creeped out by a tiny insect. She figured everyone had their issues, right?

"No problem." Millie grinned at her. "Women's

side is to the right."

"Thanks." Liz slung her bag over her shoulder and headed in. At least the place looked clean. She paid for towels and the use of the facilities and pulled out her own soap and shampoo. A half-hour later, clean and in fresh clothes, she went back out to the dining room and inhaled the aroma of succulent ham, fried potatoes, and green beans. From her seat in a corner booth, she could see all entrances but remained effectively hidden from anyone who might come in. A habit that had saved her skin more than a few times. Plus, a door directly behind her booth allowed for a quick exit if needed. She'd barely taken a dozen bites when in walked her biker friend.

"Damn," she muttered. "Can't be a coincidence." She knew Bannig probably had humans working for him, but she'd rather face a demon than this slob.

He hadn't seen her yet, so she slouched down and signaled for Millie.

"Problem, hon?"

"Not with the food, but I need it to go. And fast." While Liz talked to Millie, she kept her eyes on the rider.

Millie turned toward him, then stepped closer, effectively hiding Liz from the biker. "Got you. I'm guessing you don't want to meet. We've all been there, hon. Tell you what, where's your ride?"

"Black SUV with Pennsylvania plates sitting between the milk hauler and the Pink Lady."

"Wait 'til I've got his attention, then go out the door behind this booth. Don't worry about the alarm—been disconnected for years. I'll bring your food out as soon as I can."

"Thanks." Liz handed her enough cash to cover the bill and a good-sized tip. With Millie's help, while creepy guy studied the menu, she slipped out the side door and headed for her car. The temptation to sabotage his bike crossed her mind, but he'd parked so he had full view of the vehicle from where he sat. Millie came out a minute later with a bag.

"I can see why you want to avoid him. This job, you get to know people, and he's not one I want to know." She handed Liz a card with her food. "If you want a safe spot to sleep where you won't be disturbed, head here and give the gateman that card."

Liz took the card, and a tingle ran through her, a good one. "Thanks. I appreciate your help."

Millie went back inside, and Liz contemplated heading directly for the place Millie suggested, but she waited in the dark for a bit. This was getting to be a habit, but she didn't want to leave before she knew Millie—and anyone else working at the stop—was safe. She opened her dinner and sat there, watching while she ate. Liz could see a little better in darkness than humans, but not as well as an elf, lycan, or vamp. Still, she had enough light to spot the biker when he came out. He looked around the lot, and she ducked down. She relaxed a little when he roared off.

Liz checked the card Millie had given her, and saw the words *Selene Forest* and a map.

She decided to follow the directions on the card and took off. A few minutes later, she pulled into a nearly hidden lane. Old-growth trees lined the road, but at least they stayed where they were supposed to be instead of closing in on her. A half-mile later, she stopped in front of a heavy wooden gate. A small cottage sat next to the road. The door opened, spilling light into the darkness, and an old man limped out.

"Can I help you, miss?"

She handed him the card. "Millie sent me."

He peered at the card, then at her, and she held her breath. Then he nodded. "Welcome to Selene Forest. If you follow the lane to the right, you'll find camping sites. Help yourself to any empty spot. I'm Boreon. If you have any needs, simply ask the trees."

Ask the trees? Well, she'd experienced weirder situations. Like pieces of paper that wouldn't let you alone until you signed them. "Thank you, Boreon."

He fiddled at the side of the barrier, and the poles slid aside for her to enter.

As she went to pull through, Boreon stopped her. "Sorry, miss. I believe this belongs to you."

He handed her a creamy envelope with her name in black calligraphy. This one looked similar to her assignment envelopes but smaller and thicker. The bosses wouldn't send her on another assignment when they'd just clued her in on Bannig—would they? Not wanting to think about what the envelope held, she laid it on the passenger seat and drove on.

Liz followed the winding road through the woods. She didn't see any openings, but she did sense others behind the shielding trees. Selene Forest was an interesting place, but she did feel safe there, oddly enough. Liz finally pulled into a spot that had a picnic table and pump for running water. She turned off her car, and the air shimmered. When she looked around, the road had disappeared behind a shield of trees. But she didn't get any bad vibes like the detours in Florida.

"Interesting." Though she'd been told the place

was safe, Liz pulled out her protective crystals and positioned them around her car along with a light spell for security. Liz couldn't do heavy spells, but small ones she could handle.

After she'd taken care of her defenses, she opened the envelope. Then she laughed. The first real laugh she'd had in too long as she pulled out a jigsaw puzzle piece. Liz had gotten the first piece after she'd completed her initial assignment for O.W.L. along with a note telling her to keep them. She continued to get them with every assignment. Liz took the item to the back of her car and opened the hatch, then the wheel well. The SUV hadn't come with a spare, so she used the space for storage. The puzzle—about the same size as a small spare—had a round shape that fit nicely in the cavity. She had laid the pieces out on a thick scrap of cardboard covered with a piece of cloth.

Liz spent a couple of minutes finding the spot where the new bit went—exhaustion dulling her wits. Plus, the trees blocked out any light from the half-moon. A bright blue light flashed around the edge. The first time Liz had seen the surge of energy, she'd thought she'd imagined the flash. But the same phenomenon happened every time she added a piece. Plus, she knew if she looked, what she'd added would now be integrated into the emerging picture. All one, with no lines and no way to remove the piece once she found the right spot. She'd tried. Liz also couldn't tell what the picture would turn out to be. Every time she looked, the image changed. She had no idea what the point to the whole exercise was, but if her bosses at O.W.L. wanted her to put together a jigsaw puzzle, she'd put together a jigsaw puzzle.

Her car was a nice little SUV with four-wheel drive. A grateful client had given the vehicle to her after her second job for O.W.L. The gas mileage could be better, but it got her where she needed to be, including out of swamps. With the back seats down, she had room to sleep and space for her stuff. All the comforts of home except facilities and those she could get at truck stops and rest areas. She'd grown attached to the vehicle over the years as it became her home and office. Liz closed the wheel well.

She settled down in the back for a few hours of much-needed sleep. While not as nice as a real bed, the space wasn't bad. She also had room for a thin sleeping pad and blankets that had a lot more uses than a single sleeping bag did.

Exhaustion pulled at her, but she couldn't turn her brain off as she thought about Clear Water and her friends.

****

She must have slept, because she woke with a start to the sound of someone tapping at her window. False dawn lit the sky, but under the trees darkness still held reign. Liz grabbed one of her knives and opened the door a crack to see who was there.

"Miss?"

She opened the door all the way. "Boreon? What's wrong?"

"I apologize for disturbing you, but you have to be going. Now."

She shook her head, trying to wake up. "Excuse me?"

"You need to be there by dark."

"Clear Water's only a seven-hour drive away."

17

As she watched, his eyes clouded over, and his voice dropped an octave. "The straightest way may soon decay. When six are one, the time is come."

Chapter Three

Boreon shook his head, and his eyes cleared. Then he handed her a map. "You need to leave the main road. Though this path is longer, the way is safer."

Liz studied him and finally figured him out. He smelled of the earth and plants and all things good. Plus, even in the dim light, she could see the golden sparkles in his irises. "Elf?"

He grinned at her. "Good senses. Knew you were one too, when you came in. Only those with the blood can make their way here. Millie is a good judge."

His evaluation startled her. "Elf? Me? Nobody's ever been able to figure out exactly what I am."

"Don't know about that, but you do have some of the blood in you, else you wouldn't have been able to get in. That makes you one of us. And we watch our own."

He handed her a bag that warmed her hands as the aroma of fresh rolls assaulted her nose. "Yum! Cinnamon?"

"Millie thought you'd like some breakfast for the road. She packed a ham and egg sandwich and fresh sticky buns. Coffee in there too, light with two sugars."

Exactly the way Liz liked the potent brew. "Tell Millie I said thanks. For the food and for this place. And thank you too."

"Keep Clear Water safe. That will be thanks

enough. We need you there, miss. Troubled times are coming."

How did he know? Oh. Yeah. Elf. "Do you know when? Or what he's after?" Liz figured if Boreon knew where, he might know why.

He shook his head. "No. Even our best seers can't determine what is coming. Remember this—you are not alone. If you need us, tell the trees and we will come."

The elf disappeared into the dark. While Liz ate, she thought about him and Millie and the forest. And herself. The idea of being part elf brought a smile to her face. Some of the best people she'd met over the years were elven. Knowing this gave her a sense of belonging like she'd never had before and made her stronger for the knowledge but also a little scared. She'd never belonged to anyone. Even with Charly there was still a wariness that Liz couldn't get rid of. The last person she'd let her guard down with was Bannig, and that had not ended well. She'd decided after that encounter never to let anyone get that close to her ever again. Not even Kaeden, Charly's occasional cook—and the other friend in Liz's life. As she thought of him, her heart thumped a little harder, but she tamped the emotions down.

Liz shook her head. Definitely not going there. She needed to stick to Bannig and the trouble he would cause. As soon as her thoughts turned back to Bannig, she lost her appetite. Even the warm cinnamon buns held no appeal. Liz hit the latrine then packed up and headed out.

The way out of Selene seemed a lot shorter than the way in. Once she reached the main road, she turned into the mountains, following winding roads that avoided big cities and had incredible views of the valleys. This time of year, the mountains were decked out in their autumn finery, which added to the beauty of the drive. Looking at the scenery, Liz thought that everyone needed to get off the main highways once in a while and try a back road. Viewing such amazing sights should not be missed.

About an hour into her drive, on a particularly steep incline, her car's check engine light came on, and the power dropped off to the point where she'd have been making better time walking than driving. The car was okay coasting downhill but going up a steep hill nearly stalled the engine. And there were a lot of steep hills in Virginia. Liz chewed her bottom lip and prayed to the PTB. She grabbed a map and checked the location of the nearest town. In this day and age of GPS, she still relied mostly on paper maps. They'd never died on her or lost a signal. Or gave her strange directions like "turn left at the green house and keep going a ways 'til you reach Miller's old shed." She depended on herself and her paper maps.

"Where the hell am I?" She followed the lines on the map until she found a town within driving—if not walking—distance. Unfortunately, the place lay about five miles away, on the other side of the current mountain pass she faced. She patted the dashboard, crossed her fingers, and pressed the gas. "Come on, baby, you can do this. One more hill. That's all."

Liz could have kicked herself. She'd noticed problems after the first gas stop. Normally, she put her protective stones around her car when she left for more than a few minutes, but she'd been so frustrated when she'd pulled into the mom-and-pop store, she'd forgotten. And then at the truck stop, she'd taken time to shower, leaving her baby unattended and unprotected. Not smart.

The engine was running hot, so she kept adding water to the radiator, but the usual purr sounded…off and loud and…wrong. Liz knew from the sound that the exhaust system also had problems. When she finally made her way over the pass, she found a little hole-in-the-wall garage with a mechanic who looked as if he'd worked on Model T's—as they came off the line. While he took care of her baby, she called Charly. Unfortunately, her call went to voice mail. What could she say? "Get out of town. There's a demon coming to lay waste to the world"? Yeah, that would go over well. She briefly considered calling Kaeden, but her phone battery died. If that was Fate stepping in, Liz figured she'd thank her later. Until Charly and Kaeden, she'd never had anyone who cared enough about her for her to contact. Her bosses sent her letters, and when she needed to talk to them, she just talked.

Two hours and a couple of hundred dollars later, Liz got back on the road. She sent up another prayer to the PTB that there were no radar traps and headed to the interstate. That way, if she got stranded, she'd have some chance of getting a ride. The mechanic had assured her he'd fixed a leak in the radiator and that the power problem had been due to bad gas, but Liz had her suspicions that dirty fuel wasn't the reason, especially when the engine started running hot again and a few miles later, an ominous rattle came from underneath.

By the time Liz reached central Pennsylvania, she was running on prayers, but she also knew she had to keep going. The closer she got to Clear Water, the more urgency she felt. Liz knew Bannig had to be behind all her headaches, trying to keep her from getting to her destination, but this time, his people had messed with her car. She was not amused.

Well after dark, Liz drifted into a wide pullover about ten miles from Clear Water. A single pole light lit the area. Other than a couple of semis idling at the far end of the lot, she had the place to herself. With no buildings, no facilities, a chained picnic table, and over-flowing trash bins, this type of rest area wouldn't be popular with most travelers, including her, but she didn't have a whole lot of choice. She dug out her duct tape, scraps of wire, jugs of water, and other stuff she kept on hand and got to work.

Steam billowed when she opened the hood. "Okay, let that cool off. And the exhaust will be hot too, so time for a break." She stretched and slow jogged around the lot to kill time. Two truckers sat at the picnic table and nodded at her as she passed.

"Nice driving weather," she said. "You hear of any trouble on the road up to Clear Water?"

"Nope," one said. "Good road all the way. You got car problems?"

"Nothing I can't handle. Thanks." They nodded, and Liz headed back to her car, figuring the radiator and exhaust would have cooled off enough for her to work on the mess by then. She laid out a piece of tarp, grabbed a flashlight, and went down under to see what she could do. A handful of scraped knuckles, a tin can, wire, duct tape, and twenty minutes later, she'd fixed her exhaust system enough to get by. Next, the radiator.

A noisy bike pulled up next to her while she checked under the hood, and she gripped her screwdriver until her knuckles turned white. She recognized the bike. A dozen empty slots and he had to park here. Of course, he did. *Please, don't let this be my idiot biker stalker.*

The Powers-That-Be weren't listening. She'd have to have a talk with them later because she was not happy.

"Looks like you could use some help, little lady."

She slammed the engine hood down.

What were the odds? Her drippy friend from the convenience store in Florida stood there, paunch hanging out of a much-too-tight shirt, unwashed stringy hair, and dirty fingernails. Liz could take a lot of crap, but she could not stand dirty fingernails. She resisted the urge to use a piece of wire as a garrote. Barely.

"I'm fine but thank you." He didn't get the hint. Instead, he placed his booted foot on her fender. Not smart. Liz felt in her pocket for one of her knives. She had multiple ones in various places in her clothes. And she was an expert with them.

"Come on, baby. I'm very good at making things purr."

He still didn't get the hint. Liz was close to twisting that boot of his off the attached foot and hitting him over the head. "I don't need your help. Thank you. Now. Go. Away."

Instead of leaving, he sidled closer to her. Liz figured she was allowed to hurt idiots. She wiped her hands on her rag. "Look, mister. I don't need your help. My car doesn't need your help. And I most definitely do not need you."

He grasped Liz's arm, his oily smile turning mean. "You're here. I'm here. And I intend to have some fun.

You can give in and enjoy the fun, or not. Your choice." He licked disgusting lips.

Damn. Liz firmly believed that "no" meant "no." She smiled, grabbed his hand, twisted hard, and before he could yelp, had him down on the ground, her knee on his back, one of her knives at his throat.

"You have the wrong idea about me. A very wrong idea. An idea that you're going to get rid of right now. Understand?"

"What the f—"

"Hey, no swearing. Now, do you understand what I'm saying?" Liz pricked the skin of his neck the tiniest bit, but enough for him to get her meaning. He nodded his head. Carefully.

"And you're going to leave me alone?"

Another nod.

"And you're never going to accost another woman like this again." She added a little power to her words so they stuck in his head, along with a picture of what would happen to his private parts should he fail to heed her warning.

A nod. Reluctant, but a nod.

"And you're going to wash those filthy hands." She let him up but kept her knife visible.

"Yeah, yeah. Whatever."

The two truckers walked toward them. "There a problem here?" one of them called.

"Nope. No problem here," Liz said. "Isn't that right?"

"Yeah. No problem."

Liz got in her car. He glared at her as she backed out. "He has no idea how lucky he is," she muttered. She'd left him with all his body parts intact, an idea that had been in question. As she drove, Liz kept an eye on her rearview mirror, not surprised when she saw the single light of a bike drawing close. His placement on the intelligence scale didn't strike her as being high, more like registering as barely human. She slowed down to see if he'd go around.

He didn't. Instead, he drew up beside her and kept pace with her. There wasn't much traffic in the area, just the two of them. Liz tried stepping on the gas, but instead of speeding up, her car slowed down to the point where the engine went into stall mode, and she had to pull over. She didn't understand what the problem could be. She'd given the radiator water, so the engine wasn't running hot. And her jerry-rigged exhaust system wouldn't make the engine die. Plenty of gas. Oil levels were good. She'd even had a new fuel pump installed and the gas lines purged at one of her stops. So, what was wrong?

Unfortunately, she didn't have time to think about her car as her biker friend pulled over in front of her. Liz locked all the doors and sat tight, knives in hand, watching to see what he'd do. He climbed off his ride, sauntered back to her, and she looked down the bore of a large gun.

Damn.

Liz hated guns. Like her knives, she knew how to handle them, as well as other weapons, but refused to use a gun unless absolutely necessary. To her, there was no challenge in using a gun. Point and shoot. Plus, they were loud and needed expensive ammo. Besides, most of what she went after didn't respond to bullets unless they were silver and dipped in holy water. And even then, a clean kill shot didn't always work. She preferred her blades over a gun every time. Few—human or other—could best her in a fight with knives.

She tucked two smaller knives up her sleeves and popped the lock. He backed up enough for her to open the door without hitting him. So, he did have some minor intelligence. Rats.

With both hands raised and her blades securely hidden up her sleeves, Liz stepped out. She judged her odds, which weren't good as long as he had that blasted gun aimed at her. She needed to take care of that.

"You should have been nicer to me, Liz."

That he knew her name clinched the fact that Bannig, or some other nasty after her, had sent him. She had more than a few enemies running around out there. But she'd lay her bets on Bannig.

"My boss is pissed at you. You ignored his warnings."

"Warnings?" Liz sidestepped along the car until the open door wouldn't be a hindrance. She wanted to have a clear shot at him with her blades when she got the chance.

He nodded at her car. "You need to turn around. Do that, and your car will work fine. Well, mostly fine." His grin let Liz know he'd done more than his boss wanted. Now she was beyond pissed. Nobody messed with her car. Thunder rumbled around them, and lightning flashed. She tried hard to rein in her rage. Kind of like that comic book hero, no one should make her angry. Unlike the comic book character, she didn't morph into a monster, but anomalies tended to happen when she got angry—like lightning and thunder without a cloud in the sky. If Liz could direct the lightning, that would be useful, but she couldn't. She'd tried. She fought to not let her anger get out of control. Didn't always work, but she made the attempt. After a couple of calming breaths, the thunder died down, as did the lightning.

Liz let her knives slide from her sleeves down into her palms. Mr. Dirty Nails stood too far away for a good kick, but not for her blades. She gathered her energy and let them fly while diving sideways.

He screamed and went down. The gun went off, but the bullet didn't go as wild as she'd hoped. Pain seared across the top of her left arm. Liz pushed the burning ache away and jumped on top of her enemy, kicking the gun away. One of her blades stuck in his thigh, the other in his side. Fortunately, or unfortunately, depending on your point of view, she hadn't hit any vital organs. Liz figured that was what she got for being in a hurry. She yanked out the one from his side and held the blade against his throat. "Seems like we've been here before. I told you then I didn't like you. I don't like you even more now. And I really don't like your boss."

Liz socked him hard enough to daze him. He probably wouldn't stay down for long, but she didn't need long. She grabbed a roll of duct tape from her car and wrapped his wrists and ankles, and stuck pieces across his cuts. "That'll keep you from bleeding to death," she said to his unconscious form. She could be considerate at times. "Though they'll probably hurt like hell when you pull the tape off, so I'd be careful. Might even make you start bleeding again. Aw, shucks. Too bad for you."

She grabbed her toolbox and took out a heavy nail that she used to puncture both of his tires, pulled wires, and did whatever else she could to ruin his ride. She hated messing up such a pretty bike, but she had to be realistic. Liz reasoned someone would eventually see him, so she wasn't too concerned for his wellbeing. As she finished, she checked Mr. Dirty Nails. He'd awakened, and the string of filth that came out of his mouth rivaled the dirt on his hands. She took another piece of tape and plastered that over his lips. Then she went back to her car and took off her jacket. Blood soaked the sleeve of her shirt, but the bullet hadn't done any major damage. Probably wouldn't even need stitches. She wrapped a bandage around her arm as well as she could. Not easy with only one hand, but she had experience. Without another look at her stalker, she jumped in her car and turned the key. Dead. Not even a click. Her forehead met the steering wheel. Several times.

"Hey, Powers-That-Be, I could use a little help here. Or rather, my car could. Doesn't have to be much. Just enough to get me to the next town, okay? Please?"

Fingers crossed, she turned the key, and heaved a sigh of relief when the engine turned over. Fortunately for her, the next off-ramp led to Clear Water. Unfortunately, the dirtbag had done a number on her baby. More than what she could fix with duct tape and wire.

Sending a prayer to the goddess and whoever else might be listening, Liz kept going, though she barely limped along. She would not be discouraged. Once she decided on what needed to be done, she wasn't easily stopped.

When Liz coasted into Clear Water at just after eight p.m., most of the town was quiet, closed down for the night already. Saturday night and the only establishments open were the local big-box store, a couple of pizza places, burger joints, and the bars.

She needed a good garage, food, and at least a week of sleep. Fortunately, those were handy. When in town, Liz worked at the diner with Charly who was a witch, and a hoot and a half. And she trusted her more than she'd ever trusted anyone, with one exception, and Liz refused to think about her old friend Bannig.

When her car finally quit for good, she still had a few blocks to go, so she coasted down a nice hill and pushed the vehicle the last block to an empty parking space in the lot behind the diner and next to the garage. Liz loved her car, but not the weight when pushing. Plus, she'd been driving for two days and having arguments with fat, ugly idiots with dirty fingernails.

By the time she stood up, painful twinges that screamed bloody murder came from her back. She was cold, hungry, and tired, but as soon as she stopped, the spirit world hit her with knowledge she couldn't ignore. She needed to be there. Bannig had already arrived in town.

But why? Liz couldn't figure out what he wanted from Clear Water. A little one-hole town in the middle of nowhere. A nice place but not Bannig's usual M.O. Their last encounter had been in DC. Evil had an unbreakable hold there. Go figure. But not in Clear Water.

And what about that line Boreon had given her? "When the six are one." Six what?

Liz stared at the sky. "I sure hope you know what's going on. And if you do, I'd really appreciate you letting me in on the situation."

30

Her senses tingled as she reached for her bags in the back of the car. Liz ducked as a star blade whizzed past, thunking into her car right where her head had been a second ago. She grabbed her blades and swung around. Except for some late-evening strollers, nobody looked at her like they wanted to kill her. Unfortunately, that was the problem with evil. Even the baddest of the bad often looked innocent. Liz caught the shadow of the slightest motion across the street in an alley between the bank and a church. She figured she could ignore what she saw or go after whatever had made the shadow.

She went.

Fast as she ran, the beast moved faster. All she saw was a blob of darkness and smelled the stench of sulfur and skunk, but no ammonia. Some kind of different creature? Or did the blobs give off the ammonia scent only when dead? She needed to test her theory and let fly two blades. A high-pitched whine stopped Liz in her tracks. She recognized the sound from her encounter with the beast in Florida. She'd hit the creature but not with a kill shot. Yet.

Shaking off the creature's cry, she followed the blob into an alley that opened onto a parking lot. She skidded to a stop as one of her own knives hit the brick wall at her shoulder. Liz pulled back into the shadows. Several streetlights lit the area. Except for two cars at the far end, the space remained empty. Nothing moved. Liz inhaled deeply. The stench had faded. She had a choice—follow the smell or go back to Charly's. Before she could decide, a shadow detached from the back of the bank. This creature moved slowly but deliberately toward her. She clenched her jaw when she recognized the profile. Her heart sped up, and her mouth went dry. She stepped out.

"Hello, Bannig."

"Hello, Liz. We are met again." His voice had become deep and gravelly, not at all like the real Bannig's voice. He looked like he'd aged a hundred years since she'd last seen him. He held her knife in a hand much steadier than his voice. Liz knew better than to challenge him. She was beat, and he was a lot stronger than he looked. She'd learned that the hard way. So, she waited.

"Why are you here?" she asked after a moment of silence stretched into eternity.

He shrugged. "My business."

"Like your business in DC? I stopped you then, Bannig. I'll stop you now."

The smile on his face would have frozen lava and sent a definite chill down her spine.

"You couldn't stop me because you have affection for the one who had this body. Your emotions are your weakness, and they will be your destruction. Besides, I've expanded my resources."

"I noticed. I left one of your resources tied up on 322 about five miles south of here."

Bannig sighed. "The man has his uses, but he has no finesse. However, he is effective."

"He didn't keep me from getting here."

"No, but he did delay you."

Before Liz could ask him what he meant, a couple of drunks stumbled into the lot. Bannig and she watched them as they headed for the cars at the end.

"They really shouldn't drive in their condition," Bannig said.

Liz couldn't disagree, but she couldn't figure out his meaning. "You're not going to do anything to them, are you?" She did not approve of drunks on the road, but she also didn't approve of randomly killing someone just because you could.

"I don't have to. Besides, they are not worth the trouble. Insects." He looked back at her. "And now, I must go," Bannig said. "I look forward to our next encounter, Liz." He flipped her knife around and held the blade out, hilt first. "I believe this is yours."

Liz had no clue what Bannig planned, but she reached for the knife, half-expecting him to turn on her. He didn't. She stood there with both blades aimed toward him.

"I look forward to finally sending you back to Hell."

As he melted back into the shadows, Liz flung both blades toward him. They thunked against the darkness and dropped to the pavement. When she went to pick them up, Bannig had disappeared. She tucked her knives into her belt and headed back toward the main street.

Bannig was here. That meant a whole lot of trouble was also here. But a bigger thought bothered her. The demon had the advantage when she'd gotten there. He'd been hidden in the shadows, and he had her knife.

"So why am I still alive?" Maybe her friend still existed, somewhere inside his human body. And if so, she had a chance. A small one, but still a chance.

Chapter Four

The cold seeped into Liz. She blew on her hands to stave off the freezing temperatures and looked around. After the heat of Florida, a late October night in Pennsylvania felt downright chilly. The main street looked like every other small town she'd been in with a mixture of small shops, churches, chain burger places, and a lot of empty store fronts. But this was home, and a sense of peace always came over her when she returned here. Unfortunately, that didn't happen nearly often enough. Lately, she seemed to be away more than home. This time, she'd been gone nearly two months on various jobs.

Rather than go up to the apartment, Liz wanted to check in with Charly first, especially since Bannig beat her here. She made her way back to the busy diner. Liz grinned because that meant maybe Charly could use her help. Nerves added to Liz's shivers. After all, two months was a bit more than an overnight stay. She rarely got a chance to call and chat while on the job. Plus, she had a cheap cell phone that usually didn't work wherever she happened to be.

"No more excuses. I can do this." Liz blew out a long breath, then pulled the door open.

The first sense that hit her when she went into the diner was the noise, then the heat, and then the aromas. That mouthwatering, drool-making, stomach-grumbling scent of pizza, steak sandwiches, fried chicken, and beer. A U-shaped counter split the place neatly in two with tables and booths in the side dining areas. A half-wall behind the bar topped by a wide shelf on which the cook placed the orders kept the kitchen separate from the dining area.

Like the first time she'd come into the diner, Liz saw that Charly was trying to waitress, bus, and man the register all at the same time. Uh-oh. Not good. What had happened to her help? Liz's stomach knotted up when she saw the cook. Kaeden Pike. She'd certainly not expected to see him there making her wonder where the regular cook and waitress were. She knew Kaeden helped Charly out on occasion, but there should have been at least one other cook who could have helped. She'd hoped to put meeting Kaeden off for at least a couple of days. He looked as delicious to her now as he had the day she first met him three years ago. Back then, he'd just returned from a third tour overseas, and they'd clicked almost immediately. With sandy hair, eyes the shade of an emerald, and muscles in all the right places, he had everything a girl could want in one hunky package. Liz couldn't say for sure what they had, but hot, heavy, and intense came to mind. Unfortunately, he wanted more, and Liz didn't do serious or permanent.

Liz pulled her hungry eyes away from him and watched Charly on the other side of the room.

"If I ever see that pair of faces again, well, they'd better never show them around here." Charly slammed a tub filled with dirty dishes down behind the counter and grabbed her pad.

"Hey, Charly! You ever gonna wait on us?"

Liz glanced over at a group who looked like they had more money than brains. Two of the guys had their arms draped over girls whose tight T-shirts and tighter jeans left nothing to the imagination.

Charly glared at them. "You see anyone here but me? I'll get to you when I can. And if you see that lazy twit June and my cook anywhere, tell them they're both fired." She shoved a strand of dark hair off her face and went to a table where a middle-aged couple sat with two restless kids.

Liz figured Charly hadn't seen her yet. Either that or she was really pissed. Probably both. She noted at least six tables in need of clearing and orders up on the shelf. She hung her jacket on a nearby peg, grabbed an empty bin off the rack near the cooking area, and started clearing off tables. The sudden lack of noise in her area disconcerted her at first, but she kept going.

"Here, you don't need to do that," Charly called from the other side of the room. Liz kept working, as Charly knew she would.

"Looks to me like you could use some help," Liz called over her shoulder. Fighting back a smile, she filled the bin, wiped down the table, dumped the dirty dishes at the sink, and grabbed another tub before Charly could complain. The scene duplicated the conversation and situation she and Charly had encountered when they'd first met. They'd turned the act into a recurring joke. And yet, something felt wrong this time because the diner kept getting quieter and quieter.

"You've done this before." Charly tossed Liz an apron which she caught one-handed. She put the covering on, wrapping the strings twice around her waist, and tied them in front.

"Yep." Liz took care of two more tables while Charly put out orders.

"Need a job?"

"Could use one. Kind of between jobs at the moment."

She came over and hugged Liz, a grin on Charly's face. "Name's Charly. This is my place."

"I'm Liz. Elizabeth St. John."

"Been expecting someone with that name but didn't know when to expect her. Thought maybe she was a no-show. Nice to have you back." She glanced at Liz's arm. "But I think we need to take care of you before you keep going. You look like shit."

Damn. Liz had completely forgotten about her arm. Plus, working on her car and fighting off her stalker. She probably should have washed up first. Everyone stared at them, some with food halfway to their mouths, like a freeze-frame tableau. Charly hauled Liz back to the kitchen and to a stool. "Sit. Kae, get the first aid kit. Liz is hurt."

Kaeden already had the kit out and was next to Liz before Charly finished yelling. Liz could feel the heat from him and smell the woodsy cologne he preferred, although right then the smell of cooking overpowered his delicious scent. Still, she inhaled deeply, her senses remembering. She had to admit, the man got her heart pumping. Kaeden taught criminal justice courses part time at the local college and worked as a PI and part-time cop. And could cook like a professional chef. Gods, if she ever did stay somewhere long enough to have a serious relationship, he'd be why.

Charly unwound Liz's crude bandage, which hurt

like hell. Usually, she healed faster than normal humans, but not in a couple of hours, especially when tired. Blood seeped down her arm.

Kaeden studied the damage, then stared into Liz's eyes. "That's a gunshot wound. Fresh."

He closed down his emotions and dealt with her wound. So, she had finally returned. After two months without a word. They didn't know where she'd been, when she would be back, or even if she had survived her latest job. Kaeden had never met anyone like Elizabeth St. John. She made him madder than anyone he'd ever known. But he also couldn't get her out of his mind. She was a drink of water in a dry desert.

"She was shot?" Charly grabbed Liz's arm to look more closely.

Liz stared at Kaeden, and he stared right back.

"Yeah. Fortunately, he had a bad aim."

Kaeden kept his gaze on Liz for a long moment, then pulled out the antiseptic wipes. He grasped her arm and cleaned the gouge up. He bit back a grin when Liz gritted her teeth against the pain he knew she had to be feeling as he cleaned, salved, and bandaged her.

"You enjoyed that," she accused.

"Maybe." He cleaned up the wipes and bloody wraps.

She shrugged. "I probably deserved that and more."

"You think?" Kaeden knew he wanted too much from her. He wanted what she couldn't give him, and she'd told him so. She didn't stay in one place long enough to do a relationship. Unfortunately, his heart refused to get the message.

"Who shot you?" Charly asked.

"Some dirtbag who didn't like me saying no to him." She looked back at Kaeden. "Tell your uncle I left my attacker tied up with his bike on 322 about five miles south of the exit, though I'd be surprised if he's still there." Kaeden's Uncle Ray was the local police chief. Kaeden knew Liz and Ray went way back, and not in a good way, but he didn't know why.

"You took care of him?" Charly asked. When Liz nodded, so did she. "Good. You need to change. Can't wear that shirt out there. And where the hell have you been for two months?"

"I'm sorry. Job took longer than I thought, and I had some trouble with my car and other issues."

"You ever heard of a cell phone? Oh, wait, let me guess. Your battery is dead again. Or no signal? Which one this time?" Charly asked.

Kaeden knew Liz let her cell battery die a lot. Or didn't have service. Or just forgot to call the people who cared about her.

"Um, both? Thanks for the bandaging, but I think we'd better get back to work before those patrons out there get rowdy."

Charly sighed and shook her head, then hugged Liz and headed back out.

After escaping the kitchen, Liz dashed upstairs to her apartment, ran into the bathroom, hauled her shirt over her head as she went, and splashed water on her face. Then she saw herself in the mirror. No wonder everyone had stared at her in the diner. Mud, blood, and grease covered most of her. She added some soap to the splash, pulled a comb through her short hair, changed into cleaner clothes, then sprinted back downstairs. She didn't want to give Charly and Kaeden time to think. Or talk. She didn't have to worry as their short break had piled up orders and Charly and Kaeden were working like crazy. When Liz went into the kitchen, Charly nodded at the bins. "You bus, I'll serve."

"Works for me. What happened to your help?"

"Took off this morning without so much as a note! Eloped. Of all the... I didn't even know they were seeing each other."

Liz would bet her next pair of boots O.W.L. had their hands in the pair's disappearance, or Bannig, though she wasn't quite sure which or why.

Before long, the patrons had been served, the tables cleared, and Liz was working on the dishes in the back. Charly came in and leaned against the counter. Liz caught her lower lip in her teeth.

"I was beginning to think you weren't coming back. I'm guessing you ran into some trouble?"

"Yeah." An understatement of the decade.

"The law have anything to do with your trouble? Maybe one of the alphabets?"

"Nope." The question had become an old joke with them. Charly kept trying to figure out who she worked for and what she did. Liz kept evading the questions. Her friends knew the basics—that she worked for a group that dealt with special issues, but Liz had never given them any specifics.

"That trouble going to trouble you more?"

Liz blew out a heavy breath, dried her hands on her apron, and pushed the start button on the dishwasher. "There's a distinct possibility."

Charly studied Liz, her dark eyes so intense, they bore into Liz's soul, stripped her clean, tore her apart, then put her back together, all within the space between two blinks. Then Charly embraced her again. She was a hugger. Liz had never been hugged until she came up against Charly. She didn't quite know how to handle physical affection, but she'd figured a response out. To her, the action imitated fluffing a pillow, but nicer. She didn't know exactly what Charly's capability as a witch encompassed, but she knew Charly had powers beyond a regular witch's magic. A sensation Liz couldn't read. She'd never run up against someone like her friend before. But then again, Charly had been the one to claim Liz was part witch and then taught her simple spells.

"Well, welcome home. The rush has slowed down out there. Come on out and get some dinner. I'd say you more than earned some food."

Liz followed Charly out to the main area. Though most of the tables were empty, a good crowd still waited at the bar. "I'll help you with the bar."

Charly snorted. "I think I can handle them. Now sit." She nodded at an empty stool. "Hey, Kae. Fix our girl up with a meal. Looks like she could use one."

The gaze from his eyes could have fed Liz for a year. His face was a little too angular to be called model gorgeous, and his nose looked like he'd been in a couple of fights, but those muscles that filled out his jeans could get a girl's saliva flowing. And Liz knew for a fact what he could do with those muscles. All of them. Damn. She tamped down her libido. She didn't have the kind of life that allowed for relationships. She'd have thought two months away would cool his jets—or hers—but the heat coming from those eyes could have seared a steak faster than a bonfire.

He set a dish in front of her. "When you have time,

I'd like to talk."

Double damn. The man's voice flowed over Liz and pulled at her until all she wanted to do was grab him, haul him upstairs, and have her way with him. Multiple times. But now was not the time. Her frigging female parts refused to listen, though.

"Tomorrow. Okay? I am in serious need of a shower and some sleep."

He nodded and went back to the kitchen, but she could sense him, like he was a part of her. And that scared her almost more than Bannig.

Chapter Five

While Liz ate, she checked out her bar companions. Though they all looked *normal*, there were a couple lycans, an elf, a shape-shifter or two, as well as some regular humans. If you knew what to look for—and she did—you could tell who was what. She thought the mixture interesting. As she studied the room, she noted there were a lot more non-humans than she'd ever seen in the place before, even two months ago. More non-humans than humans? She wondered if the non-humans were building up an army, or here because this had become a good place for acceptance? She didn't get an evil vibe coming off them. No sniping at one another or wariness, just people enjoying their food. So, she sat. And watched.

Liz did feel kind of guilty sitting there eating while Charly continued to work the bar, but knew if she tried to help, Charly would scold her. She'd expected a slice of pizza but should have known better. Her witchy friend had been on her case about what she ate—or didn't eat—for five years, knowing full well that when she was on the road, she subsisted on granola bars, chocolate, and caffeine. Instead of a slice of pizza, she'd gotten a plate with grilled chicken, a delicate mushroom sauce over a mound of angel hair pasta with a side of grilled asparagus. She'd enjoyed the ham special at Millie's, but the food Kaeden made for her went so far beyond good, a priest would probably declare the dish pure sin. But he'd given her too much. She couldn't eat more than half of the dish.

"You don't like the special?" Charly asked on one of her passes. "That's one of our new dishes."

"God, no. This is incredible. I just can't eat so much."

Charly snorted, then grinned. "Well, stretch some plastic over the rest and stow the plate in the cooler. You can always reheat the dish later."

Liz tucked her unfinished meal on a shelf in the walk-in and then got back to work. By the time the diner closed, her body screamed for sleep. Her feet ached. Her back hurt. Her shoulders twinged, especially where she'd been shot. She thought even her hair throbbed. And yet, she felt good. Honest labor and decent people. Nobody shooting at her or spitting flesh-eating acid.

The diner served tasty food at affordable prices, and the tips showed client appreciation. When she counted them out, even split three ways, the sum was substantial. Liz tried to refuse a share. After all, she'd only been there a couple of hours, not all night like them, but Charly wouldn't allow that. And you did not argue with Charly.

While Kaeden cleaned up the grill and bar areas, Charly and Liz mopped the floor and finished the other cleaning that went with running an eatery. Liz stowed the mops as Charly came back and handed her one of two cold bottles of beer.

"You look like you could use this."

"Oh yeah. Thanks."

"You back for a while?" Charly took a long, slow

swig from her bottle.

Liz followed suit. That drink went down smooth and refreshing. "Don't know. Probably. But you know how my life is."

"Yeah. You ever going to tell me the whole story about what you do out there?"

"Told you. I work security."

"Uh-huh. That's a bunch of crap. You've got no calling cards, no phone—or not one that ever works—no way for anyone to contact you. I'm fairly certain you sleep in your car when you're not here. Hell, you live in your car as near as I can tell, and you're gone for weeks, or months, at a time. What exactly is this security group you work for? Some kind of black ops or something?"

Liz took another pull at her beer. "Something."

Charly sighed and shook her head. They'd been over that ground several times. More times than Liz wanted to count. She hated keeping that part of her life from her friends, but no way would they ever believe what she really did. Although…she thought about the beings in the diner earlier.

Her friend flicked her hand at Liz. "I have no clue who you work for, nor do I want to know unless you think I should, but I do know whatever you do is okay, so I won't bug you. Much."

"Come on, you know I've told you all I can. I work security, usually dealing with the stuff other people don't want to."

"Yeah, I know. But you've never come home shot before."

What she didn't know…Liz had been hurt often, but only once seriously. She didn't let Charly see all the scars. Kaeden's gaze caught hers. He had seen them all.

"Liz, if something bad is going to happen here, I'd like to know."

Who could blame her? This was Charly's home, and Liz would sure as hell want to know if something horrible was coming to her town. "When I know specifics, I'll tell you. Right now, I don't know much beyond the who and where. Who is an old nemesis. Where is here. But I have no clue when, what, how, or anything else."

"That's not much, but if you need help, all you have to do is ask."

They both jumped when they heard a loud noise from outside. The women with Kaeden rushed to the back door in time to hear a motorcycle squealing out of the lot. They stood there, staring at Liz's car. Painted across the side in bright orange letters were two words—Leave Now.

Charly turned to her. "I'm guessing this has a lot to do with our discussion."

Liz blew out a frustrated breath and nodded. "Yeah."

"You two want to tell me what the hell is going on?" Kaeden asked, and not quietly or nicely.

"I've got a little problem," Liz said.

"Would that be the same problem who shot you?"

"Yep."

He yanked out his cell phone, but before he could punch in any numbers, Liz stopped him. "Don't bother calling your uncle. He won't find anyone. I'll deal with this."

"We'll deal with this."

"Kae, I don't want to risk you or Charly getting

hurt. He and his boss are my problem. I'll take care of them."

"When are you going to understand we can help you?" His voice emerged softly, but Liz could hear the undercurrents of anger and frustration.

"He's right," Charly said. "We deal together. Liz, I know you don't like attachments. And I know you want to think you're a loner. But you're one of us. We're your friends. Let us help."

Liz closed her eyes and fought back tears. She felt a little like the Grinch whose heart suddenly grew, but a wall still held firm. Maybe with some cracks, but there regardless. "Telling you isn't that easy. There are things you don't know. Don't want to know."

"So, tell us," Kaeden said. "We probably know more than you think."

He could be right, but still... "I can't." Liz held up her hand. "Not yet. But I will when I can."

"Because of these mysterious bosses of yours?"

Before Liz could answer or Kaeden could say anything else, Charly put her hand on his arm. "Come on. Let's finish up. Liz, go see to your car and grab your gear. Come back in when you're done."

Beer still in hand, Liz went out to her car. She didn't see any damage beyond the paint. This wasn't the first time she'd been threatened. That happened on a regular basis. But this was the first time they'd come this close to her home. She grabbed her stuff, slung one bag over her good shoulder and carried her other bag in the same hand, then headed back inside. She stopped when she heard Kaeden and Charly arguing and waited outside the door, listening.

"How can you let her back in again?" His voice,

even when raised in anger, flowed like molasses—smooth, rich, and deeply sweet. "You've been putting up with this crap for five years. She takes off to God knows where, doesn't tell you—us—when she'll be back, or even if she'll be back, then she waltzes in and takes up like she's never been gone. And this time with a gunshot wound!"

"She needs us," Charly said. "And you checked her out. I know you did. And I know you're glad to have her back too."

He had and he was? Hmmm. Interesting.

"All right. Yes, I'm glad she's back. But I'm not happy. None of my contacts at any of the agencies say she works for them."

"And yet, they all knew her and said they'd take her on board any time she wanted to change bosses."

Kaeden snorted. "Yeah, but not a single one of them would say what she does beyond some kind of security."

"Not unusual for those types. Can't you accept who she is? After all, you're the one who keeps panting after her. Come on, Kaeden, you know she's good people. You know she is."

Aw gee. Charly didn't have to say something so nice. But how could she really know? Not many people would take a stranger in, give them a job, then invite them into their place as a roommate. But Charly had.

Liz decided to make an entrance, so she kicked one of the trashcans and strolled into the kitchen. "Sorry I took so long. Other than the paint, the car's okay. Well, as okay as it can be with a bad radiator, patched up exhaust, and more."

Kaeden stayed busy wiping a spot on the clean

grill, but Charly grinned at her. "Let's go. Kae? We'll both see you tomorrow."

"I hope so." He glared at Liz, then stomped out. Even mad, the man set her heart to thumping. And he had clean fingernails.

"I guess he's a little pissed at me," Liz remarked as she and Charly climbed the narrow outside staircase. Charly's apartment took up the second floor. Liz's the third.

"A little? No, he was a little pissed when you took off back in August with nothing more than a scribbled note. He was a little pissed when we didn't hear from you for weeks. Now, he's a lot pissed." She stopped on the landing outside her door. "Look, I know you won't, or can't, tell us where you go or what you're doing specifically, but we care about you. You're one of us, and I know that makes you nervous, but there you are. Even if you can't tell us where you're going or what you're doing, at least let one of us know you're alive once in a while. You can do that much, can't you?"

Liz stood there like a scolded puppy with her tail between her legs. Charly was right. But she didn't know how to do friendship. Demons she could face. Smelly blobs she could handle. Even dirty stalkers on bikes. But real people? Ones who cared about her? That was a challenge. "I don't know, Charly. All I can say is I'll try."

"That's all I can ask. You need me to look at your arm again?"

"Nah. I'm good. Night."

"Okay. I'm heading for the sack. If you need something, you know where stuff is. I haven't moved anything." She yawned widely. "See you tomorrow."

"Charly?"

"Yeah?"

"Thank you for trusting me."

She waved Liz off. "I've got a sixth sense about people. When you showed up five years ago, I had a powerful sense I was going to be the one thanking you, especially now. But I gotta tell you, this taking off and not letting me know you're alive is getting old." She closed the door, and Liz sighed before climbing to her place.

Her apartment was a large efficiency in the attic of the house. A tiny kitchenette stood at one end nearest the door, the bathroom at the other end. She'd laughed when she first saw the space. A doorstop in the sloped ceiling kept anyone from opening the refrigerator door too far and denting the ceiling. A sleeper sofa and two chairs faced an entertainment center in the middle of the area. She'd fallen in love with the place immediately. The bathroom had all the necessary elements—sink and toilet—and then there was the tub. With high sides and a higher back made for leaning against, there was nothing like that bit of claw-footed, enameled metal. People who lived on the road like she did got used to truck stop showers or the rare motel tub, which were not made for soaking. Her tub was sheer heaven. A girl could get used to that kind of luxury. She didn't know who had wrangled the monster up to the attic or how, but she blessed them every time she sank into the depths.

After dumping her bags on one of the chairs, Liz pulled the bed out, then went out on the tiny landing. The frigid air bit through her thin shirt but felt good all the same. A dim light flickered at the far end of the small parking lot below where the garage that took care of her car stood. There, a few cars sat in the lot mostly near the garage. Her gaze moved from the light to the shadows. She tried to discern if anyone lurked. Though her senses said no, her nerves remained on alert. Bannig was here. And the only way she could stop him meant she had to find out why he'd come here.

Before she went back in, she studied the sky. The town's lights all but obscured the view, but she knew exactly how to spot Orion's belt. The hunter. The three kings. Osiris. The three main stars were known by many aspects, but she mostly feared Osiris. The Egyptian god of the underworld. The ruler of the dead. Osiris was rising. And his name, this time, was Bannig.

Chapter Six

Liz shivered—not necessarily from the chill wind—went back inside, and headed for the shower. Though she really wanted to take a good long soak in the tub, she knew she'd probably fall asleep and end up looking like laundry left sitting in a dryer—clean, but really wrinkled. Instead, she pulled the curtain around and turned on the shower. The liquid heat soothed her, easing tired muscles and her mind, and she let the water run until the temperature told her she'd been in there long enough. While she toweled off, she thought she heard a noise from the outer room, but when all remained quiet, she shrugged the sound off. When Liz went out, she saw a big tan envelope peeking under her door.

An envelope that hadn't been there before she went in for her shower. And this didn't come from O.W.L. Liz opened the seal and found a blurry 8x10 glossy inside taken of her in the parking lot earlier that evening. A big red X covered her face. She snorted. Liz had gotten stronger death threats than a bad picture. She tossed the picture in the trash, set wards, said a protection spell, and flopped onto the bed, out before her head hit the pillow.

Liz had the weirdest dreams all night. When dawn lit the sky, she finally went down to the diner to make coffee. When she got there, the back door stood open, and she smelled the luscious aroma of her favorite caffeinated brew—but that puzzled her. From the sounds of the church bells in town, she knew today was Sunday, and the little witch never got up before noon on Sundays. She went in to find Charly sitting on a stool, her head on the counter, a pot of fresh coffee on the warmer. She didn't even look up at Liz. Not good. As quietly as she could, Liz grabbed some pastries from the shelves and warmed them up in the microwave. Then she poured two mugs of coffee and wafted one under her nose. Charly opened one eye and sighed.

"Thanks," she mumbled as she sniffed at the potent brew.

Liz placed a warm sticky bun by her hand. "Eat."

"Not without caffeine first. I swear I didn't sleep a wink last night."

Uh-oh. "You never don't sleep. Why so restless?"

Charly shrugged as she gulped her coffee. "Weird dreams. Like someone was trying to get me to do something. Or wanted something. And I wanted to help, but I kept running into a wall, one I couldn't even see."

Double uh-oh. That sounded like she had hit and bounced off the wards, which was good, but who or what had tried to control Charly's dreams and why? Okay, Liz knew who—Bannig. And the why was probably to get to her.

"Hey? Do me a favor?"

"Not until I have another cup of coffee."

"This one doesn't require caffeine. Go get your protection amulet. Please."

Charly put her cup down and eyed her. Liz knew she wore different crystals for various reasons—health, love, protection, and stuff like that, but she'd never asked her friend to wear a specific one before.

"You want to tell me why?"

"Let's just say I'm not comfortable with that dream you had. Get the amulet and wear it, okay?"

"Yeah. Think I will. How 'bout you? You need one?"

"I'm good. But thanks. I'm going to go for a run. You going to be okay?"

She laid her head back on the counter and waved Liz off. "Yeah. Go. Going back to bed. Maybe. See you later."

Liz nudged her friend. "Protection amulet first, then bed. Go. I'll lock up."

Charly sighed but nodded and headed up the stairs, her steps dragging. Liz watched her until she shut the door to her apartment. Then she locked up and headed out. She wanted to take a look around town, get her bearings again, and scope out the vibes, hoping she'd get a line on Bannig. The sooner she took care of his mess, the better.

Not far from the diner she found a park with jogging paths that wound in and out of the woods, next to a wide rocky river. Ripples sparkled and gleamed in the early sun and wisps of steam rose from the water, giving the area an ethereal quality. She'd forgotten how beautiful Pennsylvania could be in autumn. The trees were decked out in bright colors like someone had taken cans of paint in shades of red, orange, gold, brown, and green and splashed them across the land. A mulched path loaned itself to walking or jogging along with fitness areas. Paved bike lanes ran alongside the jogging path, and there were benches for sitting and watching the river, so everyone could enjoy the space.

Ten years ago, the park had been little more than a dumping ground for old tires, broken appliances, and used-up people. Like Liz. She knew the place well, but when she'd returned five years ago, she'd found the park had replaced the run-down area—a definite improvement.

To her surprise, a few minutes into her run, Kaeden showed up. Dressed in jogging pants and a black T-shirt, he looked positively yummy, and she bit back a sigh. She had no idea what to say. Small talk wasn't exactly her strong point, and she didn't want to get into a deeper discussion, but she didn't think she'd have the choice.

"How are your classes going?" Liz asked, more to break the silence than to talk.

"We're going to do chitchat? Liz, we really need to talk." Kaeden had been on his way to the diner when he saw Liz leaving…and followed her. Not like a stalker. He really wanted to talk to her, but she never made things easy for him.

Liz blew out a sigh. "I know, Kae. And we will. But not right now, okay? I'd really like to enjoy the park and the sun and a nice jog with nobody chasing me or shooting at me or… anything. Anyway, unless you want to chat about the weather, I'll meet you at your place later." She stretched out, then took off at a slow trot. He stayed with her.

"So, nice weather we're having," he said with a grin.

Liz stumbled, then laughed. "Yes, we are."

"You new around here?"

She glanced over at him with a startled look, and he gave her a steady stare right back. He wasn't going to let her get away without a discussion. If that meant he had to do small talk, he'd do small talk.

"Nope, but I haven't been around much."

The idea struck him that, though they'd hooked up more than a few times, he knew almost nothing about her. They weren't exactly big on conversations when they got together.

"What about your classes. Students still giving you grief?" she asked.

"Only one. Some smart-ass who thinks he knows all about forensics because he watches those CSI shows."

"Ouch. Goddess save us from television scientists. Let's see, you can get DNA samples from any tiny bit, and the same test will be processed in less than thirty minutes. And all the bad guys are caught and prosecuted within a day or two at the most."

He chuckled. "Yeah, and we only have one case at a time to work on. Nobody ever has a backlog."

"Not to mention the guns. The bad guys never hit anyone, but the good guys always do."

"Just like in training. So, where'd you get yours?" he asked, wondering how she'd answer.

Liz grinned and shook a finger at him. "Wouldn't you like to know?"

He grew serious. "Yes, I would."

Unfortunately, she refused to be baited. "How about rifle team in high school?"

"You were never on any teams. I checked. At least not here. Never did find out where you were from. Charly's known you for five years. I've known you for three, dated you for six months before you left, and I don't know you. Like where did you go to school?"

Liz stopped by a bench but didn't sit. Instead, she stared out at the river. He joined her, leaning back against the bench. "The school here was the last in a long line. By the time I got here, the academic year only had a month left, and they didn't want me. I had enough credits that, technically, I graduated, but I didn't do the cap and gown bit."

He hadn't known that. "Your family moved a lot?" He knew the answer but wanted to see what she'd say.

"Not my family. Me. I was in the system. Shuffled around from place to place." She picked up a stone and chucked the pebble into the river. The ripples flowed outward, folding back on themselves when they reached the shore.

"Oh. I'm sorry." He didn't look away from her although what she said helped him understand her a little better. No wonder she had issues with connection and commitment. She held herself so stiff, like the tree next to her. All he wanted to do was wrap her in a hug, but he didn't think she'd appreciate that.

"I don't need your pity. Not now, not ever." She hurled another stone into the river.

"I don't. I think your background made you strong." He sat on the bench more to keep from going to her than because he needed to rest.

Her shoulders dropped a little. "Non-issue. Old news. What about you? Strictly local?"

Kae bit back a grin. His turn. He'd questioned her, so she had the right to get a few in herself. "I grew up here. Most of my family is still in the area."

"I know your uncle is still around and your sister." She joined him on the bench.

He was grateful she didn't mention his folks.

They'd both passed away several years ago, killed by a drunk driver while Kaeden was overseas. The pain still hit him hard sometimes.

Kaeden breathed in her scent and reveled in the heat of her. The physical part of him really wanted her, but he tamped his urges down. He wanted more from Liz than sex. Though that seemed to be all they did when they were together.

"So, you found someone to get serious about yet?" she asked, hurting him a little. He didn't know why Liz drew him so much, but she did, and no one else could fill whatever need she stirred for him. Plus, she knew he and Charly weren't an item. They'd grown up together and were more like siblings. He could no more lust after Charly than he could his sister.

"What about that girl at the coffee shop? I know she had the hots for you."

He snorted. "Dana? The girl with purple hair, tats, and a nose ring? I don't think so." If that's what she thought he went for, she didn't know him at all. He wanted someone tall, sexy, talented, sexy, a little mysterious, sexy… He wanted…Liz.

Kaeden didn't know which view looked better— Liz or the backdrop of the river bathed in fall colors. But she had the edge. He stared right at her, a half-grin on his face. Liz swallowed. Hard. He held up his fist. The first finger came up. "No wife."

"Already knew that. Would not have hooked up otherwise. I don't encroach."

Second finger. "No girlfriend, though I'd like that to change." Her, preferably. But the look on her face didn't hold a lot of hope for him.

Third finger. "No recent breakup, at least not one I

agreed to." He wasn't above using a guilt trip on her, grinning when she winced.

Fourth finger. "No other attachments and you know I'm not gay." Or at least she ought to. He'd made damned sure when they were together that he satisfied her.

"Kaeden, you know I like you."

"I hear a *but* in there."

Liz closed her eyes, then opened them. He saw resignation on her face and knew her answer. "My job doesn't give me an opportunity for liaisons. I'm never in one place long enough."

"You've been here for five years."

"And I've been gone for two months. And before I came here, I stayed in a different town every month. I travel a lot and don't always have time to…to…" She acted like she was really stretching for excuses and running out of ideas.

"To let those of us who care for you know where you are and when you'll be back." He ran his hand through his hair. "Liz, if you don't want friends, why did you stay here?"

"I don't know. This place felt right. I'd never run into anyone like Charly. Or you. People who made me feel good. People who…cared."

Kae laid his palm against her cheek. The heat from her felt good. *Too good.* "So why not let down some of those barriers you've built up and let us in?"

Liz looked out at the river, and he wondered what she saw, what kind of thoughts ran through her head.

"I don't know, Kae. Opening up isn't easy for me. Plus, my life isn't exactly normal." She held up her hand to stop him from saying anything. "I can't tell you what I do, so don't ask. Keeping secrets is part of my life. Letting down those barriers you talk about...I don't do lightly. Can you trust me?"

He nodded, then took her hand. Of course, he could. Charly was right. He'd had her checked out by multiple groups, and although no one could tell him exactly what she did or who she worked for, they all had high praise for her. "Yes."

She laughed. "That easy? You don't even know me."

"I know more than you think. But I feel like I don't know a damn bit."

"I know you checked me out."

"Of course."

"You wanted to be sure I don't have a record like a thief or murderer or whatever."

"Or whatever. So, do you?"

Liz chuckled. "Am I what? Any of those? Nope. Didn't you find that out?" Actually, that wasn't true. She'd stolen. And she'd killed—though never a human. And all in the line of duty to the Powers-That-Be.

"I did. You're not. In fact, a couple of agents I spoke to thought rather highly of you, but they weren't exactly forthcoming as to why."

Those green eyes stared at her, one sandy eyebrow raised. She saw the questions, but how to answer them? Liz was tempted to give him a demonstration of her magical abilities, but not yet. She never had before. The subject had never come up. Paranormal talents weren't necessary when you were busy ripping a guy's clothes off.

"Your uncle have anything to say about me?" she asked, more to break the silence than to make conversation. Liz didn't have a problem with silence when she was by herself. She liked quiet. But being quiet with him was too disturbing. Too intimate. And sometimes, silence turned into an abyss. Sure, she wanted to jump his bones, but that was merely physical.

Kaeden smirked at her question. "Oddly enough, he didn't and doesn't, other than I should steer clear of you."

Liz and Kae's uncle had issues. Old ones, but still nasty. "You always have this much trouble following orders?"

He laughed and she melted. He had the most beautiful laugh. "Only when I know they're the wrong ones."

They rose and started walking again. Kae's hand brushed hers, and a tingle went up her arm. But this felt different than her danger buzzes. This one was purely physical and felt amazing. She'd forgotten how good he made her feel. He held out the hand that had brushed hers, and she wondered if he'd experienced the same sensation. A minute passed before she brought her mind back to the conversation.

Liz tried to think of something else to say, then she caught a whiff of skunk and sulfur, and her sixth sense shot arrows of warning up her spine.

Chapter Seven

She grabbed Kaeden and yanked him off the path, seconds before a large rock tumbled down the short cliff on their right. The boulder rolled past them, slammed against the bank, and splashed into the river. About the size of a large microwave, that baby would have done some damage had anyone still been in the way. While the incident got her out of answering his questions, knowing this hadn't been an accident bothered her. But who was the rock aimed at? Her? Or Kaeden?

Kaeden studied the upslope. He scrambled up a barely there path as Liz watched from below. The view of him climbing was rather heart-stopping. He stayed up there for a few minutes while Liz waited. She knew whoever had sent the rock down had run off. The frown on Kaeden's face when he came back down told her that much.

"Find anything?" Liz asked, though she knew he hadn't.

"Maybe." He didn't elaborate.

She wondered briefly if he suspected her of conjuring up the event, then dismissed the idea as ridiculous. He had no reason to suspect her of having extra-human abilities. "That was certainly strange."

"Not half as strange as you pulling me back before we knew that rock was headed our way." His gaze could have bored a hole through pure titanium, but she'd confronted worse.

"I must have seen something."

His head moved from side to side, but his eyes never left hers. "Try again. You were looking at the river."

Uh-oh. Those gorgeous greens didn't miss much. "Heard something?"

"Nope. I've got good hearing. Not a peep before you yanked. Considering what I found on my search, I'm thinking something different."

Liz was so not going there. She'd learned real young not to offer explanations when people didn't want to know the truth. "Like what?"

"What did I find? Or what do I think you are?"

"Both." What? Not who? Interesting.

"I found marks that make me think that someone pushed that rock on purpose. And I heard someone, but whoever or whatever he was, left too fast for me to go after. So, the question is—was the rock aimed at you? Or me? And why? And by whom?"

"That's more than one question."

"Do you have any answers?"

"Not to those questions."

"But maybe to my other one?"

"Like what I am? What do you think?"

"Psychic?" They reached the end of the park. Liz turned to head for the diner, but he took her arm. His strong grip didn't hurt her but let her know he was serious. "Come on back to my office. I'd like to continue our discussion."

"Do I have a choice?"

"Nope."

Liz could have easily gotten away from him, but, honestly, she didn't want to. She had questions herself about Kaeden, and all the changes in town, so she went. They both stayed quiet on the two blocks to his place. This time, she didn't mind the silence so much.

His home was an old brick house, probably built around the turn of the last century, with a wide porch hugging two sides and an honest-to-God wood porch swing. She ran her hand over the slats. He'd bought the place several years ago before his last deployment and was working hard at upgrades while keeping the old-fashioned flavor.

Liz had read about places like this but didn't think they existed until she'd come here the first time. She almost drooled over the house. This was the kind of place for families. For kids growing up and couples growing old together. If she ever settled into a house, this would be her choice. But since that would never happen, she'd enjoy what she could while she could.

From what she saw, he'd made more improvements while she was gone. The tall, wood windows that had more broken panes than solid had been replaced with well-designed energy efficient ones. And he'd replaced the worn porch floor with a wood-like composite, so he kept the flavor of the age while nodding to low maintenance. When they stepped into the enclosed foyer, closed doors graced both sides of the entry, along with a wide staircase going up to the second level, and a narrow hallway leading to the back. He opened the door on the right, and they went into his office instead of the living room on the left. Interesting. So, they were going to keep this professional. Okay. Probably a good idea. She knew all too well how soft the sofa was in the living room. How easily the two of them fit there.

Damn. Liz pulled her mind back out of the gutter and concentrated on the office. She'd been in here before, but even here, he'd made some changes since she'd been gone.

New shelves lined the walls, crammed from floor to ceiling with books that had been in boxes the last time. Plants hung from the high ceiling and sat in pots on the floor in front of the windows, flanking a small sofa. A large desk occupied the middle of the room. On the top were a laptop, printer, and all the other office accoutrements as well as a stack of file folders. Two upholstered chairs stood in front of the desk, a comfy-looking office one sat behind. Four file cabinets flanked the closed door on the back wall. This was a room for working, but also extremely organized. Liz had been surprised when she'd first seen the room. Her stereotype of PIs was that they were mostly disorganized. Kaeden Pike was without question not a stereotype.

"Have a seat." Kaeden pointed to one of the chairs as he moved around to the back of the desk. "Can I get you a drink?"

"Um, Earl Grey tea is fine. Thanks."

He strode through the back entrance leaving the door open so she could see a part of a kitchen. Keeping an ear to him, she leaned forward to see the files on his desk, chewing her lip, when she saw a thick one with her name. She inched forward and lifted the corner of the cover but scooted back when she heard him returning.

He handed her the mug, but his eyes were on the

file. He grinned as she took a sip. "Yeah, I keep checking on you. Did you get a chance to see the contents?"

"No."

He pushed the file to her and flipped the top open. She glanced down over the page. She found the usual information there—name, age, birth, places lived—a lot of them—all the stuff that makes up a person's life. Funny, there wasn't so much as a blurb about her living in Clear Water ten years ago. She figured her time there was too short for anyone to care to make note of. There were also letters of recommendation from a bunch of places and people. Cool. She hadn't realized so many people took note of what she did. She usually went in, solved the problem, and left. Liz closed the folder and nudged the file back. "So, you know all about me."

"I know as much now as I did when we first met, which is minimal at best. For instance, why are there no names on your birth certificate?"

Liz cringed, then decided what the heck. He wanted serious? He might as well know all the gritty details. "My birth parents abandoned me. My name came from the hospital where they dumped me. St. John's Hospital in Elizabethville, thus Elizabeth St. John. The longest I ever stayed with any family was my first year. After that, the time went anywhere from a day to six months." She watched his face. Most people, when they heard about her past, became more interested in studying the ceiling or floor, anything but looking at her. Other than a slight tightening of his jaw muscles, he didn't look away or flinch. His points were really starting to rack up.

"Tell me how you knew that rock was coming."

"I seem to have a sixth sense some of the time." She grasped her mug between both hands. This was where people usually got the urge to leave. Or raised their skeptical eyebrows at her. "I get lucky sometimes."

Her nerves buzzed as her intuition kicked in. For some reason, the spirit world wanted this guy to finally know all about her. Why now? Because she'd need him? "You might want to answer the phone. Your sister is going to make you an uncle."

The jaw muscles eased, and his mouth dropped open. "My what?"

The phone rang, and he stared at her, but he did answer.

While he chatted with his sister, Liz rose and studied some of the titles on his shelves. An interesting mix of forensics, criminology, and computer security as well as some good novels, mostly mysteries and adventure. What surprised her were a couple of shelves of books on paranormal phenomena. Hmmm.

As he hung up the phone, she turned and sat back down. She knew the answer but asked the question anyway. "When is she due?"

"You…? How…? They've been trying for years. How did you know?" The sense of awe and wonder warred on his face along with suspicion. Liz figured the first two were for his sister and the last one for her.

"Sometimes, I can sort of sense what's going to happen."

"Is that why you came back? Is something going to happen here?"

"I came back because this is where I live. But yes, something is going to happen here."

"What? And when?"

"I don't know. But I do know whatever happens is going to be bad."

Liz turned as someone entered the house. An older man. A memorable man. Uncle Ray Alton.

"Kaeden…"

Liz's stomach turned over, and her hands broke out in sweat as her mind went back in time. The night of her eighteenth birthday. A scared, scarred kid who'd been kicked out of her last home. She drew in a deep breath and exhaled slowly. She was no longer that frightened teen, and she'd faced down worse than Ray. And yet, her nerves chose this time to take a vacation.

"Uncle Ray, you remember Liz." Kaeden stepped around the desk to stand next to her. Funny, but that was the first time she realized Kaeden had never been around when Ray and she were together. Kae understood Ray and Liz had a past, but he didn't know why. They really didn't talk much when they got together. Today had been the longest they'd ever chatted.

"What are you doing back here?" Ray glared at her. She could almost feel the waves of anger coming off him. "I thought you were gone for good this time."

"She lives here. Uncle Ray, what's wrong?" Kaeden's gaze shifted from Liz to his uncle and back again, like he watching a tennis match.

"She's trouble," his uncle said.

"How do you know her?" Kaeden asked. "You've barely spoken two words to each other in the time I've been back. And now, you're like dogs staking territory. What the hell is between the two of you?"

"You never told him, Ray? Gee, that was nice of

68

you." Liz directed her next words to Kae but kept her eyes on Ray. "He arrested me ten years ago. When I got out, he made sure I left town. So much for my eighteenth birthday."

"He arrested you?" Though Kaeden didn't move, Liz could sense him drawing away from her.

"I found her down at the river, with a group of drug heads, next to a dead body." Ray's tone and body language showed his dislike of her, not to mention the sneering frown on his face. That hadn't changed.

"Drugs? And a body?"

Liz turned to Kaeden. "Wrong place, wrong time. I don't do drugs. Never have—never will. But your uncle wouldn't believe me until I forced him to do a test. I was as clean as the proverbial snow, but he still didn't believe me. As for the body, he was already dead when I found him. As I told your uncle and as he eventually found out."

Back in the day, the chief and his people were determined to clean up the river area. Liz had to agree, the place had been a cesspool of drugs, sex, and anything immoral. But was also the one place she could obtain a sense of peace. At least, until that night. Unfortunately, to the chief, anyone caught there was bad. Including her.

"Uncle Ray, Liz is innocent. In fact, someone rolled a rock at us on the river walk. Could have been bad if not for Liz."

"Wouldn't have happened if she hadn't been there." He said this while staring straight at her. "Lot of things wouldn't be happening if you weren't here."

"Lot of things going to happen anyway," Liz shot back. "Might be good for you that I am here."

Liz had had enough of his crap and decided she needed to get out of there—fast. Ray Alton wasn't one of her worst memories in Clear Water, but he hit near the top, and right then he was twitching that last nerve everyone talks about—the one where she usually pulled knives out and let them fly. Not a good idea.

She ignored Kaeden calling her and slammed her way out of there in a hurry.

Chapter Eight

In case Kaeden followed her, Liz ducked behind a tall, thick hedge. Sure enough, he emerged from the house and stood in the middle of the street, looking both ways. Having him look for her started a flame of warmth flowing through her, but at the same time, she had to wonder about his motives. Was he after her for himself? Or because his uncle wanted her gone?

After he went back inside, Liz returned to her apartment at Charly's. The phone was ringing when she got there. She was fairly sure who was calling, and the voice on her old-fashioned answering machine confirmed her suspicion. She made sure all the locks were secure, went into the bathroom, and filled up that wonderful tub with hot water and lots of soft bubbles. After she settled into the suds, someone pounded at the back door. Liz sank down, letting the water cover her ears, and tried to ignore the noise. She let the silky warmth surround and soothe her. Kaeden bothered her like nobody else ever had. She wanted him. But that scared her.

The tub was the perfect place for pondering her life.

Unfortunately, Liz found out quickly that Charly had given the key to the apartment to someone else. Kaeden. He strolled into the bathroom as if he owned the place and stood there looking down at her. Damn.

Catch a girl without any defenses. That wasn't playing fair. She sank as far under the bubbles as she could.

"You ran away. Again." He frowned at her, but she didn't see any anger showing on his face. Interest, yes, but not anger.

"Didn't see any sense in staying."

"You could have trusted me."

That brought her up, but one look at his heated expression had her sinking down again. "I do trust you. I told you about my talents. I've never told anyone about them. No one!"

"But you didn't trust me enough to stay. That's what you do best, right, Liz? Run?"

"No!"

"So why don't you stay? As soon as we start getting close, you leave. You used to be gone for a few days, but two months? Without a word? You are one selfish bitch, you know?"

"Selfish? Where the hell do you get off calling me selfish? I stayed away because of my job. And to keep you and Charly safe! You don't know what I deal with. If you had any clue, you'd thank me for keeping them away from here. I can't afford to get close to you. I couldn't stand that something might happen to one of you. The stuff I deal with is beyond dangerous."

"You could trust us to take care of ourselves. We're not without our own resources, Liz. We know how to protect ourselves."

She shook her head, sending droplets of water flying. "No, you don't. Not from this. Not from them. You don't know. You can't know."

He leaned over, and she fought pulling him in. "So, tell us. Let us help. Let us in."

They both jumped when Charly stepped in.

"What the devil is going on? I could hear the two of you shouting... Oh. Sorry. Continue." She backed out of the room, her face red, but a smile stretched from ear to ear as she shut the door behind her, her laughter echoing through the room.

"Kae, at least let me get out of the tub."

He grinned, grabbed a towel, and held the cloth out for her. "I'm not stopping you."

The man was almost worse than Bannig. Fine. She rose from the water and stepped out. He wrapped the towel around her, keeping his arms in place. His heart pounded beneath her ear as she leaned against his chest. He tucked the ends of the towel in and held onto her. "Liz, you can't keep us shut out, especially if there's something coming that could hurt us. We need to know so we can be ready."

Liz wanted to stay there, in the safety of his arms. To hell with O.W.L. To hell with her job. And to hell with Bannig. But she knew if she didn't move, that's exactly what would happen. Hell. She stepped away. "I need to talk to my bosses first, okay? I'm not shutting you out, but understand how hard this is for me, and how ingrained keeping secrets is in me. When I'm on the job, I can't let my guard down, and when I come back—"

"If you can't let your guard down with us, then with who, Liz? Sometimes being part of a group makes you stronger."

"I know. I'm learning. Give me time, okay? And a chance to talk with the bosses."

"Fine." He stepped back. "But no matter what, I still want you."

He left the bathroom, and Liz stood there staring at the door.

After getting dressed, she went out to the main area to think. Both Charly and Kaeden were gone. She loved them both, but Kaeden held the center of her attention. He had accepted what she could do better than most people. She guessed the rock and the phone call from his sister had a lot to do with that. But still...she thought about those books on the shelf and his uncle. She wondered if there was more to him than a cook and PI.

Liz puttered around the apartment, putting her stuff away. Doing inane chores kept her from thinking too much. From wanting too much. She also checked to see if her wards were still in place—they were. Good, nothing or no one with evil intentions could get through to do harm to anyone inside the building.

To get her mind off Kae, she sat down with her pendulum. She needed to discover background on Kaeden and his uncle and current happenings in town. As a PI and sometime cop, Kae had his ways of finding out what he needed to know. Liz had hers. Her preferred method of finding out events meant using her pendulums. She'd started working with crystals after a letter from O.W.L. told her she should. She'd discovered she had an affinity with stones. They helped her focus her abilities and enhanced them. Over the years, Liz had had some excellent training in fighting, weapons, and the occult. Though she could use multiple forms of divination, her crystals were her strength.

As Liz centered herself, she experienced a surge of energy. She'd had the sensation at other times over the years—like drinking a bottle of pure caffeine that usually meant she happened to be near a power node. A place that could be good or bad. Power had no sides. The force went to whoever had the most skill. There were places in the world where energy amassed into a small area. Like constraining a wide river into a narrow chasm, the more concentrated the area, the more powerful the force. Paranormals tended to congregate where nodes existed. Liz had sensed the force here before, but not like this. Before had been like drinking a small cup of espresso, a little bit of a buzz. Now she felt more like she'd had a double shot of super octane espresso.

That worried her. Nodes ebbed and flowed like a tide. They grew or shrank, depending on a lot of factors. She had a nasty feeling the factors weren't shrinking. And if this occurrence happened to be on the upsurge, that would explain a lot. Like Bannig.

Liz had one more job for her pendulum to do—a search. For Bannig. Doing a search worked better if you had an item that belonged to the person you were searching for. Liz dug into her crystal box and pulled out the first crystal she had ever received—a small amethyst Bannig had given her back when he'd been her friend. But she'd never used this particular one. She dropped the stone into a pendulum holder and started questioning.

She should have saved her energy. The pendulum either hung motionless or swung so wildly she couldn't get a reading. After a frustrating fifteen minutes, she realized the problem. She was looking for her friend Bannig. So, she asked one last question. "Is my friend Bannig truly gone?"

"Yes."

Liz blew out a long breath. The answer made her job easier. She could handle Bannig the demon.

After she finished with the pendulum, she went back outside. Liz wanted to see if she could find either the node or Bannig, or, preferably, both. Later, she swore she walked every street in Clear Water. The town didn't cover a large area, but it sure seemed that way while on foot. By the time she got back to her place, darkness had set in, and her feet hurt like crazy. Frustration filled her to the point where, if at that moment Bannig had shown up, she'd probably take care of him without any weapons at all.

Her door hung open when she got to the landing. Liz yanked out her knives, stepped in, dropped quickly to the side, and took a deep breath. She didn't detect any odor of skunk or ammonia. Nothing moved in the shadows. After a few moments listening to absolute silence, she flipped the lights on. She quickly saw no one was there but her. But then she saw the latest message. Lying on her table was a flower. And not just any flower. Monkshood. Also known as wolfsbane, blue rocket, aconite, and other names.

Liz knew monkshood was a pretty flower, but most types were also deadly poisonous. And there in front of her was the worst of the species, right on the table where she ate. All she had to do was touch the fibers and she'd be dead. Okay, death wouldn't be instantaneous, but the poison wouldn't take long, and the effects would be awful.

Seeing the flower there bothered her a lot. But what concerned her more was that someone had gotten in. Past a double locked door, a barred window, and her wards. Again. She needed to take more drastic measures to protect her place.

While Liz thought about her security, she pulled out a pair of rubber gloves and plastic bag and wrapped the flower up, then she got to work scrubbing her tabletop and every other surface she could clean. By the time she finished, the apartment had never looked so clean. She also disposed of every item of food not sealed—which really didn't mean much. After all, she'd just gotten home the night before and hadn't had time to go for groceries. Still, she wasn't taking chances. Every bit went into a garbage bag that she put out on the landing. She even bagged up her clothes and bedding so she could take them to the laundry the next day. By the time she finished, the clock showed well past midnight and exhaustion pulled at her mind and body. Liz went to her car and got blankets and a pillow from the back. Sleeping in her car seemed like a good idea, but she took her stuff up the stairs and spread them onto the bare mattress. She also put up some physical safeguards like trip wires at the door and windows. They weren't much, but they would get her through the night. Liz really needed some sleep. With two knives tucked under her pillow, she finally went to bed.

Pounding on her door woke her. She glanced at the clock. Seven o'clock. "Seriously? Who the hell pounds on your door at seven in the morning?" The noise started again.

"I'm coming. I'm coming. Enough already!" She jammed her legs into her jeans and yanked on a shirt. Kaeden and his uncle Ray stood on the other side of the door. Ray didn't look happy. Neither did Kae, but his look was more apologetic than anger. Ray glanced at the trip wires, stepped over them, and shoved his way into her room. She barely restrained herself from showing him back out. Forcefully.

"Are you responsible for this?" Ray demanded.

"Huh?" She shook her head, trying to fight off the last vestiges of sleep. "Responsible for what? What are you talking about?"

Liz could almost see waves of anger rolling off him. She let him stew for a bit while she scrounged in her backpack for some food. She found a partially eaten granola bar and scarfed the two bites down under the frowning face of Kaeden. "Hey, you wake me up, you should at least provide sustenance," she muttered. Especially when she'd been gone two months and her cabinets were bare.

"Responsible for what?" she asked Ray again. She didn't invite them to sit, but Kaeden sprawled on her one empty chair looking like he belonged there.

"We had a rash of break-ins and vandalism last night," Kaeden said. "And there's been a death."

His uncle glared at Liz. "Where were you last night?"

Liz forced her face to remain blank, but inside she trembled. The scene echoed the one with Ray ten years ago. "I was out. Walking. Who's dead?"

"Guy named Marvin," Kaeden answered.

"Never heard of him."

"Doesn't mean you couldn't have killed him," Ray said. The man took stubborn to a whole new level.

Liz dug a bottle of flat soda out of her bag and downed the liquid.

"Could have. Didn't."

"Prove it."

She glared at Ray. "Look, I don't know what your problem with me is, and I really don't give a shit, but I don't lie to cops. I had nothing to do with whatever happened last night, and if you weren't so busy trying to blame me, you'd go find out who really did the deed. Besides, if you check that bag on the landing, you'll see I had my own problems to deal with. I don't enjoy having to scrub poison out of my apartment at O dark thirty." Liz finished her soda, then wiped down the table with a nonchalance she didn't feel.

"Funny how every time you're around, we need a body bag," Ray sneered. "Just because you were clean ten years ago doesn't mean you are now."

"And just because you pretend to be human doesn't mean you are."

Liz had no idea where the words had come from, but as soon as she said them, she knew she'd spoken the truth. Dear old Uncle Ray was not human, though she didn't know exactly what species he belonged to. She'd seen him in bright sunlight, so probably not a vampire, though most of the ones she'd met could handle some sun for a brief period of time. From the narrow-eyed glare on his face, he resented her announcement. She rose and went over to him, standing less than a foot away, and studied him, and suddenly she knew. "Elf, but not full."

His face blanched, and he glanced at Kaeden. "You don't know what you're talking about."

She looked from Ray to Kaeden. "You never told him?" She wagged her finger in Ray's face. "Not nice, Uncle Ray. He really should know the truth."

Kaeden glanced from one to the other of them, back and forth. "What the hell are you talking about?"

"Not now," Ray said. "We have work to do."

"Liz?" Kaeden no longer sprawled in the chair. He'd sat straight up and frowned at both of them.

She shook her head. "Not for me to tell you, though I did sort of let the news slip. Give me a minute to freshen up, and I'll be right with you."

"You're not coming with us," Ray said. "This isn't your business."

Liz peered at him and saw the knowledge in his face. He hated this. Hated coming to her. Hated that he knew she could help him more than anyone. "You of all people know this is probably more my business than yours. I'll look at the body. If what I find is not what I think, the corpse is all yours. But if my guess pans out, we need to talk. You can't stop me, Ray. They won't let you."

"They have no power over me. This is my town. These are my people. I'll deal with the problem."

"If the body is nothing more than the usual, yes, you will." She left the rest of her sentence unsaid, but she knew Ray got the message.

"They? Who are you talking about?" Kaeden asked. "Are you talking about this organization you work for, Liz? Who are they? Who are you?"

Liz ran her hand through her short hair. "Kaeden, you've already heard more than is safe. But right now, I need to see this body." She went into the bathroom where she leaned against the sink and stared into the mirror. Her hair stood out in spikes, and dark circles under her eyes made her look like a raccoon, but overall, she figured she'd been worse. A quick sniff let her know the clothes weren't too rank. She ran a wet washcloth over her face and hair, taming down the worst of the spikes. Next, she unwound the bandage from her arm. The wound had already turned into a red scar. By tomorrow, even that would be nothing more than a bad memory, one more line among the dozens on her body. She waited until the angry voices from the outer room died down a little before going out.

When she returned to the living room, the garbage bag she'd put out was back inside and open. Ray wore heavy duty gloves and looked like he'd eaten several lemons, and Kaeden didn't look happy either.

"What is this?" Ray asked. "Looks like monkshood."

"Yep. Someone broke in while I was out last night and left me a message."

"You cleaned everything?" Kae asked.

"Yep. Including my mattress and furniture."

"Yeah, right. You? Clean up? That's not what you do, right?" This came from Ray.

"Okay, so you want to take me down for something I didn't do? You have a bag full of stuff possibly tainted with monkshood. Go ahead and take the mess so you can run your tests. But first think about this, last night, after walking over the entire town looking for—" She blew out a long breath. "Going over town, doing my job, I went out and killed someone, then I came back here and poisoned my own apartment, then spent the rest of the night cleaning that poison up. That about sum the facts up?"

Kaeden didn't bother to hide the smirk on his face. Ray just scowled more, but at least he stopped accusing her.

Liz grabbed her jacket, slipped on low boots, and tried to ignore the looks passing between Kaeden and his uncle. "Ready."

They started down the steps, Liz in the lead. When they got to the bottom, she glanced at the door to the diner, which stood open again. "I have to check with Charly first. I'll only be a sec."

Liz dashed in and found Charly taking inventory and doing orders. She looked like she hadn't slept in days. She probably hadn't. "Charly? Got a sec?"

"Sure. What's up?"

"Look, I don't know if this will make any sense to you, but...do us both a favor, and if you can, ward this entire building and put a protective spell around the whole place. A strong one."

She kind of peered at Liz, then nodded. "Okay."

"Thanks. I'm off with Kae and his uncle. Talk to you later."

"Damned straight."

Liz went over to her car. The guy at the garage had come in on Sunday, worked on the vehicle, and even cleaned off all the paint. When she tried to pay him, he waved her off. Said he owed Boreon a favor. From Virginia to here, small worlds, but she accepted his explanation.

She scrounged around in the back seat and found a couple of bottles of cola, downed one in a few gulps, and set the second one in the cup holder. Thus fortified, she followed Kaeden and his uncle to a place a couple of miles out of town to a ramshackle one-story cabin with weeds growing high in the yard and more junk than a junkyard. A steep hill rose sharply behind the house, leaving no room for a backyard, and a stream flowed across the front with a rickety bridge that looked like a bicycle would test the limits of support. They parked both vehicles on a grassy spot across the road. The coroner's van sat as close to the bridge as they could. She didn't blame them for not testing the stability of the span.

"Nice place," she said as she stepped over a broken shovel.

Kaeden offered his hand as they stone hopped across the stream. Slippery rocks seemed a lot safer than the alternative. "Lots of places like this in the hills, though not as many as there used to be. Most of the loners like Marvin here live deeper into the mountains."

Liz watched the coroner wheeled out a gurney. The official wore a plastic coverall and gas mask. She shuddered. If the outside looked bad, she wasn't sure she wanted to go inside.

Ray stopped the coroner. "Anything we need to know, Tom?"

She made no excuses as she stepped next to Ray and blatantly listened. The coroner glanced at her, then at Ray, who nodded at him. He removed his mask and took a deep breath. "Only odd thing was how fast the body decomposed. Neighbors saw him outside two days ago. But the body was already well on the way to rotten when we got here. Would almost make sense if this was August and hot as the blazes, but we've had freezing temps the last few nights, and his house has no heat."

"You sure the body is Marvin?"

"Yeah. I IDed him myself. You want to make certain?"

"Nah."

Liz went up the steps, then got a whiff from the inside of the house. A smell she recognized. "Ray, I need to see the body."

The coroner did a double take, then glanced at Ray who said, "Let her."

Tom unzipped the bag, then doubled over, retching into the grass. The other men gagged on the odor of sulfur, skunk, and ammonia. Liz didn't need to see what she knew. The smell told her enough. She quickly zipped the bag back up. "Do yourself a favor. Burn that—bag and all."

"I have to do an autopsy," the coroner said. "That's the law."

"There's nothing to autopsy, and whatever you do, don't let what's left in that bag touch anything organic, including you."

"Ray?"

Ray studied her, then went over to the coroner. "Do what she says. This is one of our special cases."

Tom sighed but nodded. "I'm getting too old for this crap. I guess you'll take care of the paperwork as usual?"

"Yes."

Liz strolled around the house—studying the shack from the outside rather than going in. She would avoid going inside until she eventually had to. The place barely claimed to be a hovel, so why had one of the blobs been here? She turned as Kaeden came up with a bundle he handed her.

"I guess you want to go inside? This is a plastic coverall and gas mask. Tom always has a couple extra ones on hand."

"Thanks." Grateful for the barrier, she pulled the suit on while Kaeden did likewise. Ray already wore a heavier model. She tugged on the mask and followed Kae's uncle inside, Kaeden close behind. Even with the mask, she could still taste the stench, but the smell didn't merely come from the creature that had died there. Rotting trash, food, and dead rats lay everywhere.

As she stood in the front room of the two-room cabin, a tingle ran through her, like a low-voltage electric shock, but steadier. Liz had felt that buzz before. A node, but building up energy? Or drained? With the body in the bag, she'd bet on drained, but not completely. Some paranormals could channel the energy, but doing so took a toll. Not everyone could handle the power. But she'd at least figured out why Bannig was here.

In the kitchen, she studied a circular bare spot in one corner. About three feet in diameter and the only spot in the house not covered with dirt and debris, the area looked like someone had lit a fire there. The boards were charred, and some sort of goo covered them. The remains of the blob? Keeping her plastic gloves firmly in place, she laid her hand on the floor. She felt the power. The node hadn't been completely drained. Power flowed through her and reached out. Filling her. Building until she sensed everything around. Beneath them, something else was happening. Something not good. She had to get the men out of there. Fast.

"Kaeden! Get out!"

"Liz?" Kaeden asked.

"Get out now!" She yanked at the back door, but the wood had sealed shut. Liz all but pushed Kaeden and Ray back through the living room to the front. When needed, she could be a little stronger than most people. Not superhuman, but enough to make a difference. And right then, with her adrenaline pumping and the power flowing through her, she put out some major shoving. A rumbling she could feel in her bones rose from the floor. The men stared at her as if she'd gone mad but moved toward the door.

"Not fast enough! Go!"

Chapter Nine

The rumbling grew, and the men finally understood and clambered over the piles of trash to the front. The door blew shut. All three of them yanked at the stubborn wood before the door opened. The entire house buckled and shuddered. They barely made their way to the front yard before the house caved in.

"Keep moving!" Liz urged them to the road. She didn't know how far the opening would extend, but she refused to take chances. They dashed across the two lanes as the house disappeared into a rapidly expanding sinkhole. Blue lightning streaked around the edges.

As soon as the house disappeared, the hole stopped growing, and the sparks died down a few minutes later. They stood there staring, then Ray got on his radio and called for help. Kaeden grabbed a roll of crime tape from the back of his uncle's car, and he and Liz began to cordon off the area. Fortunately, there were no nearby neighbors to gape or get into trouble. Still, a couple of cars pulled up, and people stared at the spot. Ray did what he could to move them on, telling them a sinkhole had opened up.

Once they had the area blocked off, Liz leaned against her car and studied the hole. The rim was perfectly round and nearly as deep as wide. This was no natural sinkhole. She got as close as she could, knelt, and laid her hands on the ground, closed her eyes, and let her senses take in everything. The buzz still lingered, but lower in intensity now, like a storm that had blown itself out. She drank in what was there, absorbing the power like a dry sponge does water. The buzz left her feeling as if she could do anything. But, like any storm, she knew the node had been stronger. Exactly how strong was the question.

She'd encountered nodes before, but not like this. And none that had ever caused a sinkhole or any other kind of problem. And after Boreon's warning about six are one, her gut clenched in knots.

Kaeden and Ray approached her as she knelt there, absorbing the energy. Liz rose and peeled off the hazmat suit, wondering what she would tell them.

"What did Tom haul out of that house?" Ray asked. "And exactly what happened here?"

She pursed her lips and glanced around at the growing gawkers. "A story best left for quieter places. We need to talk, but not here." She nodded at another car slowing down. "My guess is, you're going to get other spectators here."

"My place," Kaeden said.

"I'll meet you there," Liz said. She frowned when Kaeden opened her passenger door.

"I'm going with you." His tone said no arguing. So rather than do so, she went around and tossed the trash from the passenger seat into the back. Normally, she kept her car pristine, but she hadn't had the time lately. Kaeden picked up a receipt she'd dropped. The one from the little mom-and-pop store where she'd met her biker stalker. "So, you've been in Florida?"

"Among other places." Liz slid in behind the wheel and waited for him to buckle in. "Where I've been isn't important. What's happening here is."

"What is happening?"

She shook her head. "Not until we're with your uncle. He needs to know this, and there's no point in going over the story twice. Besides, I need to get some thoughts clear in my mind before we talk."

"That was no sinkhole back there."

"No."

"You felt something. A buzz like electricity, but more. Stronger. You knew what was going to happen."

She glanced at him. He described the sensation exactly. "Yes. And no. Tell me what you felt."

They were driving through a wooded area, the river on their left, a steep hill on the right. They were rounding a sharp curve when her senses buzzed, and Liz slammed on her brakes and yanked the wheel to the side. She threw the gears in reverse as a large boulder slammed down into the roadway, narrowly missing them. Kaeden swore, then held on as Liz changed gears again and sped around the rock, the side of her car scraping the guardrail on one side, the rock on the other. Ray had stopped on the back side and got out of his car.

She glanced at Kae. "Tell him to move his ass! He can investigate later. He needs to be out of there. Now."

Kaeden rolled down his window and yelled at Ray as smaller stones rained down on them. Ray jumped in his car, twisted around the rock, and both cars sped off. Her passenger stared at her the whole way to his place. Liz ignored the look, turned into his driveway, shut the car off, and sat there breathing. Too many things were happening too fast, and she was like a blindfolded man in a sandstorm, not knowing which way to go.

Liz stared at Kaeden's house. In addition to the building, he had a small barn out back that served as garage and storage. Huge trees shaded both the buildings and a large yard. She could imagine kids playing there, building tree houses, swinging from the branches. His was a house built for a family. A life she'd never have, but he deserved. And she had to give him that chance. No matter what.

"What are you?" Kaeden asked. His voice was quiet but still startling in the silence of the car.

The next few minutes were going to be rather difficult. "I'll tell you inside."

They got out, and she followed Kaeden inside where she headed for the office. She took one of the chairs in front of the desk, and Kaeden took the one behind. Ray joined them a minute later.

They all looked up as Charly strolled into the room. "Got a message that I needed to be here."

"From whom?" Ray asked.

Charly stared at him as Liz bit back a laugh. She hadn't been wrong about her boss and friend. Her witch powers only made up a part of Charly. But like Liz, her secrets were hers.

"Not important. Here I am." She curled up in a corner of the sofa. "So, you going to tell me what's going on, or do I have to get nasty?"

Liz grinned, then sobered and started the conversation. One she really didn't want to have but needed to. "Kaeden, you asked me what I am. The truth is, nobody knows, and believe me, I've tried to find out. I do know I'm part elf, part witch, part psychic, and a little bit of other beings thrown in. Basically, I'm whatever I need to be when I need to be. The only thing

I can't do is shapeshift. I'm pretty much what you see."

"You called my uncle an elf. You were being serious?"

"Yes. I called him that because he is one. At least in part. So are you." Liz didn't know why she'd never seen the proof, but then, she hadn't been looking. Usually when they were together, she had other activities on her mind.

"That's ridiculous. Fairy tales. Stuff of stories," Ray blustered.

Liz glanced at Ray who'd gone beet red. Ray had raised Kaeden and his sister after their parents died in a car accident. "You've never told him his heritage?" She turned back to Kaeden. "What your uncle never thought to tell you is that there are more beings in this world than humans. There are elves, lycans, vamps, shape-shifters, witches who can do magic, and more. That creature the coroner took out of that house did not belong to the human realm."

She glanced at Charly. "Does he know about you?"

Charly shrugged. "I've never kept my background a secret, but most don't understand, or believe. But I'm happy to know you're one of us, even if only in part."

Kaeden did a double take on Charly, then glared at his uncle. "All those special cases. You knew and you never told me."

He snorted. "Need to know basis and you didn't need to know."

"I didn't need to know that I'm not human? What else don't I need to know? Becky's pregnant. Is her baby going to be weird? Is she part elf too?" Kaeden jumped up and paced the floor from door to desk and back.

"Your sister is fine, and so is her baby. Doc Andersen is keeping an eye on her," Ray said.

"She knows," Kaeden said. "And so does Andersen."

Ray nodded. "I told her before she got married. And Andersen has to. He's the town doctor. Some of our citizens require special care."

Kaeden sank down on the sofa. "So, when were you going to tell me?"

Liz could see every emotion crossing his handsome face—horror, betrayal, confusion, and more.

"If you'd ever gotten serious with anyone but her, I'd have told you." Ray spat out the word *her* like he'd bitten into a piece of rotten meat. *Gee. Nice to know his real feelings about me. Ha.*

She turned her chair around to face Kaeden. "Family issues aside, we've got a bigger problem. That hole back at Martin's was a power node—a drained one. That's what happened to that *thing* the coroner took out. The *thing* tried to contain the power and couldn't. I'm also afraid there are going to be more nodes." Liz didn't tell them she'd been able to absorb the rest of the energy. They didn't need to know that.

Ray snorted. "That's ridiculous. Even if there was one, and I'm not agreeing with you about that, there's never more than one in any area."

"When six are one, the time is come," Liz intoned. She noticed Ray's face had gone from red to snow white.

"Where did you hear that?"

"Boreon told me. And from the vibes I'm getting from you, you've heard that saying before."

"An old fairy tale," Ray grumbled. "Nothing

92

more."

Kaeden snorted. "Like elves and werewolves and vampires are tales. Enough, Uncle Ray. Tell us what you know. I've got a feeling—gee, maybe my elf senses are finally kicking in—but I think Liz needs to know." He turned back to her. "That's what you do, right? You deal with problems like this. You're some kind of superhuman agent."

"She is not!" Ray paced the room. "She's an anomaly. Dangerous. Unpredictable. I told the council she should never have been—" He stopped in mid-stride, his mouth hanging open, his eyes wide.

"Never have been what?" Liz asked quietly. She'd never heard anyone say anything about her origins. "Born? Or created?"

Ray didn't move. Not so much as a twitch. Liz rose and strode over to him. She waved her hand in his face. Not a blink. She pinched his hand. Nothing. She glanced at Kaeden who'd joined her. "Seems like Uncle Ray has said more than he ought to."

"What happened? Is he all right?"

"Yes. He's spelled. You can think of what happened as sort of like hypnosis. There's a suggestion that when he's about to reveal something he shouldn't, he stops."

"How long will the…this…spell last?"

"No telling. My guess is a few minutes. Long enough for him to realize what he almost did. Charly, you're probably more adept at this than I am. Can you tell?"

Charly rose and approached Ray. She laid her hands on his shoulders, closed her eyes, and blew out a deep breath. A moment later, she opened her eyes and shook her head. "Strongest spell I've ever encountered. Nothing we can do until the enchantment runs its course."

She went back to the sofa and curled up again.

"Can he hear us?" Kaeden asked.

"I don't know. Depends on how deep the spell is, but my guess is, yes," Liz answered.

Kaeden faced his uncle. "I hope you can hear me, Uncle Ray, because I don't want to have to say this again. I appreciate everything you did for Becky and me. You were there for us when our folks died, but you are an ass. You had no right to keep this information from me. And you had no right to treat Liz the way you've been treating her. When this mess is over, you will tell me everything. Everything. Or you are out of my life. I cannot forgive you for this."

He went to the sofa and sat down next to Charly. Liz studied Ray. A single tear tracked down his lined face, and she almost pitied him. Almost. Kaeden got one thing right, Ray was an ass, but she understood trying to protect family. Okay, she didn't really understand since she'd never had one, but if that kind of closeness came anywhere close to what she felt toward Charly and Kaeden, the emotion went beyond strong. "I think he got the message."

"Now, about these power nodes," Kaeden said.

Liz dragged her chair to sit across from him and Charly, the coffee table between them. "You've heard of ley lines?"

"Yes. Lines of energy that crisscross the world," Charly said.

"Sometimes when multiple lines cross, they form a power node. Doesn't happen all the time. If so, we'd really be in deep shit. But once in a while, when the circumstances are exactly right, they do. A power node is like a battery. If you have the right connections, you can tap into the energy and drain the force, taking on that power for yourself."

"What kind of beings can drain a node?" Charly asked.

"Some witches, some elves, demons. And me. There are probably others too, but those are the ones I know for certain."

"Some? Not all?" Kaeden asked.

"No. Not everyone is power sensitive. You obviously are, or you wouldn't have been able to sense the buzz back at the house. But you did, didn't you?"

"I felt something—like if I put my hand on a piece of electrical that's got a short somewhere in the line."

"A heavy buzz."

"Yeah."

They all looked as Ray stumbled, then caught himself. Kaeden glared at him but didn't say anything. Liz nodded and went back to her explanation. Ray wouldn't tell her anything else about her background, she knew that, so there was no point in questioning him. But she would get to the truth eventually.

"How do you absorb the power?" Kaeden asked.

"There are a couple of different ways, but the easiest is to stand dead center and draw the energy into yourself. Problem is most people can't take on that much pure energy without serious consequences."

"Like what?" Charly asked.

"Like killing them," Ray said.

"Thought you said they were a fairy tale," Kaeden sneered.

Ray blew out a long breath. "I may have misstated." He turned to Liz. "But six? That's unheard of."

"So now you believe." She stared at him and then understood. "Had a little talk with the Powers, did you? Or rather, they talked, and you listened."

"Powers?" Kaeden asked.

Dang. Liz sighed. The explanation got more complicated with each word. "Another long story for another time. We've got enough to deal with right now. If what I think is happening really is, things around here are going to get real bad—real fast."

"Who do you think is the problem?" Ray asked.

"My old mentor. Bannig." Liz noted that Ray didn't flinch, so maybe he didn't know about Bannig. "When you kicked me out ten years ago, he recruited me for my bosses. Taught me everything I needed to know. And yes, Kaeden and Charly, I am an agent. I work for an organization that deals with these types of situations. The only thing is, I've never seen my bosses. Only my trainer, Bannig. Unfortunately, three years ago, a demon took him over."

"You've met him since as the demon?" Ray asked.

Liz barely kept from wincing as she thought about the scar across her ribs. "Several times. Most recently, here in Clear Water. I don't believe in coincidences. Bannig is here for the power nodes. If the demon in him drains the rest, he'll be unstoppable."

"Which means what?"

"All hell breaks loose, Kaeden," Charly said quietly. "My coven divined that something bad would happen this week, but none of us could figure out what. Then when Liz showed up, hurting and a mess, I had a sense her appearance was connected."

"So, we need to keep him from the nodes," Kaeden said. "Where are they?"

Everyone looked at Liz. She really hated letting them down, but she had no choice. "Therein lies the problem. I have no clue." She glanced at Ray. "You wouldn't by any chance have a ley line map, would you?"

"No, but I might be able to get one."

"Charly, can you sense the lines?"

"Yes, but not as easily as you. I'd have to be standing right on top of one before I can sense the energy, and even then, my awareness is weak. I'm not attuned to that kind of power."

"Ray, what about you?"

"About the same as Charly."

"Okay. In that case, Kaeden, you're the next strongest besides me. You and I need to go for a long walk."

"Excuse me?"

She could see the confusion on his face and didn't blame him. Finding out he wasn't completely human was bad enough, but then to have to deal with a whole bunch of non-human crap on top of that while facing the possible apocalypse would be a lot for anyone. She had to give him kudos though. He appeared to be handling the situation better than most people would.

"We can't find the lines from a car—too much metal around us, so we're going to need to walk the streets and discover what we can sense. Charly, you and Ray see if you can come up with a map of some sort. We'll—"

Charly interrupted. "We'll go back to my place and get some food into you."

Liz shook her head. "I'm good."

Charly snorted, and Kaeden raised his eyebrow at Liz, and she knew she had lost the argument before she even started.

"So far today, she's had a granola bar that contained more sugar than nutrition and three colas," Kaeden threw out.

Charly blanched. "When you come down off that sugar-caffeine high, you are going to be hurtin'. Food. Real food. Now."

"Tattletale," she mouthed to Kaeden. He grinned back at her, completely unrepentant.

****

An hour later, full of steak sandwiches, fries, and salads, Kaeden and Liz headed out on their walk.

"Which way?" Kaeden couldn't believe that he was out here, trying to find something called ley lines—which he seemed to be sensitive to. *Because he was part elf!* Like his uncle and his sister. And Liz... Liz was some sort of super-agent. And Charly was a real witch with magic. And someone named Bannig, a real demon who was determined to kill Liz and take over the world.

Chaos filled so much of Kaeden's mind that he forced himself to shut down that part of his brain and concentrate on the matter at hand. Although, when he glanced at Liz, all that he'd learned sort of made sense concerning her. Okay, so he still didn't know everything about her, but he knew more than he had, and knowing even what little he did made her more intriguing.

He watched as Liz stood in the middle of the street, eyes closed, ignoring the traffic coming. Kae dashed out and tried to direct the cars around her. *Was she insane? Or was he?*

Finally, she opened her eyes and shrugged. "I'm not getting anything, so one way is as good as another."

Back on the sidewalk, Kae watched in amazement as Liz sat down and pulled off her boots and socks, stuffed her socks in the boots, tied them together, and slung them over her shoulder. "Are you nuts? You'll freeze!"

"This is also the best way to sense what's underground." She raised an eyebrow at him, glanced at his shoes, then back up, a smile on her lips.

Kaeden sighed. This clinched the earlier insanity thought, but he joined her. The pavement felt damned cold, but also kind of invigorating—at first. Twenty blocks later, his feet sore from stones and other stuff he'd stepped on, he wouldn't be surprised if he had a touch of frostbite.

They'd done a five-block square, ending up back at the diner, and he'd sensed nothing. Neither had Liz he guessed from the frustration he saw on her face.

"Guess we'll try a wider search," Liz said through chattering teeth.

Kae could barely hold back his own shivers, but at least he'd had on a heavy jacket, hat, and gloves unlike Liz in her light windbreaker. She had to be freezing because he certainly was. He steered her toward the back of the diner and the steps up to her place.

"We need to get warm. And think this through. There has to be a better way to do this." They sat on the bottom steps and put on their footwear, then went up the metal steps. Kae stood close to her while she unlocked the door, blocking the breeze that had sprung up. When she opened the door, he stopped in shock and grabbed her before she could go in.

Everything not nailed down in the apartment had been piled on her sofa bed and covered with filth, red paint—he hoped that red stuff was paint—and what smelled like oil.

"What the hell!"

Kae held onto Liz, turning as he heard Charly calling them. She climbed the steps and held out a large Kraft envelope. "I came up to tell you my wards had been breached." She glanced inside. "But I guess you know."

"Any idea when?" Liz asked.

"Probably while we were at Kae's. Whoever did this is good. I didn't even know until a few minutes ago when I went to strengthen them and found them gone." She pointed at the mess. "Any idea who did this?"

"Bannig. Or more likely someone working for him. You'd need him to get past your wards, but I doubt he did the actual work." Liz pulled away from Kaeden and entered the apartment. "He wouldn't be bothered with something this dirty. This isn't his style. I'll bet you a week's worth of tips my stalker friend did this. He and I are going to have a long discussion one of these days, and he isn't going to like the outcome."

Kaeden could almost feel the dark anger rolling off her. Thunder rumbled loud enough to shake the building, but when he glanced at the sky, there weren't any clouds. Then he studied Liz with her clenched fists. Her? No. Couldn't be. Could it?

Liz ducked past Kaeden, holding her nose against the smell. The odor almost had him gagging. He studied her closely. She seemed calm. Too calm. But he could also see a tightening around her eyes, the clenched jaw. She had to be beyond angry. He certainly would be if someone had done this to him. Plus, she didn't really have much in the way of belongings. And now…she had nothing.

"Garbage bags are under the sink."

Kaeden stared at her. "We need to call Uncle Ray. He should see this. At least report this."

Liz pulled the box of trash bags out along with a pair of rubber gloves. "No point. We both know why they did this. They want me out of town. Not going to happen. They tried several times to stop me on my way here, yet here I am. And here is where I'm going to stay. I've got a job to do."

"Liz?" Kaeden gaped at her. She couldn't be serious. But just in case, he grabbed his phone and took multiple shots of the damage.

Liz sighed and put down the *Grateful Dead* T-shirt she'd picked up. She'd picked up the old T-shirt at a used clothing shop for nothing—a cast-off, like most of the rest of her stuff. Like her. And now, the shirt belonged in the garbage. Like her. "It's like this. You said I'm some kind of super-agent. Well, I am. And I get death threats all the time. This isn't the first and won't be the last, though this is the first time they've come into where I live. They were sending a message. And I'm going to send one right back. I am not leaving. This is my town. They are not welcome here."

Liz grabbed the envelope Charly still held and ripped the seal open. Sure enough, she found another picture inside, this one of Charly and her in the diner. She didn't care about herself. She could handle most anything Bannig and his minions threw at her, but she would not let anything hurt Charly. Or Kaeden.

Kaeden stared at the picture, his eyes wide and mouth opening and shutting. "You've gotten other pictures like this? When? Why didn't you report them?"

"Report them to who? Your uncle? Yeah, like that would have worked." Kaeden's anger was nothing compared to Liz's. The pictures were her problem to deal with, and she would. She knew if she opened her mouth, something nasty would come out. Something she didn't want hanging in the air between them, so she turned around, stormed out the back door, and down the steps. In the few minutes since they'd come in, rain had started falling. Hard. As she left, she could hear Charly telling him to let her go. Smart woman.

Too bad he wasn't a smart man.

Chapter Ten

"Liz!"

She ignored him and went to her car. Climbing inside, Liz locked the doors and sat there, her hands on the steering wheel, hair dripping, wet clothes, and all. The temptation to turn the key in the ignition and drive away pulled at her. She should turn her back on this place and not look back. Let whatever was going to happen here, happen.

Except she couldn't. She cared about these people. About this place. She couldn't unleash Bannig on them. And now Kaeden was standing outside, in the pouring rain, staring at her.

"Open the door, Liz."

Liz closed her eyes and leaned against the back of the seat, trying hard to ignore him.

Then she heard a noise at the passenger side window and the sound of the lock popping. That's what she got for falling for a cop. They knew how to break into cars. She kept her eyes closed, trying not to pay attention as Kae climbed in. At least, that was her plan. He was one hard-to-ignore hunk. The scent that belonged to him filled her nose, and she breathed deeply. Gods, what would life be like to wake up every day to that aroma?

She shook her head. Dangerous territory there. She was a nomad. No roots. Unfettered. Footloose and fancy free. A rolling stone. A tumbleweed. Could she come up with any more clichés that meant no commitments? She mentally started to make a list and had barely gotten six when she heard him shift in the seat.

"Liz, we need to talk."

"I don't need to do anything. You want to talk, talk." Liz still hadn't opened her eyes. She was afraid if she did, she'd melt or some other such nonsense.

"Nice ride. How's your mileage?"

That got her eyes open. She hadn't expected him to ask about her car. She'd expected recriminations about running away, but he asked about her car. He was devious. "Not great, but not too bad."

He glanced in the back where she still had her sleeping pad laid out, along with a couple of boxes of odds and ends, all neatly labeled. "So, you really do sleep here when you're away?"

"Yep. Sleep. Eat. Live. This is my home away from home."

"Not that I blame you, but why this and not a van?"

"This was a gift."

"Whew! What'd you have to do to earn this?"

Liz stared at him, and he grinned back, unapologetic. "I helped a family get rid of a nasty spirit."

"A ghost?"

"No. Ghosts are disembodied spirits stuck here either because of unfinished business or because they refuse to pass over. There are other things that go bump in the night, and some of them are definitely not friendly."

"Some? Not all?"

He turned to her, and she shivered. She told herself the chills were because of the temperature. Yeah. Right. Her feet were cold, but other parts of her were heating up. "Absolutely not. There are spirits who exist to help us poor lowly humans. Most people generally refer to them as angels."

"Angels are real?"

"As real as you are."

He moved closer. Unfortunately, with the gear shift in the center, he couldn't get next to her, but he came as close as he could.

"Are you real?" he asked. He touched her hand, but she refused to move. If she did, she wasn't sure she'd be able to keep from jumping his bones.

"As real as can be." Why did her voice sound so deep and breathy?

His hand moved up her arm. "I don't think so."

His breath tickled her ear. "You don't think so. What? That I'm real?" Yep. Her voice. She never knew she could sound like that.

He reached across and pulled her closer to him. By then, her brain had ceased to function.

"You're like this car."

Oh great, just what a girl wants to hear, that she's like a car. Thanks a lot.

"You're all hard and polished on the outside, and warm and comfortable on the inside."

Well, he got one thing right. Her insides were definitely warm. Much warmer and she would self-combust. Especially when he started nibbling on her earlobe. Then he moved lower, and she was lost.

Things were getting really interesting when a bolt of lightning struck almost in the middle of the parking lot. They jumped apart as if they'd been shot.

"We should get upstairs," she managed to say. "Charly is probably wondering what happened to us."

"Yeah. Right."

So, they headed back up the steps double-time because of the storm. When they pushed open the door, Charly stood to the side of the pile, a plastic trash bag over her clothes and a bandana tied over her mouth and nose. She had on rubber gloves and held another trash bag nearly as big as she was. She looked so silly in her getup, Liz couldn't help but laugh. Then something happened, and Liz couldn't stop laughing. Then she started crying. She did not cry. Ever. Crying meant she had a weakness, and she refused to allow weaknesses in herself. She'd been weak the last time she met Bannig. If she hadn't been, they wouldn't be facing him now.

But she couldn't stop. Kaeden came over and folded her into his arms, and she continued to sob until there were no tears left.

"Better?" he asked when she finally calmed down.

"No. But thanks." Nothing had been resolved. Nothing settled, and she knew they were going to have one heck of a discussion one of these times, but not now. Now they need to clean up. She pushed away from him and grabbed another bag.

Charly held up a pair of shorts that weren't too badly stained. "Some of these things can be cleaned."

"Toss 'em," Liz instructed. "I think I know who did this, and I don't want to wear something he touched." This was something a human would do. A human with dirty fingernails and injuries where her knives had hit their marks.

Charly nodded. "Got you."

When Kaeden held up a lacy black thong, embarrassment heated her face, but she shrugged and held the bag open. She knew for certain she'd never wear any of the clothes again. Maybe some could have been salvaged, but she didn't care. Besides, all this was merely stuff. She didn't need stuff. She was an agent for O.W.L., and agents didn't put down roots. This was what happened when they did.

The three of them made quick work of cleaning up the place. By the time they finished, the apartment looked like no one had ever stayed there. Everything had been stripped bare and scrubbed down. Kaeden hauled five bags of trash down to the dumpster. She got the one remaining bag out of her car. It held one change of clothes along with a few toiletries. The pile looked pitifully small, but at least those items were clean.

"You're not thinking of staying here," Charly said.

"Of course, I am. This is my apartment."

"Liz, you can't," Kaeden said. "What if they come back?"

Faster than they could blink, she yanked two knives from her boots and let them fly at the door, both hitting at nearly the same time in almost exactly the same spot. A second later, two others joined them. Charly and Kaeden stood there, mouths agape. "They didn't come while I was here. And if they do, I'll be ready."

"Fine," Charly said. "But I'm going to cleanse this place and set stronger wards all the way around. I should have done so earlier like you said, but I got busy at the diner. If I'd known…"

"Not your fault. I should have set stronger ones of my own—a mistake I won't make again. You take care of your place and the diner. I'll set my own here."

"You okay with a cleansing? Or do you want to take care of that too?"

Liz could have, but she knew Charly needed to do something to help. "I'd appreciate if you did. I'm not exactly flush with herbs at the moment."

"Be back up shortly."

After Charly left, Kaeden faced her. "I don't care how formidable you are. You're not staying here by yourself."

"I'm perfectly capable of taking care of myself."

"Yeah, I can see that. What if you'd been here when they came?"

"Then they'd be dead, and I'd still have my stuff."

"Are you so sure of that? That bullet wound says otherwise."

She yanked the dressing off her completely healed wound. "This? Less than a scratch, which I can handle. What I can't handle is if something were to happen to you or Charly."

"We can take care of ourselves. We're not helpless, Liz. We may not have your powers, but we know how to protect ourselves."

"No, you don't. Not from this. Not from the things I face."

"Tell us. Let us in, Liz. Let us help."

"For now, will you settle for some advice? Don't get in my way if something happens."

He glanced at the knives still stuck in the door, then held up his hands in a surrender motion. "If that was a demonstration of what you can do when you're merely pissed, I will definitely stay out of your way. I'm going to run home to get some things, but I'll be back."

"Fine. But be sure to knock and do not come in unless I tell you."

He glanced at the knives again. "Understood."

Charly made quick work of cleansing the small apartment, leaving behind the scent of sage and other herbs. Once she left, Liz went around the place, checking the windows, especially the one at the fire escape, as well as the lock on the door. Whoever had broken in had been good. She didn't find any signs of forced entry—almost as if they'd had a key or were exceptionally good with lock picks. Or used magic. She bet on the last. Demon magic.

Liz set her wards around the room, then, at each opening, she added salt and other herbs Charly had given her. Then she set some manual traps and added a spell that would stop anything from coming in unless she invited them. By the time she finished, the place was a fortress. An empty one, but still a fortress.

Finally, she sat down on the sofa—a sofa that no longer even had a mattress as that had been covered in filth as well. Liz stared at the bare place. The room looked the same as when she'd moved in. She'd had a little more than what she had now—her backpack and an overnight bag. The bags held everything she owned. Not even blankets to sleep in. Bannig's minions had done her a favor. They'd taught her a lesson she needed to remember. No attachments. Nothing to tie her down. She didn't need things. Or people. Or anything. She was an agent on the job. Her job was her life. Period.

Liz jumped as a heavy knock sounded at the door, then settled back down. Minions didn't knock. She didn't even bother to get up. "Come on in, Kaeden."

He pushed the door open with one foot and hauled in two huge suitcases and had a backpack over his shoulders. In other words, he had more with him than she even owned at that moment.

"What the hell? You planning on moving in?"

"If I thought you'd let me, I would." He dumped the suitcases on the sofa. "I'll be right back."

When he came back, he had a handcart that had a large, plastic-covered object strapped to the handles. "Give me a hand."

Puzzled, Liz went to him. "What do you need me to do?"

He unstrapped the object and laid the thing on the floor. "Take one of those knives of yours and carefully slit the plastic."

When she did, the bag opened, and a thick foam mattress began to unroll and expand. "A mattress?"

"I ordered this for my guest bedroom but haven't put it up yet. Obviously. So...here you go."

Liz laughed and shook her head. "I don't believe this. You brought me a mattress."

"And more." He went to the suitcases and opened them. Inside were pillows, blankets, sheets, towels, and more. "Thought these would come in handy too."

His thoughtfulness touched her. A moment later, she heard another knock. "Come in, Charly."

Charly pushed open the door, her arms full of bags. "Thought you could use these."

She emptied out containers of food that she stowed in the refrigerator and cabinet as well as a six-pack of cold beer.

"Definitely could use this," Liz said as she grabbed one of the bottles. "Thank you."

"No prob. Kae, you staying here?" Charly asked.

"Yep. Don't care how talented our agent is, I am not letting her stay here alone tonight."

"Looks like we're having a slumber party then," Charly commented. "Unless you don't want me here?" She wiggled her eyebrows at Kaeden.

Liz tossed one of the pillows at her. "Doesn't matter what he wants. My place, my rules. And I say you stay." That cold spot inside her that she kept trying to grab onto warmed up. She didn't need anybody, but she wanted these two people here.

They chatted and drank until the wee hours of the morning. Charly fell asleep first, curled up on the end of the mattress. Kaeden nodded off shortly after—his head on Liz's lap, his arm draped across her legs. She sat there, Charly at her feet, and wondered when she had turned into this person who had a home and friends. The change had happened so gradually, she hadn't noticed, but the change had happened. She leaned against the back of the sofa and sipped her drink.

She'd never had a problem dealing with the entities she dealt with. Went in, did the job, and left. No emotions. No ties. But this time, what they'd done was personal. And she'd be damned if she'd let anyone, or anything, hurt these two people.

Chapter Eleven

Well after dawn, Liz carefully climbed out of bed and headed for the shower. She leaned against the wall, letting the water sluice over her. Out in the other room rested two people who had worked their way into her soul. Charly had become the sister she'd never had. And honestly, better than a sister. She was the friend Liz had dreamed of when she was a kid. Charly accepted Liz, faults and all. She yelled at her when she needed it and held her hand when she needed that too.

Then there was Kaeden. Much more than a one-night stand, he was the embodiment of everything she wanted in a mate, but she kept pushing him away. Why?

"Because he scares me," she told the water. "I want him so much, I can't breathe, but look at my life. I never know when I'll have to leave, how long I'll be gone, or even if I'll live long enough to come back."

"And I get that, now."

Liz opened her eyes to find Kaeden standing there, his head at the edge of the shower curtain. He swept the material aside and stepped in. His scent reminded her of clean mountain forests. She eyed him from head to foot and back up again, enjoying the view. "Awfully brave of you to come in like that," she teased.

"Figured you wouldn't have any knives on you in here."

He might have figured that, but he didn't know her as well as he thought. She had at least one within easy reach, plus her razor. "I have other ways of dealing with problems that don't involve weapons."

"I know."

Kaedon picked up the soap, one eyebrow raised. What could she do? Kick him out? No way. She nodded and surrendered.

Liz leaned back against him as he ran his hands over her chest and abdomen, working his way down. Damn that felt good.

By the time they turned off the controls, the water had gone cold. They had played each other like fine-tuned instruments, and both reached release. Liz had never had a partner who could satisfy her like Kaeden did. She'd had liaisons before she met him, usually short, as in one-hour types of hookups—not even one-night stands—but nobody had ever touched her like he did. She didn't know why she didn't feel the need to hold back with him, which made all the difference. And even more so now that he knew about her.

When they left the shower, they were alone in the apartment. "Guess she figured we didn't need any help," Kaeden snickered.

"No, but I could use a couple urns of coffee."

"Agreed."

They headed down to the diner, grinning when they walked into the aroma of freshly brewed coffee, bacon, eggs, and home fries cooking on the grill. Charly sipped from a mug while she cooked. "So, you two have fun?"

"Don't know what you're talking about," Liz deadpanned as she grabbed a mug and plates.

With a grin as big as the sinkhole, Kaeden took the

spatula away from Charly. "Definitely."

What was this thing about guys and their sexual egos? Still, Liz couldn't help the grin on her face either. Best shower she'd had in a long time, if ever.

"'Bout damn time," Charly said. "So, what's our modus operandi today?"

Liz held out the plates for Kaeden to fill. "You talk to your contacts and try to find a ley line map of the area. Kaeden and I are going hunting. We'll start at the source of the last node and work outward on a pattern from there."

"That makes more sense than randomly walking the streets," Kaeden agreed.

"Charly, I know you don't open for a couple of hours, and you've got a lot to do, but is there any way you can use your resources to see if any of them can sense ley lines?"

"Will do. I'll call Kaeden if I find anything."

"Great. Thanks."

They finished their breakfast in companionable silence, cleaned up the area, and headed out. "My car or yours?" Kaeden asked.

"Mine. I've got some equipment we can use, plus more…uh, resources."

"You mean weapons."

"Yes."

"Works for me." He climbed into the passenger side. "Let's go."

They drove back to the sinkhole. Not that there were a lot of choices, but Liz took a different route from the original one they'd used, one that didn't go between the river and cliff. She figured there was no reason to invite trouble.

"So, who do you think trashed your place?" Kaeden asked.

"The same dork who dogged me all the way from Florida. And yes, the same one who gave me my newest scar. I should have taken care of him the first time I saw him."

"I'm surprised you didn't."

That he thought so little of her hurt. "Whether or not you believe me, I'm not some bloodthirsty killer. I take care of the job. If I have to kill something or someone, I will, without hesitation—usually. But if I don't, I don't. And I don't kill humans. At least, not ones who don't need killing. I might make an exception with this one, though."

"So, what is Bannig to you, and why didn't you kill him the last time?"

Liz pulled into the grassy area across from the sinkhole, shut off the car, and leaned against the steering wheel, her chin on top, and stared out the windshield. "That was the only time I hesitated. I had him dead to rights, and he knew it, and I stopped. He's the one who gave me that ugly scar across my ribs."

Kaeden winced. "That could have been a killing slice."

"Almost was. Took more than a few stitches to take care of." The scar remained as a reminder to Liz never to hesitate, no matter what—or who—she was up against.

"Still, you couldn't kill someone you knew so well. Someone you cared about. There's nothing wrong with that."

She sat up straight and glared at him. "Yes, there is! If I'd taken care of him then, we wouldn't be in this mess now."

He stayed calm in the face of her anger—which irked her even more.

"You don't know that for sure. If a demon took him over like you said, that thing would have taken over another body, right?"

"No. Not if I'd done my job right."

"Liz, you can't blame yourself. What's done is done. We need to figure out the current problem and deal with the situation we have now. Can you do that?"

Funny man. "Better than you. Come on. Let's see what we can find."

As soon as they got out of the car, the buzz hit her, but this one contained a different quality than the sinkhole. More like a rope attached to her insides and pulling at her. "You feel that?"

"I think so. Have there ever been two power buildups in the same place before?"

"I'm sure there have, but this doesn't buzz like a power node. Close your eyes and really try to sense the energy. Do you sense a buildup of power, or a tugging, like you want to follow the pull?"

Liz watched as he did what she asked. With his eyes closed, he turned his head, like he sensed a strong ley line and the power building. Kaeden opened his eyes and looked at her. "Should we follow?"

"Yes. And I think we can even keep our shoes on," she added with a grin. Liz went back to her car and tucked several more blades into her clothing, adding to the ones already there, then she handed Kaeden a gun.

He shook his head and pulled one from the inside pocket of his jacket. "Got my own."

She offered hers again. They were both the same

make and model, but hers didn't use regular ammo. "You might want to keep yours as a spare and use mine. The bullets are specially made and dipped in holy water. Don't waste them. They cost me a fortune."

He took the piece and checked the load. "Your bosses don't pay for them?"

"My bosses don't pay for a lot of the stuff I use. Which is fine. They don't care what I do, just that I complete the mission. Besides, they pay me well including some expenses usually."

The path of the power led toward the woods. "It figures following this wouldn't be an easy walk," she said as she climbed over a large windfall. "If we were to follow this direction for any length of time, you have any idea where we would come out?"

Kaeden stopped and studied their surroundings. "Downstream. This will eventually cross the southwestern part of town. Should we go back and try to find the pull from there? And how do we know the path will stay straight?"

"Ley lines are always straight. Can you get a bearing on our location on your phone now and pull up a map?"

Kaeden pulled his phone out, then shook his head. "No signal out here. I'm not surprised up here in the mountains. Even the best phones have spotty pickup around here."

Liz laughed. "Gee, no signal? Go figure."

"Yeah, but at least my battery is charged." He smirked at her.

She just shook her head and pointed at the car. "You go back to town and see if you can pick the buzz up. I'm going to follow the path from here."

"I don't like leaving you alone."

How sweet. She smiled at him, then patted her pockets. "I'm not without my resources. I can take care of myself."

"What happens if you get into trouble?"

"I'll ask the trees for help." When he frowned at her, she chuckled. "Long story. Go on. I'll be fine."

He did as Liz said, and she studied the mountain. The incline looked steep, but no worse than anything she'd done before. Bad guys tended to hide in one of two places—in big cities where they remained anonymous, or out in the middle of nowhere. She had extensive experience with both. Liz took off at a pace that wouldn't tire her but would cover ground as quickly as possible. When she reached the top of the rise, she stopped and stared at the rough trail that cut through the woods. A trail that followed the line.

As she followed the trail, she stretched her senses out. She didn't want to be caught unaware. Less than a half mile into her search, she stopped, her senses tingling. She knelt and touched the ground. The buzz felt stronger, but not node strong, and she knew that wasn't the problem. She ducked behind a large tree, pulled her knives out, and waited.

Liz didn't have long to wait as three men stepped out from the trees. One of them held a rifle cradled in his arms. The other two didn't appear to be armed, but that didn't mean they weren't dangerous. Both were tall and muscular with an air that said *not human*. From the looks of them, they were either lycan or shape-shifters of some sort. The one on the left sniffed the air, then pointed directly at the tree where she hid. She shrugged, and stepped into view.

"Nice of you to make this easier for us. You must be truly stupid." The man with the rifle brought the barrel up. "We keep sending you messages, yet you're still here."

She kept her blades in plain view and moved closer. "I'd say you're the one not getting the message. This is my town, and you are not welcome."

"Not yours anymore. Leave now and we might let you live."

"Not going to happen."

As he squeezed the trigger, she ducked and threw a blade. At this close range, she couldn't miss—and didn't. Unfortunately, neither did he, but her injury was nothing more than a flesh wound—in almost the same place she'd been wounded before. Liz's assailant went down with barely a sound. The other two stared at her, then attacked.

Unlike the movies where the bad guys attack one at a time, the two ganged up on her. She was fast, but not fast enough as they got in more than a few punches, but she did some major damage with her blades. She took out another one, and the third shifted into some sort of canine, turned tail, and ran into the woods. Liz considered going after him but decided not to. She was bruised, bleeding from being shot—again—and had some cuts, but she came away from the fight in better shape than her attackers were. She looked down at the scum. "Can't say I didn't warn you."

She froze when she heard clapping, and Bannig stepped out from a large tree. "Very good, my dear. Thank you for disposing of those worthless ones for me."

"You won't win, Bannig."

He laughed, and Liz shivered at the cold sound.

"I already have. The signs are written in the stars. My people fight on multiple fronts, and you fight for the losing side. Join me and know real strength."

Liz grabbed her knives and flung them, missing Bannig when he ducked behind the tree again. She advanced, but when she got there, he'd disappeared.

Why am I still alive? What does he want from me?

Liz retrieved her other knives from the bodies, flung the rifle into the woods, and took off without a backward glance. Fifteen minutes later, she met Kaeden.

"What happened to you? You look like you were in a fight." He pulled out a kerchief and wrapped her upper arm, then checked her over for other hurts.

"Yeah." She told him what happened. "I guess you should tell Ray about the bodies."

"As in plural?"

"Killed two. Third one got away."

He stared at me. "Three? Plus Bannig? And you're—"

"Alive. I guess you didn't find the node?"

"Didn't get a chance to look yet. The car died on me. I just got here myself."

Liz stared at him, her gut churning. "Damn. They've been delaying us. Come on!"

She took off running, Kaeden right behind her. They vaulted over fences, through backyards and alleys, staying as close to the line as they could. A few times, they were forced to go around buildings, picking the path up on the other side. They were nearing the far side of town when the ground rumbled, making them stumble. Liz skidded to a stop on a boat ramp at the edge of the river. In the middle of the river, a large eddy swirled around a jutting rock, all that remained of a small island that had been there. A speed boat rocked in the waves. Two of the passengers clung to the sides as if holding on for their lives. A third stood at the stern, his arms raised, sparks of lightning flying off him. Liz didn't need to see his face.

"Bannig."

Chapter Twelve

"What? You mean that's him? He found another power node in the middle of the river?"

"Yes. We were too late." Lightning struck the beach a few feet from where they stood. Kaeden jumped, but Liz just stood there. Bannig was playing with her. She figured he didn't want her dead, or she would be. But why?

The boat took off, heading upriver. Laughter floated back to her. She bent down and sensed the residual energy, but not anything else.

"Okay, I don't think he got the first one, but he did get this one. That means he'll be even stronger. I have to stop him before he finds the others."

"Let's go back to my place and see if Charly or Uncle Ray has a map for us," Kaeden said. "Plus, we need to take care of you."

"Can we go pick up my car first?"

"The engine is dead."

Liz snorted and headed toward her car. "I bet it'll work just fine now. Trust me."

"You're not going to let me say no, are you?"

"Nope."

Kaeden sighed and shook his head but did as she asked.

When they got to her car—which started just fine as she'd said—she thought hard on how to find the nodes. At Kaeden's house, they grabbed some food, and she went to his bathroom to clean up while Kae called his uncle. A few minutes later, Ray walked in, several rolls of maps under his arms. Close behind him came Charly and two other men. Liz sensed a full elf and a shape-shifter of some sort, probably canine, as that was the scent she got from him.

"This is Tobias and Ulrick," Ray introduced the strangers. "They know the ley lines better than anyone in the area."

Liz nodded at them. They studied her, then Tobias bowed his head to her. "We are honored to have you here at this difficult time. Our people are gathering. We will be at your service when needed. The time for waiting is done. You are the one who will contain the darkness."

"I am honored for your help," she returned, though his words bothered her. Usually, the only people depending on her to do something were the local cops. But this mess was even bigger than she thought if they were calling in the troops.

"Back in the woods, three men attacked me—one human, one a canine shifter, and one…I didn't get a chance to figure him out, but definitely not human. I left him and the human dead. The canine turned tail and ran. Tall, muscular, wore a black T-shirt with a Nazi symbol."

Ulrick snarled, his teeth bared, and Liz thought she saw the beginnings of claws on his hands before he reined in his anger. "Anders. He will be taken care of, my lady. You have my word."

"Good enough for me."

Liz told them what she knew, what she suspected,

all the while, keeping his words in her mind. *She would contain the darkness. What did that mean? And why call her lady?*

Tobias unrolled the maps on Kaeden's kitchen table. The largest turned out to be a topographical layout of the area. Over that, he laid a clear sheet of acetate that had been marked with a multitude of lines. Kaeden placed an X over the spot where the first node had been. Another in the river for the second.

Liz stared at the lines. There were dozens of intersections. Possibly hundreds. "I've never known an area to have so many in one spot."

"There are others around the world," Ulrick said. "But this large a confluence is rare. That is why many of our kind have been moving to this area. We are drawn to the power of this place."

"Plus, this is a small town, not as built up as many places are," Tobias added. "With so much of this area still forested and the nearby river, the power is more available."

"Which is why Bannig is here instead of in a big city," Liz said. "But there are hundreds of intersections. We have no way of knowing which one will turn into a node."

"You knew about the power yesterday when you warned the others to get out," Charly put in. "And when you went back today, you knew something else was coming."

"Yes, but not until I got there and felt the buzz," Liz said.

"So, go out to the river spot and see if you can sense something there now."

"If we're going to go out, we should go now,"

Kaeden said. "It'll be dark soon."

"We can get Alex to go with you," Ulrick said. "Darkness is his home."

"A vamp?" Liz asked. Though she knew a couple, something about them creeped her out.

"The ones here are…civilized," Tobias said. "They do not drink that which is not freely offered, and Doc Anderson always keeps a supply of other blood on hand for them."

Liz held back her shudders. "Fine. Let's go and get this done. I want to find that next node before Bannig does."

Ulrick made a couple of calls, and within fifteen minutes, the group gathered at the same boat dock she and Kaeden had been at earlier. Deep shadows already darkened the lower part of the surrounding mountains, though the tops still shone in the sinking sun. A short, pudgy guy with spiked hair who looked to be barely out of his teens met them there. He wore low-slung jeans, a ragged shirt, an army surplus jacket, and high-top sneakers. Next to him, a sleek speedboat bobbed in the water.

"Hi. I'm Alex. Rick said you needed a ride out to that rock."

Liz snapped her gaping mouth shut. This kid was a vampire? "Uh, yeah. Shouldn't take us too long."

"No problem. Climb aboard, though I can only take two of you."

"Kaeden and I will go," Liz said. She thought Kaeden had been taking all this weirdness rather well. Not only had he learned about his elven blood, but that the people he knew and dealt with on a regular basis weren't always human. That alone would be enough to send anyone off the deep end, but he kept hanging in there with her.

The others nodded their agreement, so Kaeden and Liz climbed aboard, and Rick pushed them off. A minute or two later, the current had them next to the rock. Liz leaned over the railing, trailing her hands in the water. She wasn't sure what she expected to feel, but nothing was there. Not even a twinge. In the lowering sun, Alex circled around the rock with Kaeden and Liz both dangling their hands in the cold water. Finally, Liz pulled back. "This isn't working."

"You want to go back to shore?" Kaeden asked.

"No." As fast as she could, Liz tugged off her shoes, jeans, and shirt. "I'm going in."

"Liz! Wait!" Kaeden made a grab for her, but she jumped before he could stop her.

The icy water set her teeth to chattering almost immediately. Every cut and scrape on her abused body burned. Liz shook off the pain and dove under the surface, running her hands along the rock. The buzz was there, but like the old cabin, this was almost an afterthought. Lines of light power radiated out from the rock, but no single one seemed any stronger than the others. Someone tugged on her arm, and Liz swung around to find Alex grinning at her. He pointed up, and she surfaced, gasping for air.

"Get back in the boat. I'll search more. Cold doesn't affect me, and I don't need to breathe."

Duh. With Kaeden's help, Liz climbed back aboard the boat.

"What the hell did you think you were doing? You're freezing! And you were down so long, I thought you'd drowned or gotten caught in an eddy or current or something." Kaeden wrapped her in his flannel shirt and almost rubbed her skin raw.

Liz stopped him and put her clothes back on. "I had to be sure, and we weren't finding anything up here."

He placed his arms around her, warming Liz. "That was probably one of the dumbest things you've done. Alex could have gone in for you."

"Know that now." She glanced up as the subject of their conversation climbed over the back of the boat.

"Nothing there but the usual lines."

"Might as well take us back then," Liz said. "No point in staying out here."

"Me and my buds might come back out to, you know, keep an eye on things," Alex said. "In case something develops."

"You don't need to do that," she said.

He grinned. "Gives us an excuse to have a beach party. Beautiful night for skinny dipping."

Liz shivered, then laughed. "Fine. If anything happens, call Kaeden or Charly."

"Will do." He dropped them back at the dock, then sped off into the night.

She watched him go, a little bemused.

"Not your stereotypical vampire, is he?" Tobias asked, a smile in his voice.

"Not at all," Liz agreed as she thought about the young-looking man. She briefly wondered about his real age. She told the others what they'd found—or hadn't found—and they all headed back to the diner where Charly set out hot chocolate and beers. The place had officially closed down an hour ago—but Kaeden and Charly set to work putting together a meal for everyone. As they cooked, other people showed up.

Liz sat back in a corner with her beer and watched most of the crowd as they greeted Tobias and Ulrick with the respect usually given leaders. So that made Ulrick the alpha of his group and Tobias the head of his. By the time Charly and Kaeden finished cooking, a dozen beings had joined them. Charly seemed to know what each one wanted, from rare steaks to vegan platters and everything in between. She handed Liz a bowl brimming with a thick beef stew and hot rolls dripping with butter. Though she hadn't known at the time, that hot, thick meal was exactly what she wanted, and she dug into the delicious fare.

As they ate, the group discussed what to do. "We don't have enough people to put someone at every intersection," one woman commented. "But we can cover a lot of them."

"I'd concentrate on the ones that intersect with the two that have already been drained," Liz said. "Those two were connected, so maybe the others are as well."

"Good idea. We'll set people on as many as we can."

"Thank you."

The group discussed what else to do, but Liz knew the conversations were mostly just talk. None of them could handle a demon growing in power like Bannig. She wasn't even sure she could. While the others talked, she rose from the table and went to the front double glass doors. Streetlights lit the town at regular intervals, but in between were shadows, and that was where she looked.

"Problem?" Kaeden's soft voice tickled her ear.

"No. Well, no more than usual. Just restless, I guess. I hate waiting."

"I get that. But there's not much we can do until we know where the next node will be."

Liz didn't want to disagree with him, mostly because he'd probably misunderstand, but he was wrong. She could do something, and as soon as she could, she would go on the hunt.

She backed away from the door as a new set of people arrived, and except for Charly, Kaeden, and Tobias, the others left. A moment after, a tall, older black man with graying hair and wire-rimmed glasses strutted in as if he owned the place.

He wore a brown suit, bow tie, a cool old-fashioned hat, and carried a cane that drew her eye like nothing else. From his solid gait, the man obviously didn't need the cane for walking support, so only for show and what a show. The piece was made of polished ebony, inlaid with gold-and-silver etching down the length, and topped with a silver claw holding a crystal ball. An honest-to-God, palm-sized crystal ball. Liz had an almost identical one on her dresser.

He stood there inside the door, and the place got quiet, but nobody moved. So, she did.

"Hi. I'm afraid we're closed, sir."

"I know, but thank you, Elizabeth."

His use of her proper name drew her up short. Everyone in the diner, even some of the regulars who were getting to know her, called her Liz. Only a handful of people knew her as Elizabeth.

"My name is Jacob. Jacob Smith."

Well, at least he wasn't John Smith. But still, could a name get any more generic? "Pleased to meet you, Mr. Smith."

"Please, call me Jacob. I'd like a chance to speak

with you if I may?"

"Concerning what?"

He gazed at the gathering. "In private, please."

Liz glanced at the others—who still hadn't really said or done anything—then nodded and took him to one of the back booths in the area away from where everyone else gathered. They slid into opposite sides of the booth. "How can I help you, Mr. Smith?"

He grinned at her. "Again, Jacob, please. And I may be able to help you."

"In what way?"

He laid the fancy cane on the table. She could barely take her eyes off the beautiful piece of work. Even though they were in a darkened corner, the crystal sparkled, and she'd never seen anything so beautiful, so mesmerizing.

"Twist and turn, turn and twist. Time and place do not exist."

Liz heard the words in her head but still couldn't pull her gaze away from the cane. If Bannig came in at that moment and surrendered, she wasn't sure she could do anything about him.

"Liz?"

She shook her head and looked up to find Kaeden and Charly frowning at her. Jacob had disappeared, but the cane still lay there.

"Where were you?" Charly asked. "We called your name a couple of times."

"Where'd he go?"

"Who?" Kaeden asked.

"Jacob. The old man who came in with this cane."

"I don't know what you're talking about. You waved at us and came over here for some reason.

Where'd you get the cane? That workmanship is beautiful." Kaeden reached for the staff, but she blocked his hand.

"Don't. No one touches this. And you didn't see an old black guy come in? We came over here to talk. He looked like Morgan Freeman."

"I think I'd remember someone like that," Charly said. "Nobody's come in except my group for several minutes."

What the...? Something wonky was going on here. Who had she been talking to? And which side was he on? "Charly, without touching this, can you get anything from the cane?"

Charly held her hands over the cane and got such a beautiful look on her face. "It's amazing. All white light." Before Liz could stop her, she picked the staff up and handed the wood to Liz. "But this isn't for me, or anyone else. This is for you, Liz. Only you."

Liz took the cane, reluctantly. Almost gingerly. Yes, the staff called to her, but caution kept her from full acceptance.

Then her brain flashed, and she understood. She glanced at the door, knowing her jaw was open.

"Liz?" Kaeden looked at her.

"The old man I saw? Jacob Smith?"

"Yeah, what about him?"

"I think he's one of my bosses."

Chapter Thirteen

Both Kaeden and Charly stared at the door then
back at Liz. "No wonder nobody else could see him,"
Charly said. "So, what's with the cane?"

"No clue."

"Maybe they wanted to give you a gift," Kae
suggested.

"I doubt it. The bosses never give gifts. Everything
always has a reason, but what is the reason behind
this?"

"Can we figure out the cane later?" Charly asked.
"The others are waiting for us."

"No problem but let me secure this first." Liz ran to
her car and tried the spare tire area with the puzzle, but
the length didn't fit, so she tucked the cane under where
the seats folded down and covered them with a blanket.
Satisfied that she'd hidden the cane sufficiently, she
rejoined Charly and the others.

Several women and a portly geek arrived. They
took a variety of bags and satchels to a long table, then
opened them. Liz watched as they laid out scrying
bowls, herbs, crystals, Tarot decks, and more. She
grinned when Charly waved her over.

"Thought we could use some specialized help, so I
called in the troops. Everybody, this is Liz. Liz, this is
my coven. The new people are Chris, Debra, Misty,
Sue, Ann, and Gabby."

"I am honored," Liz acknowledged them.

"Are we setting up here?" Debra, asked.

"I think we'll go up to my apartment," Charly said. "It's more comfortable."

They quickly set the diner to rights and trooped up the steps to Charly's. The entire place had been decorated and furnished with a nod to nature. Earthen shades dominated the apartment, and plants abounded. Charly cleared off the dining room table and laid a white silk cloth over the wood. Liz finally understood why she had such a large table for only one person. Each of the newcomers went to a specific spot as if they'd done so many times.

"We know you're looking for a person named Bannig," Debra said. "We're going to try to locate him for you, but the search would be easier if we had something of his."

Liz shook her head. "I tried my stones. They didn't work."

"Do you have anything else?"

She couldn't exactly come up with hair strands or anything like that. "I don't…wait. I might." She ran out to her car and dug through her possessions until she came up with a book of monsters and mythical creatures. Something so impersonal wasn't much, but better than nothing. She took the book back to the group. "He gave me this when I finished my training. He signed the first page. Does that help?"

Debra took the book, held the tome between her hands and closed her eyes. A moment later, she opened them and shook her head. "No. There's nothing here."

That didn't surprise Liz. After all, her search had told her there was nothing left of her friend Bannig. Just the shell the demon was using.

While they chatted, Liz studied the group. Chris went to the tray of cookies and started wolfing them down like he hadn't eaten in days. His girth said differently. The women looked to be a mix of ages from one in her late sixties to a youngster who looked to be in her late teens. The other three were close to Charly and Liz in age. At least that was her assessment.

"Are all of you witches?"

Charly grinned. "Well, not Kae, but the rest of us, yes. Though we all practice the arts and have different powers, not all of us have the ability to cast spells."

"But a group of seven? Isn't that an odd number— no pun intended?"

"There are many theories," Charly told her. "We believe thirteen is an unlucky number for us. Three holds much better karma. Our schedules don't always coincide, so the number isn't usually an issue. Tonight's the first in over a year we all had the evening free."

Coincidence? Liz didn't think so. There were too many of those. "So, by my count, you've got five too many."

"If you count again, you'll see we have nine, a triple three, much more powerful than a single triad. Though Kae's technically not a witch, as we've seen, he's still someone with power, and you...well, we all know you've got power by the boatloads." She handed Liz a tightly wound bunch of sweetgrass and sage. "Would you light this, please?"

Liz walked around with the herbs and chanted a spell for protection. She could sense Kaeden watching her, but he had his own chores. Everyone had a job to do.

Two of the women set out glass bowls and containers of herbs on the low coffee table in front of the sofa. They mixed and spoke words over the bowls. Liz couldn't hear what they were saying but knew their actions. Like her, they were asking for safety, for clarity, for help. Liz added her own pleas to her bosses, just in case.

She sat back and watched as the group got to work. Witches. Here in Clear Water. In the open. Ten years ago, this wouldn't have happened. Even five years ago, she would have been surprised. How had Charly kept this all from her? She'd never had a clue. *Some special agent I am.*

Finally, Charly announced that they were ready to begin.

Over the course of the evening, Liz found out Debra and Sue specialized in herbs and oils. Ann read Tarot like nobody's business and could also read runes, I Ching, and other divining objects. But she had no talent with crystals and pendulums. The cookie-scarfing geek was precisely what he looked like. Liz knew about not stereotyping people, but he had an affinity with machines, especially electronic systems that went way beyond the norm. Gabby worked as a massage therapist and with personal energy and could also scry.

Liz glanced at Misty, the only person not working with something. "What's your specialty?"

Misty beamed then snapped her fingers, and sparks flew. "I seem to have this thing about energy, especially fire." She glanced at the unlit candles sitting in the middle of the table, blew at them, and they flamed to life.

"Cool!" Mild envy hit Liz. Okay, she could make thunder and lightning, but she couldn't control them. Seriously, what she could do with a power like Misty's.

These people weren't merely saying they were witches. They were the real deal. They had moved to Clear Water at various times over the past ten years. All for different reasons, but still, they were here. Now. Liz found that incredibly interesting.

"We know you're here because of Bannig and the power nodes. Is there anything else we need to know?" one of the witches asked.

"That pretty much covers everything. Death and destruction on a cosmic level if I don't find and stop him."

The group got to work. They laid out cards, threw runes, burned herbs, and consulted stones. If there was a way to do divination, they did, unfortunately with no results. Frustration showed in frowns, chewed lips, and clenched jaws. They were being blocked, but how?

"Let's try something else," Debra said, and everyone sat back to listen. Kaeden beside Liz. She leaned her head on his shoulder, and he wrapped his arm around her, pulling her close. She inhaled his essence. How had she never noticed his distinct elfism? She had to struggle to concentrate on Debra's words in order to get her mind off him.

"We've been going about this separately," Debra said. "One thing at a time. What if we combined our powers and did a search that way?"

"Combine them?" Liz asked. "How?"

"There are several ways, but the easiest is sort of like a séance. There are nine of us, a triple triad. We can use the unity of the circle and increase our power by channeling everything through one person. The most logical person would be you, Liz."

Liz definitely did not like where this was going, especially with the itch of power from the first node still singing in her bones. "Why me?"

"You're the one with the connection to the spirits," Charly explained. "No one here has your kind of power. We read tea leaves or spark candles, but not what you do."

She sighed. What could she say? These people were trying to help. Could she do any less? She rubbed her arms as she thought through everything that could go wrong—and there were a lot of things. The power coursed through her. Along with something else. Something with the prickle of evil. And that something was in the room. Liz studied each of them, but she couldn't read auras. And Charly trusted them. She didn't like the idea but couldn't sense anything other than her angst.

"Liz?" Charly prompted.

She decided to agree. If holding a séance would help her find Bannig before he drained the next node, she'd handle a little discomfort. She mentally armed herself to be ready for anything. "Yeah, fine. Let's do this."

While the others prepared, Liz rose and paced the room, trying to rub the itch off her arms. They set up the table, enclosed the area in a salt circle and set wards and other protection spells around. Funny how all the precautions didn't make her anxiety lessen. Her senses were all saying this was a really bad idea. She jumped when Kaeden came over to her.

"Liz? What's wrong?"

"I've got a really bad feeling." That covered a lot of area, so she let him interpret the words however he wanted.

"Should we forget this?"

His trust gave her a warmth that helped with the cold spikes. "If I said yes, would you?"

He turned away and called across the room. "Charly? Liz isn't sure about this."

Charly came over to them, and the others paused in their preparations. "Liz, we've taken every precaution possible."

"Have you ever done this before?"

"Yes. Several times. And it always worked like a charm, no pun intended. You're jumpy because you're not used to working with a group. That's all. You'll see. Trust me."

Trust her? How could she not? This was Charly. The person who'd taken her in, fed her, befriended her. Liz had never met anyone like Charly, and maybe that was part of her problem. She'd never met anyone so completely good. Even Kaeden had his dark side, but not Charly. She was pure light. Liz nodded, and they joined the others. Kae was on her right, Charly on her left, the rest arrayed around the table. All the lights had been turned off, but a single candle flickered in the center of the table.

"Grasp hands and do not let go," Debra instructed.

Kaeden's hand surrounded Liz's, warm and strong. She gripped his like a lifeline. Charly's felt cooler, but still welcome.

"I call upon the spirits of the universe to hear us. I call upon…"

Debra's voice droned into the background as Liz

stared at the flame. The level of light in the room increased and flowed until the brightness engulfed everyone. Sparkles danced over their skin. Liz glanced at the others to see if they saw the glow, but they all had their eyes closed. She nudged Kaeden, but he just gripped her hand tighter. She tried to speak but couldn't. Something blocked her.

Debra's chanting barely sounded above a whisper. The candle flared to nearly a foot tall and pulsed. As the flame increased, the pattern worked into a face. At first, she thought the image looked like Bannig, but then he changed into something else. No human face looked like that. How could something so incredibly beautiful fill her with such dread? Evil flowed from the light like a living thing. Oily. Heavy. Searching for an outlet. A portal. Testing each of them. Liz blew at the candle, trying to stop the entity, but the blaze burned even higher. She tried releasing her hands, but couldn't, as if they were bonded to each other.

"You are mine." The voice sounded guttural, a thing born of nightmares.

"I belong to no one," Liz all but screamed.

"You were created to be a vessel. My vessel. None will stop me. I will be invincible."

The flame drew closer, the heat scorching her fingertips. She had to move. Fast! Liz rose and backed away as far as she could with her hands firmly clenched by Kaeden and Charly. Still the flame advanced. Inhuman laughter came from the blaze, and she knew she had to get free. Break the circle free. If that thing got to her, he would feed on the power, and they would have a being even worse than Bannig. And Liz refused to allow that.

The flame moved closer. All the light concentrated on her. The others sat there, as if in a coma—breathing, living, but nothing else. She did the only thing she could think of and hoped Kaeden would forgive her. Liz hauled back on Charly and Kaeden until their chairs tilted and they fell over. When that didn't release them, she twisted, raised her foot, and kicked Kae's crotch. Hard.

He jerked, blinked, and looked up at her—confusion and pain on his face. Once he woke up completely, she found her voice again. "Kaeden! Let go!" Getting free took some hard pulling, but they managed to release their hands.

Next, she turned to Charly. Girls may not be as sensitive as guys in that part of the anatomy, but they do hurt if you kick hard enough. And Liz did. She didn't even have to tell Charly to let go. She did so on her own. Liz guessed that breaking with Kaeden had weakened the link.

A scream filled with frustration and hatred surrounded them, and a bolt of lightning jumped to the other six, leaving a stench of sulfur behind. And six slumped bodies.

Chapter Fourteen

Kaeden and Charly hunched over, gasping, but at least they were awake and alive.

"What happened?" Charly sat up, a puzzled frown as she took in the scene.

Liz eyed Kaeden, still prone on the floor, pain etched on his face. She helped him sit up. "You tell me. What do you remember?"

"What's to remember? We just sat down. Kaeden? Are you all right?"

"Get him an ice pack. And Charly? We sat down a half hour ago."

"Huh?"

"Go. Ice. Now."

Kaeden glared at her. "A simple *let go* would have been preferred."

"You think I didn't try? Kicking you was definitely not my first choice."

"Nor mine. What happened?" He took the ice from Charly and placed the pack on his tender groin. The others were slowly waking up and staring around like they were in a daze.

"Charly, are you all right?"

"Yes. Damn. What did you hit me with? My crotch feels like shit."

"I'm sorry. Honest. But I couldn't think of any other way to get your attention."

"So, what did happen?" Debra asked. Everybody eyed the singe marks on the tablecloth, a path leading directly to where Liz had been sitting.

"Tell me what you remember," Liz repeated as she occupied herself with cleaning up the mess. The task kept her busy, so she didn't have to look at them.

Kaeden blew out a hard breath. Liz hoped from frustration and not pain, though she knew better.

"Not much. I remember sitting down to start the séance and Debra beginning her chant. Then nothing until you were standing over me yelling, and I was in more pain than I care to think about."

Liz looked at Charly. "Same here. Nothing."

Everyone else shook their heads as well.

"Damn. I was afraid of that." Liz told them what she had seen and what had happened. "I guess this isn't what went down the last time?" she asked when she finished.

Charly shook her head. "We never had anything like this happen before."

"You said you'd done a circle of nine before."

"We did. Once. We were looking for a lost child and found him quite quickly."

The bad vibes she had were amping up. They'd done this before, but not with her, especially not her buzzing with power. Plus, she'd bet her best knife they weren't here in this building the last time. "Where were you when you did this before?"

Charly frowned. "I think we were at Gabby's. She lives on a farm a couple miles east of town."

Liz's stomach clenched. "You were away from here. I should have known better. I should have listened to my twinges. I should have stopped you."

"That's an awful lot of should haves," Kaeden said. "Care to elaborate? I know you were concerned earlier. Why?"

"The power buzzing through me. The veil between here and the demon world is thinning, and the power nodes are drawing them here. When we opened the portal to the spirit world, we allowed that thing through."

Charly gave a shiver, like shaking off a chill. "The thing you saw. Do you think he was Bannig?"

"Maybe. Maybe the one inhabiting Bannig. He was definitely some kind of demon."

"What did he mean when he said you were a vessel?" Kaeden asked.

Liz shrugged. "I have no idea. Why don't you ask your uncle? He seems to know more about me than anyone else."

The others packed up their gear and headed out, all of them moving slowly as if they weren't quite there, but the demon hadn't gotten them. They hadn't been taken over. Just dazed.

She hoped.

A minute after they left, lightning lit the sky, followed immediately by a huge clap of thunder that shook the building. The others barely got to their cars before the clouds opened and a deluge poured down. Lightning strike followed lightning strike, as if all the forces of nature were being unleashed at the same time.

"I didn't know the weathermen predicted rain," Liz said.

"They didn't," Kaeden replied.

Liz studied the sky. She'd bet her car this wasn't a natural storm.

"You two might as well spend the night here," Charly said. "Nobody's going anywhere in that storm, not even upstairs. Besides, your place is still rather empty."

She wasn't wrong. Even though they'd brought sheets, towels, and some food—not to mention, a mattress—Liz still didn't have more than what could be packed in a backpack and overnight bag.

Liz took the guest room as Kaeden stretched out on the sofa. Even if they had been inclined to do something, getting hot and heavy didn't feel right in Charly's place, plus Liz's recent boot placement pretty much assured Kaeden wouldn't be doing anything for a while.

She kissed him and headed to bed, but the last thing she wanted to do was sleep. She sat cross-legged in the middle of the bed. At other times, when she'd needed to make personal contact with O.W.L.—something more than talking to the air—she'd been able to do so by putting herself in a light trance. Coming so close to what had happened earlier, opening up to the spirit world caused a few nerves, but she needed answers.

Liz closed her eyes and calmed her thoughts. Moments later, the nothingness surrounded her. She could see, hear, touch, taste, smell. All her senses worked. But there was nothing there. Nothing to see but grayness all around her. Nothing to smell, not even her own aroma. Nothing to hear except her own voice and even that was muted. Nothing to touch since nothing else existed.

The first time this had happened to her, she'd freaked out. The sensation was like sensory deprivation, but in grayness instead of darkness. Liz still didn't like the lack of…everything, but at least she knew what to expect. She settled to a sitting position though she didn't know what she sat on here in the nothingness. Nothing else, including her perspective, changed. Liz rested her hands on her knees, palms up.

"I call to the spirits who empower me. I call to the spirits who guide me. I call to the spirits whose names I do not know but who live in my heart. I call to them to speak with me now."

Liz closed her eyes and waited. She never knew how long the spirits talked with her. She had no sense of time there. She could have been there seconds, or decades. Liz tried to keep time by counting, but her mind wouldn't stay on task. Her thoughts kept going off in other directions.

She sensed a change and opened her eyes. Instead of gray, her surroundings were now pure white with no discernible walls, floor, or ceiling. Liz waited there, lost in time, until a man appeared in front of her, surprising her. None of her bosses had ever appeared to her before. She'd heard them, sensed them, but had never seen them. He appeared short, chubby, with red cheeks and a white beard and wore a white robe.

"You have questions."

"I do."

"You understand I may not be able to answer them?"

"Yes. First, has anybody ever told you that you look like Santa?"

He chuckled. "I get that question all the time. You can just call me Nick. But I think that is not your real question."

"You're right. Do you know where Bannig is hiding?"

"No. Like you and your friends, we have not been able to search him out. Powerful shades are protecting him. All we know is what you know, he is in Clear Water."

"Do you know where the next power node will be?"

"No."

"What am I?"

A slight widening of his eyes and hesitation was the only sign that her question had startled him. "You are an agent for good."

"That is what I do. What am I?"

"You are many things."

"You're not answering my question." Liz did what she had never done before. She rose to stand in front of him. "What am I? What is my purpose? Why was I created?"

He backed away from her, his ruddy face going even redder before he disappeared. She sat back down and spoke to the emptiness. "You might as well answer my question because I'm going to stay here until you do."

A jolt of electricity went through her, and she opened her eyes, finding herself back in her room. She snorted. "Okay, you won this round, but as you know, I don't give up easily. In fact, I don't give up, period. So, you'd better decide to let me in on the secret."

Liz lay down on her bed, a small smile on her face. She really hadn't expected an answer, but she'd confirmed something. She'd been created for a purpose. She wasn't an accident of birth who nobody wanted.

Sure, she didn't know who or why or how, but for the first time in her life, the hurt she'd grown up with thawed a little.

Liz wanted to hold onto that good emotion.

While the storm raged outside, Liz slept, probably better than she ever had in her life.

The next morning, she woke and stretched out the kinks. The sky outside was clear, and when she opened her window, she breathed deeply of the crisp air. She followed her nose out to Charly's kitchen where a pot of coffee dripped, and Kaeden stood at the stove flipping pancakes.

"Good morning." She wrapped her arms around him and kissed him on the back of his neck. "How are you doing this morning?"

He turned around in her arms, kissing her gently. "If I wasn't still sore, thanks to you, I'd show you. But…"

She stepped away. "I really am sorry."

"I know."

"Charly already down in the diner?"

"No. She had some errands to run and a couple deliveries to make. Said she'd be back later."

Liz frowned. Charly not opening the diner was like the IRS not collecting taxes—something that never happened. But the diner business belonged to Charly, not Liz. Still, she'd check to make sure Charly had help. Even hunting for Bannig and the ley lines, she could still bus tables and help. "So has anyone checked in on the ley lines yet?"

"Had to call the night watch off. That storm was too nasty. But they're all out checking now." He handed her a plate with strips of bacon, a small stack of pancakes topped with melting butter, fried apples, and cinnamon. She dug in, sighing in ecstasy.

"How come you're so giddy this morning? You're not usually a morning person." He sat down across from her and attacked his own platter. He knew that about her. That said something about how much time she'd been spending with him before she took off. That mote of warmth inside her grew a little more.

"Let's just say, I had a good night." She went on to tell him what had happened. "So, I know the Powers-That-Be did something to make me the way I am. I might not have been wanted by any families, but I wasn't a throwaway."

"Oh, darlin'. You are very much wanted."

Liz nearly choked on her breakfast, the heat from his eyes burning her. She resisted the urge to fan herself. "Um, yeah. Well. I think I'm going to grab a shower." A cold one. "Want to meet up to go on the hunt for ley lines ourselves?"

"Sure. Give me two hours. I could use a shower, and I have some things to take care of."

"No problem. I'll take a look around and see what I can find. Might be able to narrow our search down a little." Liz had an idea she wanted to try out but wanted to do it on her own.

"Liz, be careful. We know something else is after you. Whatever that demon is wants to take you over."

"And now that I know, I'll be extra careful. No worries. Go. I'll take care of the dishes."

"I can do them."

"Nope. You cooked. The least I can do is clean up. Besides, the sooner you're out of here, the sooner we can get back together." She gave him a peck on the cheek. "Plus, I need to run to the store to get some new duds. Seems like most of mine met with an accident."

"Some accident."

"Yeah, well, I'll deal. Go. I'll see you later." She all but pushed him out the door.

Liz cleaned the kitchen in record time, grabbed a jacket, and climbed into her car where she found a picture of her taped to the steering wheel, once again with an X drawn over her face. This time, they'd shot from the shore when they'd been searching for the second node. The picture didn't bother her, but the implications did. She knew everyone who had been standing on the bank waiting for Kaeden and her. Granted, a couple of them she'd just met, but still, they'd been presented as friends, and she'd trusted them. "How's that old saying go?" she asked the universe. "Keep your friends close and your enemies closer? Looks like I need to do some digging around to see who is what."

Liz grabbed a dowsing rod from the back of her car. There were several to choose from—willow, hazel, and copper. She chose the copper one and closed her mind to everything but the pull of power. She let the rod pull her wherever, sweeping across the parking lot, but the metal just pulled her in a circle. She walked all over the parking lot but kept coming back to the diner and circling. Frustrated, Liz put the rod away and headed for the local discount store. At least she could buy a new pair of boots and some necessities.

An hour later, when she opened the door to her place, she stopped. Liz knew her mouth was hanging open. Kaeden and Charly spun around, their faces reddening, their hands full of boxes and more food.

"We didn't expect you back for a while yet," Charly said. She finished slicing the loaf of French bread on the cutting board in front of her.

"What are you two doing?" Liz stared around at the apartment. Curtains hung at the windows, plants sat on small tables, books on bookshelves—when did she get bookshelves—and more?

Kaeden grinned and led her to a chair. "We thought we'd surprise you by putting stuff back in your apartment." He opened cabinet doors. "Look. You even have pots and pans and dishes."

"I don't cook," Liz said.

"I know. But I do." Kaeden stirred whatever simmered on the stove. The aroma set her mouth to watering and her stomach to grumbling.

"And you have real food," Charly added as she opened the refrigerator door. "Which is much better than those pull-the-tab-and-nuke-me things I see in your bags."

Liz didn't know what to say. Their thoughtfulness overwhelmed her. "I…um, thank you."

"Hey, Kae, I think we've got our girl speechless," Charly said with a smirking grin.

"May have to remember that," he said. "Give her a plant or two and some food, and she's helpless."

Liz tossed a new throw pillow at him. Which he threw right back, missing her as she ducked behind the sofa-bed. Soon, the three of them were tossing pillows, laughing, and having fun. She couldn't remember the last time she'd had fun. If ever. Their merriment continued as they sat down to steaming bowls of minestrone and fresh garlic bread.

Unfortunately, their fun came to a screeching halt when a frantic knock on rapped against the door.

Chapter Fifteen

Liz opened the door to a boy she didn't know, who looked to be in his early teens. Kaeden obviously did as the boy went straight to him.

"What's wrong, Micah?"

"We got a buzz out near the river. Mom said to come tell you fast."

Kaeden handed him a glass of water, which he gulped down. "You did good, Micah. We're going there. You want a ride?"

"Nah. I'm good. Practice for the cross-country team. Thanks."

Liz strapped on her knives, then pulled on her new hiking boots. "Ready."

"Charly, you coming?" Liz asked.

The little witch glanced at the clock and frowned. "Can't. I've got to interview a new cook and waitress this afternoon. But you'd damn well better let me know what's going on."

"Will do." Liz grabbed her backpack and followed Kaeden to the car, and she jumped in on the passenger side.

They sped down to the river where several people gathered on the bank, all of them facing the same direction, kind of like seagulls on the beach.

The car had barely come to a stop before Liz jumped out and ran for the spot. She didn't have to touch the ground to feel the buzz. "Kaeden?"

"We'll follow this one together." He turned to the group. "Thanks. We'll handle this from here." He tossed his keys at an older man. Liz recognized him as one of the mechanics from the garage behind Charly's. "Derek, can you make sure my car gets back to the diner?"

"Not a problem."

"Thanks."

Kaeden and Liz took off. The power sang through her body. This one felt even stronger than the first two. Which disturbed her. Knowing there were probably going to be six of these things was bad enough, but if each one became stronger than the last, that would be even worse.

Liz's self-appointed protector easily kept up with her ground-eating trot, but she wished she had eaten less. As good as the food had tasted, going for a jog right after eating had her stomach roiling. Once again, they climbed hills and ran through meadows. Their path took them directly into town, then back out to the outskirts. The buzz got stronger. She gathered her energy and put on a burst of speed, arriving at an old sawmill as the ground trembled and the buildings swayed and shook.

She skidded to a stop as she saw Bannig standing in the center of the area, arms stretched high overhead. Lightning surrounded him as he absorbed the power. Two of the three men with Bannig rushed her when she raced toward the demon, hoping to stop him from taking all he could from the node. She fought the men, barely noticing when Kaeden took on the last man. She needed to get to her nemesis. The men were stronger than they looked and nearly outdid her, but she finally had them down and out.

"Enough." The voice rising from Bannig's body belonged to her old friend, and yet not. She heard a deeper undertone along with a reverberation that sounded like he stood in a huge room and not the middle of a destroyed mill. The men backed off as Bannig strode over to her and Kaeden.

Liz cringed upon getting a closer look at Bannig. He looked like he had aged even more than before. His once powerful body now gaunt and gray, and his hair had thinned to almost nothing. Killing him would be a blessing for her old mentor. She gripped her knives, then his eyes changed from red back to the pale blue of the man she knew. Liz hesitated the merest fraction of a second, before letting the knives go.

His eyes changed back. Bannig laughed, then flicked his fingers. The knives stopped in mid-air, as if they'd hit a wall, then thudded to the ground. "You cannot stop me, Elizabeth. You should know that by now."

"Maybe not, but I'll keep trying."

"If you could only feel the power! Join me. Let me show you. We can do marvelous things together. Open yourself to me. Come to me. Be with me. You were meant for this. Only you and I are strong enough to control all the nodes. Come to me. Come to me."

Liz took a step forward. Then another. She wanted... Liz didn't know what she desired at the moment but knew if she got to Bannig, the power would be hers. She needed this. She could handle the power. Somewhere inside her, Liz knew the demon was right. She had been created for this. And yet, a part of her knew it was so wrong. She fought the pull. Fought the need. Then Kaeden touched her, and that was enough to break the demon's spell.

"No!" Liz stepped back, away from Bannig. And back again. "No. I will not join you."

"Then you will die!" He flicked his fingers, and a whirlwind struck her. Kaeden grabbed her and hauled her to the ground a millisecond before lightning struck the spot where she'd been standing. She struggled to sit up.

"Let me go. I need to handle this."

His arms dropped away, and she stood. Liz lifted her arms and channeled everything she had into controlling the small tornado and turned the wind back against Bannig. Everything he threw at her, she threw right back, but the fight was one she couldn't win. She knew that. And so did Bannig.

Then the loud retort of a gun sounded in her ears, and Bannig stumbled. The storm died down. Another shot and he stumbled back again. The storm disappeared. Liz advanced on him as Kaeden kept shooting. She had nearly reached him when he stepped backward and dropped into the sinkhole that had opened with the quake. Liz dashed to the edge but didn't see anything. She was tempted to jump in after Bannig but was in no condition to follow him down to wherever that hole went. And she was beyond starving. You'd never know she'd eaten a full meal less than an hour ago.

Tired beyond measure, she collapsed onto the ground.

"Liz? Are you all right?"

Kaeden knelt next to her. She glanced up, noting

the shiner on his right eye and the bruise on his jaw. "Yeah. Just great. Where did our two thugs go?"

"Not sure. I was watching you and Bannig. I guess they took off. What happened? From where I stood, I thought you were going to go to him."

"I was."

"What?"

She looked up as a half-dozen cars, including Kaeden's uncle, pulled into the area. "Looks like the power junkies are here along with the law. Any way we can get a ride home? I'm not sure I could get there on my own at this point."

"Kaeden?" Uncle Ray came over to them.

"We missed him," Kaeden said. "But not by much. We were so close this time. Next time, we'll be there. Uncle, any way you can give us a ride back? We're beat."

He tossed Kaeden the keys. "Wait in the car until I get things cleaned up here."

Kaeden and Liz climbed into the front seat of the cruiser. She chuckled when she thought about the last time she'd been in this car. Or maybe not this one, but an identical one belonging to Chief Ray.

"What's so funny?" Kaeden asked.

"Just thinking about the last time I sat in your uncle's cruiser. I was definitely not invited to sit in the front seat."

When his uncle joined them, Kaeden flashed her a cocky grin and then climbed into the back seat. The gesture wasn't lost on her, or his uncle.

Ray dropped them off at the diner, and they trudged up the steps to her place. Exhaustion filled Liz, plus a hefty dose of frustration, and seriously pissed off.

She wanted to fight something. To kill something. Preferably Bannig. When they opened her door and the aroma of broiled steaks wafted out, her mood mellowed—a little. Charly grinned at them from the table where she put a large salad.

"I think I love you." Liz followed her nose to the stove where two beautiful steaks sizzled and popped. "How'd you know when we'd be back?"

Charly just grinned.

"Oh. Yeah. Witch."

Then she laughed. "While I'd love for my powers to take the credit, this time all I used was the phone. Heard the sawmill went down and almost took you two along." She waved a large steak knife at them. "If you ever scare me like that again, Bannig will be the least of your worries."

Wow. Just wow. Liz didn't know what to say, so she followed Kaeden's lead and sat down. Charly kept up a running commentary as she served the steaks and dished out the salads. When she ran out of breath, they filled in the gaps as they scarfed down that delicious food.

"So, he got away with another one," Charly said.

"Yep."

"And now he's stronger than ever."

"Yep."

"And we have no clue where the next one will be."

Gee, why don't you drag me down lower than I already am? "Nope."

The three of them sat there staring at one another, then Charly cocked her head and pursed her lips. A look that meant she was thinking something over.

"Liz, you still have those maps? The ones with the

ley lines?"

"Yes."

"Get them."

Charly and Kaeden cleared off the table, and Liz laid out the maps. "Where was the first one?"

Kaeden placed the saltshaker over the spot where the house had disappeared. Pepper went in the middle of the river, and a shot glass over the sawmill.

"A triangle," Charly said. "So, the next three could be another triangle? What about an inverted one, like the Star of David?"

Liz shook her head. "I don't think so. This town has changed a lot since I first came here. The people—the town—is more paranormal than normal now. What if that's not a coincidence? What if all the changes are about the power?" She took away the condiments and grabbed a pencil and started drawing. "What about a pentagram?"

"That only gives us five reference locations," Kaeden pointed out.

"With the sixth at dead center." She took her steak knife and stabbed the end in the middle of the diagram she'd drawn. All three of them stared at the central spot, then at one another. The point of the knife centered on Charly's diner. Exactly where Liz's dowser had said the node would be.

Charly's face went pale. "You mean I'm going to lose this place?"

Damn. "No. I will not let that happen."

"What can you do, Liz?" Kaeden asked. "He's gotten too powerful for us."

"Maybe for the three of us, but what if we had more people? Like a small army? You've already got some people." What she hadn't told Kaeden or Charly was how badly she'd wanted to join Bannig. His body couldn't handle the power, but the demon had taken over a human body. And she wasn't human. Liz knew she could manage the energy. Knew she could take the power in. She also knew the demon would want to join with her if she did, and there was no way in Hell would she let that happen. She'd die first.

"We can pull in some more people," Kaeden said. "But which spot do we go to?"

"If the next one follows the same pattern, we've got twenty-four hours to figure that out and two places to check. We set people at each spot, and the rest of us stay here until someone lets us know the power is building, then we head there. Where are the next two spots?"

"The river bridge," Kaeden said. "And…damn."

"What?" She peered at the map but didn't know the town well enough to know the spot he pointed at.

"It's the gas depot. Big tanks of natural gas, at least a dozen of them."

Damn was right. She studied both areas. Both had their advantages and disadvantages. The bridge would prevent anyone from getting into town unless they took the long way through the mountains. Not impossible, but definitely more difficult. The gas depot would be a spectacular spot. If all those tanks went up, the explosion would leave a sizable crater, though the sinkhole part might take care of that.

Another thought struck her while she studied the map. Where was Bannig? He had to be staying somewhere nearby. If she could take him down, they wouldn't have to worry so much. But where could he be staying? There was one small inn on the square and a couple of bed-and-breakfast places. "Charly? Where's the fanciest place in town to stay?"

"You mean besides these lovely digs?" She glanced at Kaeden, then pointed at a spot where two ley lines intersected. "The Reynolds mansion. But the place has been abandoned for years. Nobody lives there, but somehow the place always seems to be in pristine condition."

"I've never heard of the mansion," Liz said.

"No reason you should. After that, the inn, then the two B-and-B's."

Liz held her hand over the map and closed her eyes. Moving her hand around, she sensed a slight tingling. When she opened her eyes, her hand lay over the mansion. "That's where he's at." She grabbed her jacket as lightning flashed and thunder boomed loud enough to rattle the windows. When she looked out, no clouds showed in the clear sky.

"Where do you think you're going?" Kaeden asked.

"After Bannig." Thunder crashed again.

Chapter Sixteen

"You're not going out with that storm coming." Kaeden crossed his arms over his chest. Impressive, but not enough to stop her.

"That's not a natural storm. I'm going to go see where the center is." Though Liz had an idea Bannig needed to bleed off some power. Either that or something had pissed him off.

"You can't be serious," both Charly and Kaeden said at the same time.

"Why not? Bannig is the one causing the chaos. If I can get to him, I can stop him before something happens."

"Something's already happening," Kaeden said. "He's powerful enough to cause this much nastiness. You know he's got more power than you do right now. Wait until we call in help. Please, Liz. Give us a chance to get more people here."

Liz hesitated. He made sense, but she itched to go. She needed to be out there hunting him. "Fine. But I'm still going out." She held up her hand to stop any arguments. "Just for a minute and only as far as the front of the diner. I'll be right back."

"I'll go with you," Kaeden offered.

"No. You. Won't." She blew out a frustrated breath. "Seriously, I'll be gone two minutes. Max. All I want to do is talk to some trees."

Both of them looked at her as if she had gone over the edge, and maybe she had. "Don't ask. But I promise, I'm okay and I'll be right back."

Liz left before they had a chance to stop her. She glanced at the sky. A dark swirl of clouds hung over the northeast corner of town. Lightning flashed inside the swirl. Right over where the mansion would be. And Bannig. She knew that with everything in her.

She ran around to the side of the diner where a couple of huge oak trees stood and laid her hand against the bark of one. Liz felt a little silly, but there was nobody around. "Hey, Boreon, I don't know if you'll get this message, but we could use a little help up here in Clear Water. Send whoever you can as soon as you can. Thanks."

She patted the tree, then turned to head uptown. She figured she'd apologize to Kaeden and Charly later, but she needed to see Bannig that night. Unfortunately, she realized her jaunt would have to wait.

Kaeden leaned against the other tree, one eyebrow raised. "Interesting."

"Thought I told you to stay upstairs."

"Yep. I took a lesson from you and didn't listen."

She really hated when the things she did or said got thrown back in her face. He followed her as she trudged back up the stairs. At the top, Liz swung around to look back uptown. The clouds were gone, and a bright moon shone down on town. The fireworks were done for the night.

Charly sat at the table, talking on her phone. She snorted when they came back in. "She was going to go, wasn't she?"

"Looked that way to me," Kaeden admitted.

"I was talking to the trees." Even to her ears that sounded lame. Liz blew out a frustrated breath and flopped down on the sofa. "Fine. I'm here. What's next?"

"We've already got people set up to watch both sites," Charly said. "Next, we figure out how to fortify this place. If this building is node central, we're going to need to get out the big guns in protection."

"I'm not sure there is any protection from this," Liz said. "But we'll do what we can. Besides, we don't know the exact spot. The node could be here at the diner, or out in the middle of the parking lot, or next door. The map is too small to pinpoint anything beyond this general area."

"This is going to be bad, isn't it?"

"Yeah, I'm afraid so. Look, Charly, I'm used to this. I've dealt with Bannig before. Why don't you go away for a few days? Far away. Somewhere warm and sunny, with sand, sea, and cabana boys to serve you silly drinks with umbrellas."

Charly was shaking her head before Liz had finished talking. Her reaction didn't surprise Liz but did settle a heaviness on her shoulders. She didn't want to see anything happen to Charly. Or Kaeden. Or anyone.

"I'm not going to run. Tell you what, after this is all over, why don't we both go find those cabana boys?" She grinned at Kaeden sprawled on the sofa bed and raised her eyebrow at Liz. "Although, I don't think you'll need one."

Liz didn't know whether to be happy or run screaming into the street. These emotions were all so new, so raw.

They spent the rest of the evening doing what they

could to protect Charly's building. They poured salt, set out wards and crystals, and even did a super-duper, over-the-top, you-ain't-getting-through-this-no-way-no-how protection spell. By the time they finished, this world had never seen a more guarded place.

Charly headed down to bed. Kaeden peeled off his shirt and opened the sofa bed. Looked like she had a roommate. Not that she'd complain, but his being there did put a crimp in her usual style.

"Liz, if you want me to leave, I will."

Did she? Yes. And no. And...damn. "No. Stay. Thanks."

They curled up together and scratched a couple of itches—several times—before Kaeden dropped into a deep sleep.

She didn't know how much later Kaeden and she awoke to the sound of a phone ringing, well before dawn lit the eastern sky. He grabbed his, but before he could answer, Liz got a tingle. "Tell Ray we'll be there in ten."

Kaeden answered while Liz hauled on her jeans and a shirt. He quickly followed suit after ending the call.

"How did you know?"

She shrugged. "I don't know the specifics. I just know I have to be there. What did he tell you?"

"A break-in at the local farm supplier. So why do you have to be there?"

"Don't know. Just that I do."

They jogged down the stairs, and Liz grabbed some supplies from her car along with her special coat. Her coat was ankle length, black leather, and fitted with a high collar, a double-breasted front, narrow sleeves, and a boatload of handy pockets. She'd bought the castoff from a thrift shop with money from her first job with Bannig. The piece fit her like a glove and served as a reminder that affection was fleeting.

While Kaeden drove, Liz tucked a variety of knives and other weapons into her boots, belt, and pockets. She also tucked a heavy, unbreakable vial in a special pocket inside the top of her left boot. Kaeden eyed her as much as he could while driving.

"You already know I'm good with them," she said to his unasked question. "Besides, I don't like guns. They need ammo and require licenses and are expensive. Knives are cheap. You can pick them up anywhere, or even make one out of scraps." Next, she strapped a blackjack to her left wrist.

"You look like you're getting ready for a war."

"I am. Tonight is a practice run to get something they need, or even a diversionary tactic. We might see two or three thugs at the most."

"So why the hardware? Between you, me, and Uncle Ray, we should be able to handle two or three."

"I believe in being prepared."

He stopped the car in front of the local farm supply store. A black-and-white, lights flashing, sat there with Ray and another man standing in the light. They stared as she and Kaeden got out.

"What's she doing here?" the man demanded as soon as he saw her. Liz got strange vibes from him. She sensed he wasn't what he seemed. And he smelled dark. Oily. With overtones of skunk.

"She's a special investigator," Kaeden said. "She's been looking into problems like this in other towns. Liz, Bruce is the store owner."

Bruce glared at her. "Could be she's the problem."

"Now, Bruce," Ray said. "You know that's not true. How about if you finish that list of what's missing for her? Kaeden, I'd like to speak to you and Agent St. John."

The three of them walked over to Kaeden's car, out of earshot of Bruce, though the guy tried to listen. Liz moved so she could keep an eye on him and held her knock-out stick in the folds of her coat, handy but out of sight.

"What's wrong, Uncle Ray?"

"I'm not sure yet. Do you?" He looked at Liz, and she understood. He might not like that she was here, but he knew he needed her.

A frisson of energy went down her spine. As calmly as possible, she unbuttoned her coat and slipped the material off. She also palmed one knife. Kaeden eyed her but didn't say anything. Bruce chose that moment to rush them. Before either Kaeden or his uncle could move, Bruce attacked Ray. Liz kicked at Bruce's head, but he moved fast for an old man. Too fast. He spun and took off. Uncle Ray lay on the ground, blood staining his head, but Liz didn't have time to check him over. "Take care of your uncle."

She chased after Bruce. Liz could move fast, but that thing moved faster. And he knew the ground. She didn't. Plus, although a nice full moon and one streetlight illuminated the area, darkness still obscured the perimeter. Liz lost him in the shadows. "Damn."

Liz headed back toward the cars then a small noise to her left made her duck. A bullet whizzed over her head.

Old Bruce jumped her. In close quarters, Liz could

hold her own against almost anything, but this guy gave her a challenge. She pulled out every trick she knew, and he kept swinging. Until she went for the obvious. Knee to the groin, clenched fists on the back of the neck. Even with that, he kept going. Damn. What was this guy? Then she knew. A shade. Definitely not one of the blobs Bannig had been throwing at her. Shades were almost unstoppable.

Liz backed off as much as she could, with him following. She only needed a few seconds. She flicked her best knife at his heart, and he went down. The blade was a special one with several spells. While the knife and spells wouldn't kill a shade, they would hold one immobile for a few seconds. And that was all she needed.

She sat on Bruce and pinned his clothes to the ground with her other knives in strategic spots. Then she pulled the vial from her boot. By now, Kaeden and his uncle had joined them, flashlights and guns in hand.

"Liz, we can take over now," Kaeden said.

"Yeah. I don't know what got into him," Uncle Ray said. "Bruce may have an occasional temper fit, but he's basically a nice guy."

She shook her head. "You don't understand." She opened the vial and held the container over Bruce's chest. "This isn't the man you knew."

She pulled her knife from his chest and used the blade to slit open his shirt. No blood flowed from the wound. Only an open slice where her weapon had gone in. He bucked and squirmed, but Liz held on tight. Then she dumped the vial of holy water over the cut.

The scream that came from him was beyond human. Liz jumped back as his skin began to blister, as if he'd been hit with a strong acid, and a stench of ammonia and skunk roiled off him.

Kaeden snatched her as she jumped back. "What the hell did you pour on him? Are you trying to kill him?"

She grabbed Kaeden's hand and upended the last few drops of water. He jerked back, then stared at his hand. Fortunately, nothing happened. "It's holy water. And I hope he does die. Or at least the thing inside him."

Ray stepped toward Bruce, but what he saw next had him scooting back. Even in the dim light, they could see the dark shade rising from Bruce's chest. The thing writhed in the air, its face contorting like the painting *The Scream*, then burst into pieces and disappeared, and the shell that had been Bruce dissolved into nothingness.

Liz retrieved her blades, careful not to touch the gore on them. She jabbed them into the ground several times until they were semi-clean, then she pulled a heavy cloth from a pocket of her coat and wrapped them.

Ray and Kaeden stared at her.

"What happened?" Ray asked. "Was that Bruce?"

"Yes, he *was* Bruce. At one time. The man you know as Bruce has probably been dead for a couple of days. Shades like that always use up bodies fast. What you saw was nothing more than animation. The same as the guy from the cabin a couple of days ago." She turned and strode back to the car. She had a nosebleed, a split lip, and would have a shiner in the morning, not to mention assorted aches and bruises in other places. Getting beat up was for the birds. She knew she healed fast, but sheesh.

"Here." Kaeden gently cleaned the blood off her face. "You were amazing out there. I've never seen anyone fight like that."

"Yeah, well, you learn fast in this business, and I've been doing this for a long time." She sighed and leaned her head back. "Can we get out of here yet?"

"Soon. Why don't you get in the car? I'll handle things with Uncle Ray." He opened the door and helped her settle in, then brought her coat. He tucked the collar around her neck and smoothed the rest down over her like a blanket.

The welcome warmth enveloped her. Now that the adrenaline had worn off, the cold air got to Liz. She knew most of the shivers were from reaction. Liz really wanted a drink. Something measured by proof not the amount of chocolate.

While Kaeden and his uncle talked, she glanced at the sky. "Hey, Powers, you got a mess to clean up down here. Unless you're planning on waiting until this is all over. I think your cleanup crew's going to be busy around these parts. And I could really use some help. Got anyone else like me sitting around?"

Personally, she didn't care what happened to the blob. She just wanted to go. If Kaeden didn't finish soon, she'd start walking. Fortunately, less than five minutes later, he climbed into the car, and they took off.

"You, okay?" he asked.

"Yeah. Just great."

"Uncle Ray wants to talk to us both tomorrow."

"Fine." She wasn't in the mood for chitchat. Thank the PTBs, the man took a hint occasionally.

When they got back to her place, Liz headed for

the bathroom. One look in the mirror had her wincing. Absolutely not a pretty picture. And by tomorrow, she would look even worse. She stripped out of her clothes, got into the shower, leaned her head against the wall, and let the hot water ease some of the aches. Although she healed fast, it would take a bit of time.

The door opened, letting in chilly air and something else. Or rather, someone else. She opened her one good eye and looked Kaeden over. The man stole her breath. Muscles that looked like a sculptor had carved them, and the lightest touch of fur covering his chest. And even more interesting lower down. The fact that her eyes closed again showed how crappy she felt.

"What…?"

"Shhh."

The next thing she knew, he was massaging shampoo into her hair. Then soap over her shoulders. Down her back. Oh, goddess, that felt so good. Liz let him do his thing. She certainly felt warmer. And from the hardness poking her in the back, so did he. When he turned her around to soap her front, she reached for him, but he shook his head and put her hand on his shoulder.

"This is for you. Relax."

And she did. Sort of. But when he started massaging her lower parts, she went limp. Who knew soap, hot water, and someone else's fingers could do so much? When the orgasm hit her, her legs turned to rubber.

He held Liz until her heart returned to normal. Then he turned off the water, grabbed a towel, and dried her off. She stood there, wrapped in that big fluffy towel while he dried himself. She didn't think her brain was functioning. He did some quick first aid to her face and hands, then led her out. The bed had been turned down, and a steaming cup of something that smelled decadent sat on the side table.

"What's that?"

"My special hot chocolate." He pulled her ratty nightshirt over her head.

She poked her head out. "Um, no offense, but I could use something stronger than a mug of cocoa."

"Uh-huh. Into bed. You need sleep." He held up the blankets while she crawled in. Then he fluffed the pillows so she sat against the back and handed her the cocoa.

Liz took a healthy swig and nearly choked. Then took another, slower sip as the smooth cocoa laced with something that tasted like hundred proof soothed edgy nerves. The nerves edged back up as he crawled into the bed, next to her. She leaned her head over on his shoulder, listening to him breathe.

Between the shower and the special cocoa, and his soft breaths, she began to get drowsy and slid down into the blankets. Kaeden kissed her forehead before curling up next to Liz. Nobody had ever done that for her. Cared for her like he did. She thought she fell in love with him at that moment.

And that scared her more than the shade and the nodes and even Bannig.

Chapter Seventeen

By the time Liz woke up, the brightness and angle of the sun told her she'd slept most of the morning. The aroma of coffee must have brought her out of sleep. She managed to open one eye to see Kaeden sitting at her table with several books and maps strewn across the surface. "Mmff?"

Her mumble was enough to get a mug of coffee in her hand. Several gulps later, she opened another eye. "Reading?"

"Yeah. Trying to learn about what I've seen and heard over the last couple of days. Figured I should understand what the hell I am and what's going on."

A quick glance from Liz showed the books were all on paranormal beings and activities. They were public library types with nothing more than surface info. She pulled out the second chair and sat, mug in hand. "If there's something you want to know, you can ask. I've seen most of the things in those books. And a few that aren't."

"You look like shit."

Okay, that didn't help. But he spoke so nicely, almost like a compliment. "Thanks, I think."

She nodded at the books. "So, what do you want to know?"

"Would you like something to eat?"

Liz didn't bother to look at the clock. Her stomach

told her all she needed to know. Breakfast was long gone with lunchtime currently on the menu. That must have been exceedingly good cocoa Kaeden had given her. She'd never slept so late. Her stomach rumbled, answering his question before she could. "Sure."

"Food first, info second. Give me a minute."

For his food, she'd wait. Liz went into the bathroom and took inventory of her hurts. Soreness, cuts that were already scabbed over, a whole lot of bruises, but nothing serious. A glance in the mirror showed the worst. Her left eye was nearly swollen shut and already a lovely shade of dark purple. Her bottom lip was twice the normal size. She would never be a contender for a beauty pageant, but at that point, she thought she looked more like a Picasso portrait.

But she'd looked worse. And hurt worse. Kaeden's special cocoa had done the trick.

Liz returned and sat down to look through the books. The first five, she laid aside as basically useless. Then she got to the one at the bottom of the pile. That one had definite possibilities. The brown leather binding crackled as she opened the cover. The pages were yellow with age. She couldn't read the title, and a few pages were missing at the beginning, but the information was mostly intact. And what information there was. She'd never seen a book so in depth about the powers of evil. There was even a chapter on shades like the one she'd fought. But nothing on Bannig. Or power nodes. Or canes with strange writing.

Kaeden came back with a plate steaming with fluffy waffles topped with thick whipped cream and blueberries—delicious and easier to eat. God, she loved this man. As the thought ran through her brain, Liz nearly choked on the food. *Love.* Something that did not exist for her. But this man had her thinking about staying. About loving. About belonging.

She swallowed her terror and attempted to put on a calm face. Fortunately, her years as an agent for O.W.L. helped in that department.

"Nice book," she said to cover her lapse. Even though the waffles melted in her mouth, the act of eating still hurt. Much more of this kind of tasty food, and she'd have to update her duds to a larger size.

"I found that one on your shelves. By the way Uncle Ray wants to talk to you as soon as possible."

"Call him. I might as well get this over with."

"What was that thing last night?"

"They're called shades. They take over a willing body and can only be killed with holy water, like I did last night."

"Willing? You mean Bruce let that thing take him over?"

"Not quite the way you mean. The act is sort of like making a contract with the devil. You make a wish. Or say a prayer. Something important to you. Then someone shows up and offers to make your wish come true, for a little favor in the future. They prey on the desperate or the greedy."

"Bruce had a greedy streak. He always wanted more than he had."

"Then that's your in. He probably agreed to something that would make him a lot of money, never thinking of payback. Or betting on sometime in the distant future. People like him rarely think of the here and now. Unfortunately, what usually happens is the wish is granted, and payback is extracted in the same week. Sometimes the same day."

"So, in that way, he was willing," Kaeden said.

"Yes."

"What else will we be up against?"

"Lower-level demons, a ghoul or two, some rogue elves, vamps, or shape-shifters, weres. Those are mostly corporeal problems. They're fast and strong but can be destroyed. Like any human, you go for the kill, and they stay down. The problems are things like shades. The things without bodies." As Liz talked, his eyes got wider, and she sighed. Shocking a hot bed partner is never a good thing to do.

"But there's no telling what we'll face." She glanced around. "Answer the phone and tell your uncle he can come any time."

The phone rang as she carried her dishes to the sink, washed and dried them, and cleaned up what Kaeden hadn't, which didn't amount to much. But the task gave her something to do until he finished.

"Uncle Ray will be here shortly. How are you feeling?"

"Like I've been beaten up."

He got an ice pack from the freezer, wrapped a towel around it, and gently laid the pack against her face, followed by a kiss on the tip of her nose.

Liz held the ice against her cheek while he checked the cuts on first one hand, then the other. She guessed she fidgeted too much because he sat back on his heels and smiled up at her.

"You're not used to having other people do things for you, are you?"

"That obvious, huh?"

He smiled and gently touched a spot on her face

that didn't hurt. "Sort of. I'm done with your hands, and I don't remember cuts anywhere else, but a lot of bruises." He handed her a couple of extra-strength pain killers. "You might want to take these."

"Thanks." She swallowed them as two people came in the door. Kaeden's uncle she expected, but Charly? The diner should have been open.

"Charly?"

"Got some new help in, though I'll have to let the cook off for a few days around the full moon." She shrugged. "Hey, who doesn't get cranky once a month? Equal opportunity here." She studied Liz. "Nice face. Kaeden told me you ran into a little trouble."

"A little."

"Hope the other guy looks worse."

"He does."

"Good. Now, tell me what happened last night."

Kaeden and Liz brought her up to speed.

"This really is serious, isn't it?" Charly studied Liz's face and hands.

Each and every one of those bruises and cuts hurt. The pain pills had yet to take the edge off. "Yeah, I'm afraid so."

"You kids have been dabbling in things you shouldn't," Ray said when they'd finished.

"Uncle Ray, I haven't been a kid for ten years," Kaeden said. "And you can't deny what we saw last night. That…thing might have looked like Bruce, but we all know it wasn't. Or the one we found at the cabin."

Ray's shoulders drooped, and he sighed. "You're right. I know." His cell phone rang, and they got quiet while he answered. "Got a bad accident out on Newport

Road. Could use your help, Kaeden."

They both took off, leaving Charly and Liz to talk.

"Charly, I'd like to make some suggestions," Liz said.

"Like what?"

"You should carry protection. Nothing fancy. Regular stuff will do, like holy water. Keep a vial with you at all times."

"No silver bullets?" Charly asked, a grin peeping from her lips.

"Nah. Too much trouble and too expensive. Though wearing a silver cross wouldn't hurt."

"You don't wear one," she pointed out.

"Too dangerous in a fight. I used to wear one and almost got choked once."

"Might make some of the vamps a little uncomfortable," Charly said.

Liz thought about Alex and how he'd helped them at the river. "How about you carry a small spray bottle of holy water. But keep the bottle handy." Charly nodded and Liz relaxed. "Have we heard anything from either of our groups at the sites?"

Charly shook her head. "Nothing yet."

"I'd like to go out to them. I know the people there are sensitive to the nodes, but I'm probably more attuned than anyone."

"Which one first?"

She closed her eyes. Which one? Bridge or gas dump? She played a hunch. "Bridge."

Just then, someone knocked at the door. Charly answered, and Misty stood there. "Charly, Walt cut himself bad. We need help."

Charly dashed out. After they left, Liz blew out a

sigh, glad for the chance to be alone for a few moments. There were way too many people around her of late, though some of them she didn't mind, but she still missed her solitude. She also thought about what she had to do. She knew Kaeden wouldn't agree, but he didn't have a choice. The job belonged to her alone.

She went down the steps. Charly stood outside the back door, staring up the steps as if she knew Liz was going to come down.

"Going somewhere?"

"Yes. I have to go. You know that."

"Yeah, I know."

"How's Walt?"

"Already healing. Cut wasn't as bad as Misty thought, but we needed to take care of him." She glanced at Liz with that *stripping you down to your soul* look she got. "You shouldn't go alone. Call Kaeden."

She shook her head. "No. He's needed at the accident."

"You can barely move."

Her friend had that right, but she had to go. "I'll be fine. Besides, nothing is probably going to happen until evening."

Charly wrapped a hand around Liz's arm. "Be careful."

Wow. More warm comfort. Much more of this and Liz was going to start feeling…she didn't know what, but something good. "I will. Thanks."

She took off and headed for the bridge. If she could beat Bannig to the node, then maybe she'd have the edge over him. Besides, she had to deal with her former mentor by herself. Nobody else could help.

When Liz got to the bridge, she didn't see anyone

around. She'd expected some of their people to be there. And there wasn't any traffic, an oddity for that time of day. As soon as she got out of the car, she could sense the power. The node hadn't reached full strength yet, but the energy was there. But where exactly?

Liz circled around the car searching for the strongest vibe. She'd parked on the town side of the bridge but sensed the pull farther out. The span was one of those old-fashioned metal kinds with an open grid base and huge side girders that arched over the river. As she neared the middle of the span, the pull grew stronger until her body hummed. She passed the halfway point, and the sensations lessened, so she turned around and went back to where they were the strongest.

If asked, she'd have had a tough time describing what she was experiencing. A part of her wanted to stay and drink all that energy in. Absorb the power. Be the power. Another part of her wanted to run screaming from that place. The power didn't project good or evil, but a combination of the two. Like a yin and yang. Perfectly matched. She stood there, eyes closed, letting the force wash over her. That is, until an entirely different tingle had her ducking as a bullet pinged off the girder next to her.

Liz jumped behind the beam as another shot rang out. They were coming from the area where she'd parked the car. She couldn't see anyone, but someone was there and probably more than one of them. Liz didn't have too many alternatives. Standing out in the open, she did the only thing she could think of.

She jumped.

Chapter Eighteen

Liz dropped feet first into cold rushing water. Fortunately, the river ran deep around the bridge. As she went under, she knew the power had nearly reached a peak, almost ready to burst. Unfortunately, so were her lungs. She came up on the town side of one of the supports. She couldn't stay there long. The strong current pulled at her, and she didn't have anything to hang onto. Liz took several breaths and dove down, swimming with the current. When she got to a spot where low-hanging trees and shrubs offered ample concealment, she climbed out on the opposite side of the river from town and her car. Unfortunately, the far side offered almost no protection. Chief Ray had done a good job of cleaning up the river area with an eye to beauty but not hiding. She carefully made her way up the bank, listening as well as she could for anything that sounded like someone looking for her.

"Do you see her?"

The question followed by breaking branches and swearing had her scrambling for cover. She sank into the muck and underbrush. They drew closer, and she held her breath.

"Bannig's not going to be happy about this," one of them said.

"We did what he said and kept her away."

Liz recognized that second voice. Mr. Dirty

Fingernails. The temptation to climb that bank and have a go at him nearly got to her, but they had the advantage. She might not like hiding from a fight, but there were two of them with guns. She was wet, cold, nearly blind in one eye, and already hurting. Not great odds.

"She's gone," he said. "Let's go."

"What if she comes back?"

"We'll be waiting. You stay on this side of the bridge. I'll watch the other."

Their voices faded back in the direction they'd come from. Liz stayed crouched where she was, shivering, covered in muck, twigs poking her in places she didn't want to be poked, and tried to figure out her next move. She didn't have a whole lot of options. They'd be waiting for her on either side of the bridge, and Bannig would be here soon.

As quietly as she could, she climbed out. A barely-two-lane road wound along the bank between the trees. She'd have an easier time walking the road, but she'd be in the open. Liz climbed uphill away from the river into the tree line and followed the road as well as she could. She realized being quiet in the woods when dry leaves are underfoot and freezing your ass off wouldn't win her any prizes in the easy category. But either she moved better than she thought, or the man on this side had no senses. Considering who he hung out with, she leaned toward the latter.

He stood there, in the middle of the road, away from the bridge, kicking at stones. The guy never knew what hit him.

And yes, she felt some major remorse for taking out a human, but the guilt lasted only long enough for him to melt into a blob. Not human. Not on her side. No remorse. Liz retrieved her knife and ducked back into the trees as she tried to figure out her next move. She couldn't exactly walk across the bridge. She didn't have a whole lot of time as the sun crept nearer to sundown. She had run out of options.

Liz picked up the rifle from off the road. Fortunately, the weapon had fallen away from the ooze. Liz checked the load and sighting. If she liked guns better, this would be one she'd pick. She saw a shadow where she thought her stalker stood and fired.

The string of filth that drifted across the river told her she'd either hit him or come damn close. Liz smiled and stepped out onto the bridge, firing as she went. She used the girders as much as she could for cover, but she was still in the open. When Liz reached the center, all that power pulled at her like no other time. A large whirlpool formed under the bridge. She also saw a boat coming downstream. A boat carrying one person, and Liz knew him. She also saw a couple of cars coming down the road from town. One belonged to Kaeden, the other to Chief Ray.

She knew they wouldn't get here before Bannig did, and she had to stop him from getting this node, so she performed an encore. She dove into the water right into the middle of that whirlpool. As she did, something burned her side and chest, and she knew her stalker had gotten in a couple of good shots.

Liz didn't know what dying felt like even though she'd been close a couple of times. But she'd never experienced this euphoria. This sense that she was a part of everything. The water pulled her under, but she experienced no fear. Instead, she'd finally found peace.

She felt happier than she'd ever been in her life. Liz knew when her feet touched the bottom, and she knew she wasn't breathing, but she still wasn't afraid. She pulled all that power into her and held the energy inside for the briefest of seconds. She could see everything, past and present. But not the future. Funny how she found that interesting.

She saw Kaeden standing on the bridge, looking down while he stripped out of his clothes. His uncle had her shooter in cuffs. Bannig's boat circled the spot where she went down, then took off like all the demons from hell were on his tail, and maybe they were. Liz reached out her mind to his boat and thought the word *stop*, and he did. She enjoyed watching him drift toward the rapids with no power. Liz didn't know what she could do with this new power of hers, and the temptation to find out intrigued her, but something inside her knew this wasn't the right time. She understood that when Bannig gained control of the boat and took off at high speed.

As Kaeden hit the water, Liz rose to the surface. When she got to the top, Kaeden swam toward her, but she stopped him. "Don't come any closer and don't touch me. Not yet."

"Not yet? Liz! I thought you were dead. Are you okay? I saw blood—"

"I know. Please. Wait."

She hung there, treading water, fighting the current, but Liz knew she was doing the right thing. She closed her eyes and envisioned all that beautiful power flowing from her, dissipating in the water. Electricity sparked around her, so she grabbed one of the supports that ran down into the bedrock, kind of like a grounding wire, and let go of the energy. Between the water and the grounding, the universe reclaimed all that lovely power. Well, almost all. After all, she wasn't stupid.

She dog-paddled over to Kaeden. "Now you can touch me."

"Are you hurt?"

"No."

With his help, Liz got back to shore where they had quite an audience now. Ray stood there, along with Charly, most of the members of the coven, and a few dozen others. She must have looked a sight because when Kaeden hauled her out of the water, dozens of eyes went wide and jaws dropped. Liz looked down to find her shirt sporting two holes, one near her chest, the other on her right side, both stained heavily with blood. When she pulled the material up to check, there were two well-healed scars that looked as if they'd been there for ages.

And maybe they had been.

Charly wrapped a blanket around her. Liz could still sense that core of energy inside her, but not enough to keep her warm in the falling temperatures. Kaeden yanked his clothes back on as Liz strode over to her stalker who sat in the back of the chief's car.

"Guess this finally puts you out of the picture."

"You don't know nothin', bitch. You think you won? We'll be back. You can't stop us."

"Actually, I can." Liz turned and strode away from him. Then she saw her car.

All four tires had been punctured, the windows broken out, and deep gouges marred the exterior. Inside, the seats were slashed to ribbons and her stuff strewn all over and trampled into the ground. A quick glance told her the cane had disappeared, but for some reason, they hadn't touched the puzzle.

Thunder rumbled in the cloudless sky and lightning flashed. This time, she was seriously pissed.

"Liz." Kaeden came to her, but she waved him off. She'd never been able to direct her anger before, but she aimed her gaze at Dirty Fingernails and let fly. Lightning flashed right next to the car, and everyone scattered. Everyone except Kaeden and Charly.

"Liz!"

Liz barely heard him, but she felt him when he pulled her to his chest. "Liz! Look at me."

He swung her around in his arms, but all she wanted was to get to her stalker. Then Kaeden kissed her.

Damn. That man knew how to take a good piss off and deflate her anger like a popped balloon. But she wouldn't complain. Besides, he replaced the rage with something else. Between the buzz from the node and the lightning, Liz was so stoked she could barely keep from stripping him down and having her way with him right there, audience and all.

By the time he backed off, the only evidence left of her snit was a scorch mark next to the chief's car and a white-faced stalker in the back seat—one who smelled like an outhouse. In the summer.

Tears leaked from her eyes. Kaeden reached out and wiped them away with his thumb. She jerked away. "I don't cry."

"I know."

"I never cry." Although she seemed to be doing a lot of that lately.

"I know."

He wrapped her in his arms, holding her close while she wept. But her tears didn't last long. Her rage still simmered. Kaeden must have sensed something because the next thing she knew, he'd bustled her into the back seat of his car and climbed in next to her. He tossed the keys to Charly. "You drive."

"Got you."

They headed back to the diner, Liz's head on Kaeden's shoulder. Nobody said anything on the short drive back.

"You. Get a shower." Kaeden aimed her toward the bathroom.

"You don't want to join me?" She gave him what she thought was a come-on look and beckoned with her finger toward the bathroom.

"Not right now." He all but pushed her into the bathroom, then closed the door.

Damn. Then Liz got a good look at herself in the mirror. Double damn. And wow. All signs of her fight with Bruce were gone, and her skin had a sheen she'd never noticed before. Liz shucked off her clothes and checked. She had those new scars, but nothing else remained. Even the scar across her ribs from Bannig was gone. And she felt wonderful. Liz also noticed something else. All her senses seemed like they had been turned up to high. The light was brighter, and she could hear Kaeden moving around in the outer room. In fact, she could hear people in the diner two floors down, not exactly what they were saying, but she knew they were there. And she smelled all those lovely aromas as well.

After a quick shower, Liz donned her old nightshirt she'd left hanging on the back of the door and went out.

With her heightened senses, even the soft cotton abraded her skin. Kaeden had his head buried in the fridge, and Charly was nowhere to be seen, but Liz smelled something wonderful coming from the dishes with lids on the table. She closed her eyes and inhaled deeply. Fried chicken, mashed potatoes, corn, and apple cobbler for dessert. Her mouth watered, and her stomach grumbled before Kaeden even noticed she had come out.

He straightened up and produced two beers. "You hungry?"

"Starved." And yet, also still buzzing and she didn't know which she wanted more—him or the food. Since her stomach wouldn't shut up, she settled for the food.

"I had the tow truck take your car to my place. It'll be safer there in my garage than out in the open."

Aw. Sweet. Liz knew Kaeden had all kinds of questions for her, but he held them off until they finished—which didn't take her long. She polished off her dessert before he'd finished half his meal. He kept looking at her like she was something strange, and maybe she was, but she didn't care. She felt too good to care. And too buzzed to sit still. While he finished, Liz prowled the apartment. Confined. She needed to get out. But clothes were kind of an issue. When she'd gone shopping, she'd picked up undies, boots, and things like soap. The basics. She hadn't bought an entire wardrobe. Liz had figured what she had in her bags would do for the time being. What she hadn't figured on was Mr. Dirty Fingernails turning everything into sludge.

Liz jumped when someone knocked at the door,

and Charly came in bearing two bags. She dumped them on the couch into a pile of material that was quickly separated into skirts and tank tops. "There's no way we're even close in size for jeans, but I figured you could do something with these skirts. They're both too tight on me but should work for you—with a belt. And the length will probably come to right below knee-length on you, but they're better than nothing."

"Wow. Thanks." Liz didn't know what to say. These two people took better care of her than she did. She grabbed one of the skirts and pulled the dark blue flowy material on. The loose elastic waist drooped a little. Skirts were so not her style, but she figured the old saying about beggars being choosers fit. Besides, the flowy material covered the necessary parts and would do until she got something else. Liz turned around and pulled off her nightshirt and replaced that with one of the tanks. When she spun back, Kaeden was gaping at her as if she'd sprouted horns.

She patted her hair, thinking she'd mussed the short curls when she changed shirts. "Is something wrong?"

Charly chuckled. "Always knew I had a reason to be jealous of you, but wow. If I wasn't solid straight, even I'd be tempted. Hey, Kaeden, maybe we should thank those demons for giving us a girl."

Liz had absolutely no idea what Charly meant.

"And the best part," Charly continued, "is that she has no clue. Liz, a word of advice—when all this mess is over, get yourself some girly clothes and wear them."

"Um, okay." She still had no clue what they were talking about, but she'd play along. In the meantime, she needed to get out of there. "Speaking of that, I'm going shopping. You want to go with? Oh. Wait. You need to. Or you need to let me borrow one of your vehicles. Or…"

"Liz!" Kaeden put both hands on her shoulders. "Stop. Before we go anywhere, I wish you'd tell us what happened."

She pulled away, ignoring the hurt in his face. If she stayed close to him, she was going to jump his bones, but she preferred to do those activities without an audience. "Look, can we talk while we drive? I really need to get out of here."

Kaeden stared at her for perhaps a minute, then nodded and grabbed his keys. "You coming, Charly?"

"Can't. Have to get back downstairs to show the newbies how to close things down, but I'll talk to you both later."

Liz nearly flew down the steps to the parking lot and paced around the car until Kaeden got there and let her in. She knew he was worried, especially after he'd glanced at her for the millionth time. They did a whirlwind shopping trip and headed back with numerous bags of clothes for her, including a skirt that fit her. She liked the way Kaeden looked at her when she caught him looking.

Back inside, Liz peeled out of her borrowed clothes, doing a naughty dance for Kaeden. She didn't know why her libido wouldn't let go, but she really needed him. Liz saw his eyes go wide, but he kept backing away. She thought she had him when he pulled off his shirt and tossed the top in the bathroom.

"How 'bout a shower?" he asked, his voice low and oh, so sexy.

"Oh. Yes. A shower! That would be wonderful. All

that lovely water cascading over both of us." Liz finished stripping and headed in. And realized her mistake when she heard the door slam and something being wedged under the knob.

"Kaeden?" She jiggled the knob, but the door wouldn't budge. "Kaeden!"

"Make that a cold shower, Liz. I'll wait."

She kicked. She screamed. She yanked. She swore. She stomped. She cried.

She eventually wound down, then got in the shower and turned the tap to barely warm. By the time the water turned cold all on its own, the buzz had settled down to a nice, even high. The door opened, and Kaeden came in with towels and her new fluffy bathrobe.

"You okay now?"

"Better. I'm, um, sorry about that." And a part of her was. But a part of her wasn't.

"What happened to you? If I didn't know you better, I'd say you were on some kind of drug or something."

"The power node happened. At least I think so. Man, if that's what Bannig's been feeling, no wonder he's hot for these nodes. What I don't understand is why nobody else is hanging around to absorb them. The energy is like a high you wouldn't believe."

Kaeden handed her a mug of tea, and she curled up on a corner of the sofa, though she still had more energy than she knew what to do with.

He stared at her as if she was some sort of freak, and maybe she was. "So, you and Bannig are two of the few people who can absorb this energy but not end up dead."

"I'm beginning to think only I can. I'm feeling really energized, but Bannig's not looking so good lately. So, you're saying I'm a freak of nature."

"Not a freak. Someone special. With special abilities. You said so yourself—nobody knows exactly what you are. Maybe this is why."

"Yeah. Right."

"What if you asked your bosses? Would they tell you if you guessed?"

They'd always put her off when she asked them before. "Not a bad idea. I wonder—"

"Just ask. What do you need to do?"

"I need to meditate, go into a trance. I prefer using crystals but can sometimes go into a trance without them." Her stomach grumbled. She'd eaten not long ago, but she felt like it had been days not hours. She figured all that power burned up a lot of calories.

Kaeden grinned. "Why don't you do your thing while I go downstairs and get you some more food? You want anything in particular?"

"Something with a lot of protein and carbs. I think that's what I'm going to need. But no caffeine or sugar, please. I'm buzzed enough."

He laughed and headed down while Liz tried to find a comfortable position and center herself. After several tries, she finally sat down on the floor with candles surrounding her inside a circle of salt. Liz closed her eyes, cleared her mind, and waited.

The white room appeared right away instead of the gray nothingness, but this time, the whiteness had definition. There were actual walls and a floor and ceiling. And a door. While Liz waited, she wondered if she could do more. Before long, soft carpet appeared underneath her, then a window, and pictures on the walls. And a fireplace. The room kept evolving, then stopped when the door opened, and Nick walked in along with a woman and another man. The man who had given her the cane.

He stood slightly behind the other two and caught her eye and shook his head. Interesting. He wanted her to stay quiet. Hmm—a PTB that went off the grid? Now she had leverage.

All three of them stared at their surroundings, then back at her. As they did, everything faded away and they were left once again with the empty room. The woman smiled at her.

"Your powers are developing quickly."

"Probably thanks to the power node I absorbed this afternoon." That got startled looks from all of them.

"You were able to absorb a node? And you had no effects?"

"Interesting. So, I guess you aren't all knowing. Yes, I absorbed the power, and beyond feeling like I'm on the highest high ever, I'm good. And there are two more to go, if I understand correctly what's going on. So, my question to you is, what am I that I can take on this power, hand the energy back to the universe, or at least, most of what I took on, and still be standing? Am I some kind of demon like Bannig?"

"No," all three of them answered at the same time, which settled that worry.

"What am I?"

They glanced at one another, then shook their heads. "We do not know," Nick said.

She hadn't expected that answer. "What do you mean you don't know?"

The woman stepped forward. "Just that, Elizabeth. We don't know. We saw your birth in our readings and knew you were going to be special, but we didn't know how special."

"You saw my birth? Then you must know who my parents are."

Again, a combined shaking of heads. "We do not."

Well, that sucked. Then she studied them. She didn't know who or what they were, but even angels could lie. Couldn't they?

"But we cannot," the woman said, as if answering her silent question. She held up her hand to forestall her next question before she asked. "Agreed, we may not always tell you everything, but we cannot lie."

"Okay, so you can't—or won't—tell me about myself. What about this ability of mine to handle the power. Did you know about that before this?"

"Not exactly. We had an idea, and all the prophesies say the…you…will be able to hold back the dark, but the proof is a most interesting development," the woman said.

"And you can't tell me any more about how to stop Bannig or when the next node will blow or anything else."

"You have all the knowledge you need, Elizabeth. Follow your heart and your instincts. They have led you on the correct path so far."

The woman jerked a little and glanced at both men who nodded at her. "I am sorry, Elizabeth, but we must leave. Be careful with Bannig. He is so shrouded in darkness, even we cannot pierce the veil."

And before she could blink, they were gone, and she sat in the middle of her apartment with Kaeden at the table. She rose to her feet and joined him. "That was interesting."

"What happened? Did you find out anything?" He uncovered a plate holding a steak sandwich filled with onions and mushrooms, fries on the side, and a large glass of milk. She laughed at the milk, then downed the entire glass.

"Hey, you said no caffeine or sugar," he said as he drank his own.

"Works for me." As she ate, she told him what had happened. "So, I don't know any more now than I did before."

"Not true," he said. "We know where the next node will be and approximately when, and we know you can handle the energy. But we have to make sure you're there and not Bannig."

"And that, as they say, is the rub." She yawned widely. Although Liz still sensed the energy within, she also felt tired beyond measure, an odd combination.

Kaeden pulled out the bed and motioned her in. "Sleep. We'll work the details out in the morning."

She glanced at him, judging his mood. His answer to her unspoken question was to crawl into bed with her and show her that he really did care by holding her until she fell asleep.

As Kaeden watched Liz sleep, he thought about the events of the past few days. Blobs and shades and human-like things that weren't human—and Liz had handled them all with barely a blink. But when he'd seen her go into that river and not come up—he'd been ready to tear her shooter apart himself.

But she had come up, healed. And changed. Like on the highest high ever and almost glowing. She'd absorbed all that power and…

And what?

"What are you?" he whispered. "I should leave you, but I can't. You are someone—something so special, I can't even begin to understand. But I know you hold my heart. I can't let you go, even though I should. Who knows what you can be? What you can accomplish. I'll just hold you back. And yet, I love you, Elizabeth St. John. So there. I said so. I'm yours until the end." He chuckled quietly. "Which may be a lot sooner than we want."

He sank down, pulled her to his side, and slept.

****

The next morning dawned gray and damp. The kind of day that made a guy want to stay curled up in bed with a beautiful woman, hot chocolate, and no cares.

Shame life didn't work like that.

Kaeden and Liz were finishing up breakfast when there was a knock at the door.

"Come on in, Charly," Liz called.

The door opened, but Charly wasn't standing there. Misty was. And she didn't look happy. "Misty? What's wrong?" Kaeden asked.

"Charly's not here?"

"Um, no. Isn't she down at the diner?"

"No. And nobody's seen her, and she isn't answering her door or phone."

Before she finished talking, Kaeden grabbed his keys and bounded down the steps. Liz followed close behind. Inside, Charly's apartment didn't look any different. Nothing was out of place, except no Charly. This was so unlike her as to be weird. In all the years he'd known her, she'd never missed a day at the diner. Not even when sick. She might leave for a time during the day, but opening and closing were her things. She did not miss those. Ever.

"Misty, do you know how to open?"

She nodded, though Kaeden could tell she didn't want to.

"Open and get things going like normal. If anyone asks, Charly's out running errands. Okay?"

"Yeah." She disappeared down the steps.

When Liz turned around, she saw an envelope propped up on the table. On the outside of the large cream envelope, Liz's name stood out in black calligraphy.

Chapter Nineteen

Liz opened the envelope. Inside she found the usual sheet of heavy cream paper. Heart thumping, she read the words: *The cane is of utmost importance. Finding Charly will lead to the cane.*

Finding Charly?

"Liz?" She handed Kaeden the letter. She'd never given anyone one before. She'd never gotten more than one per job before. And they always disappeared after she signed them. She'd never had one like this. No signature needed. And no disappearing.

"Where are your crystals?" Kaeden asked.

"Most of them were destroyed at the river by my stalker." Then she got an idea. Liz ran for the door to Charly's bedroom, Kaeden on her heels. "Charly's. I can use hers. Better anyway to find her."

They double-timed into her room, and Liz pulled a good quartz pendant from Charly's box. They went into the living room, and she got to work.

"Is Charly in trouble?"

Maybe.

"Is she lost?"

No.

"Okay, that can mean two things," Kaeden said. "Either she's out running errands and doing fine, or she's been kidnapped but knows where she is. You need to be more specific."

"Yeah. I know." Liz tried again. "Has Charly been kidnapped?"

Maybe.

"Maybe? What kind of an answer is that?"

"Easy, Liz. The stones won't answer if you're agitated. You know that."

She did. She took several deep breaths, grounded herself, and tried again. "Is Charly safe?"

Maybe.

"Damn. This is getting us nowhere."

Kaeden took the crystal and headed back upstairs. "Come on."

"But—"

"That wasn't a request."

Nobody ordered her around. Even gorgeous men who served amazing food and drinks. Still, she followed.

Kaeden aimed her toward the sofa. Liz sat down on one end and watched as he went around the place turning off all but one of the lights. Next, he lit several candles and turned off the last lamp. Her irritation melted away. She refrained from fanning herself. Did the man honestly not know how hot he looked? Especially in candlelight?

He sat on the opposite end of the sofa, and she waited to see what he would do next.

"Give me your feet."

"Huh?" There came that brilliant conversationalist again.

"Your feet. Put them up here. Please."

Liz scrunched around until she could lean against the arm of the couch, her feet on the cushion between them. He took both and laid them in his lap. Then he started rubbing.

And she died.

Right there. In her attic room. She died.

How had she gone her entire life and never had a foot massage?

She forgot about O.W.L. And Bannig. And the nodes. And Charly. Her entire existence came down to the sensations this incredible man gave her. She nearly had an orgasm right there. Fully clothed. Her eyes closed, and incredible pleasure flowed over her.

"Liz?" His voice sounded low and mellow, like warm honey pouring over her.

"Hummmmm?"

"I want you to listen to my voice."

"Okay."

"Be quiet and listen. I want you to keep your eyes closed and draw a picture in your mind. A picture of a feather gently floating to the ground. Slowly. Softly."

Liz knew what he was doing—a form of hypnosis. But she'd never heard of a hypnotist who gave a great foot massage at the same time. They all should.

She followed his instructions, picturing the feather, relaxing, opening herself to his voice.

"Now, hold Charly's crystal in your hand."

He shifted, and the pendulum draped over her palms. She wrapped the stone in her hands and centered on the crystal, rubbing her fingers over the smooth coolness of the facets.

Kaeden's voice continued, "Now, think about Charly. Do you see her?"

"Um-hummm." And she did. She could see Charly as clearly as if she was sitting across from her.

"What is she doing?"

"She's in a car. And she's mad. And a little scared."

"Do you know where she is?"

She tried to concentrate on Charly, but her image grew blurry. "No. And the image is fading."

"Okay. Relax. Can you tell me anything else?"

"The car is a junky, older one, two-door. One of those awful pine air fresheners hanging from the knob on the radio." She sighed. "The vision's gone. I can't see her anymore."

"No problem. You did fine. You can open your eyes when you want."

She did and studied him. "How did I do that? Scratch that. How did you do that? Because I know for sure I never have."

He shrugged, which would have bugged her if he hadn't looked so cute. Besides, he was still rubbing her feet.

"An idea I had about you. You're so tuned to crystals, and they're good for seeking things out, so I thought I'd try taking you deep, like you do with your bosses. So, we know Charly's mad, but okay. Unfortunately, we don't know where she is. I shouldn't have asked you. You don't know this area well enough to recognize landmarks. Have you ever used crystals with a map?"

"For places, yes. Lots of times. But not often for people. I've tried to look for Bannig several times with no luck."

"He's not human. Charly is. I'll get the maps."

Liz sighed when he put her feet down, and he laughed. "Why do women love foot massages so much?"

Women? As in plural? She saw red. Okay, enough. Charly. She had to concentrate on her friend. "Hey, you try wearing three-inch stilettos while dancing backward. Or spending the day on your feet serving customers."

He patted her knee. If she hadn't been so relaxed, she'd probably have slapped him. The gesture came across as condescending. Liz was losing her objectivity. The man turned her on, but some things he did confused her. Should she jump his bones or slap him silly? She could go either way. She had to get a grip. He grinned at her, and her mote of irritation fled.

"You'll get more later. Charly first, then massage." He left the room to get the maps.

Massage? As in more than her feet? That settled her completely. She didn't care how patronizing some of his actions were— she'd died and entered Nirvana. Her mind was wavering from one extreme to the other. A side effect of the node? If so, an irritating one. This had to stop. She forced her muddled brain together as he returned and spread a map of the local area over the table.

"Center the crystal here at the diner."

She cleared the crystal and did as he asked, and the crystal started swinging in a wild arc, then the pendulum stopped and hung straight down. At the diner.

"Here? Charly's not here."

She tried again, with the same results. And again.

Then they heard a noise on the stairs. Liz ran to the door, Kaeden on her heels, and there below them stood Charly, dripping wet, scraped, bruised, hair a mess, one shoe missing, stockings torn, and her jacket hanging off one shoulder.

"Charly? What the hell happened?"

Kaeden and Liz dashed down to Charly's level. While he opened the door, Liz wrapped her arms around Charly's shoulders. Once they were inside, she steered Charly toward her kitchen where Kaeden had a chair pulled out for her.

"I'm gonna kill him." Charly stumbled to the chair and sank onto the seat, shoulders stiff, mouth clenched.

"Who?" Kaeden took her jacket, wincing when she cringed.

Liz dug out ice packs, got a towel wet, grabbed the first aid kit, and a blanket. She might not be able to boil water, but bandages she could handle. She didn't know whether that was a good thing or not, but she did have plenty of experience. To each, her own strength. Liz's happened to be fighting and handling blood.

Charly had nasty scrapes on both hands, both knees, and a bad cut down one shin. Her face showed scratches, but no bleeding, so Liz handed Kaeden a wet cloth and wrapped the blanket around her shoulders. "Clean up her face while I deal with her hands and legs."

"Tell us what happened." The quickest way to get someone's mind off what you're doing to them is to get them concentrating on something else. Liz cut off the rest of Charly's stockings above the knees. "You look like you were thrown out of a moving car."

"I jumped out when the bastard slowed down at Murphy's Curve. Ow!" She tried to back away from Liz, but she wouldn't let her. She had to see how deep the cut went to figure out if Charly needed stitches.

She didn't, thank the goddess, but Charly would

probably have a scar.

Kaeden had finished with her face and started cleaning up her hands. "Charly, you need to tell us exactly what happened."

Charly took a deep breath and exhaled slowly. "I was driving along old Route 5 to make a delivery when my truck died. So, I started walking."

"Why didn't you call me?" Kaeden asked.

Charly's face infused with red, and Kaeden shook his head. "Let me guess. Your cell phone battery is dead. You're getting as bad as Liz. What gives with you two and dead batteries?"

Liz glared at him.

Charly nodded and held up a bandaged hand. "I know. I know. I'll be better. I promise. Anyway, I could still see my truck when a car came by, and the driver offered me a ride. Unfortunately, the driver was Harry."

"Harry? You mean Harry Carter?" Kaeden asked. Liz heard astonishment in his voice—and not the good kind.

"Yeah." Charly hunched over, shrinking into the blanket as if to hide there.

"But you hate him," Kaeden said. "With good reason. He's a real bastard."

Charly nodded. "Yeah, I know. But a ride is a ride. He said he'd bring me home."

"And you believed him?" Kaeden shook his head. Liz had a feeling he would have *tsked* but held back—a good thing. Keeping Charly from hitting him might have been difficult if he had.

"No, but I didn't have a lot of options. Especially out there." She jumped as Liz hit a particularly bad spot.

"Sorry. I'm almost done." She applied antibiotic cream and butterfly bandages over the worst of the cuts and wrapped Charly's leg in gauze. Liz grabbed a flashlight from the counter by the door and checked Charly's eyes. "Did you hit your head? Are you dizzy or anything?"

She still considered a run to the emergency room if necessary. And Kaeden was watching, checking her out as closely as Liz.

"No. I'm fine. Not dizzy. Not nauseous. No headache. No double vision." She held up her leg. "Thanks. You're good at that."

"Lots of practice. Unfortunately."

Liz cleaned up the supplies and stowed them back in the cabinet. Kaeden sat down next to Charly. The white bandages around her hands stood out against her olive skin. "Okay, so you decided to take Harry up on his offer."

"Yeah. I figured a short ride, no problem, right?" She sighed a long, drawn-out breath that spoke more than her words did.

"So, what happened?" Kaeden asked.

"Big mistake. He made up some story about needing to stop by his folks' place. That's when I started to get a little nervous. I mean, his folks live out past the school." She glanced at Liz. "That's in the wrong direction from here. On the north side of town."

"How'd you get away?" Liz asked.

"We passed his folks, and he was driving like a maniac. I asked him where we were going, and that's when he got really weird. He started muttering something about Bannig and that I had to be the one. He scared me. I saw a big stick like a cane rolling around on the floor, so when he slowed down for the curve, I grabbed the staff and hit him. He slowed down to stop me, and I shoved the door open and jumped out."

"You could have been killed!" Kaeden's voice emerged rough with emotion.

"Yeah, well, I decided jumping would be better than staying with him, especially if he was taking me to Bannig. He was acting like he wasn't himself."

"He didn't stop?" Kaeden asked.

"Yeah, he did, after I jumped out. I guess I didn't hit him hard enough. But you know how thick the woods are there, and since the sun was barely up, I hid in the dark under the trees. I made damned sure he didn't find me."

Liz stood with her back to the fridge, a bad idea settling in the pit of her stomach. She recognized the sensation. "Charly, what's the distance from where you jumped out to here?"

"About two miles. Why?"

She checked the clock. "It's nearly seven. A good walking pace is three miles an hour. You were in bare feet in the near dark, so drop your speed to one to two miles an hour."

"And?"

She shook her head and sighed. "Do yourself a favor and write down everything you told us and put a time scale on it if you can."

"Liz?" Kaeden stared at her. She didn't know what to tell him.

"I've got a bad feeling she's going to need a timeline and evidence. And we need to write down our statements as well."

"Statements? That doesn't sound good," Kaeden said.

"This doesn't feel good."

"Should I take pictures?" he asked.

"Might not be a bad idea." She handed Charly the notepad by the phone, then took the paper back. "You can't write with those hands."

"Use my phone," Kaeden said. "At least my battery is full."

He set the phone to record. As Charly got ready to talk, he held up his hand. "Wait." They waited while he called his uncle and told him about Charly. When he finished, he set the phone up again. "Tell, us again, exactly what happened. Don't leave anything out."

Charly repeated her story.

"Was there anyone else around?"

"No. Can I go change?"

Kaeden shook his head. "Not yet."

A knock at the door interrupted them, and Kaeden let his uncle in.

"I need to talk to Charly," Ray said.

"I'm here."

He glanced at her and raised one eyebrow. "Can you tell me where you were at approximately six o'clock this morning, Charly?"

"Walking home. My truck broke down."

"Uncle Ray? What's this all about? Why are you questioning her?" Kaeden asked. "Harry Carter kidnapped, assaulted, and hurt her."

"About an hour ago, a trucker found Harry Carter in his car in the middle of the road. Dead. Beaten by a cane or large stick from the looks of his injuries. We also found Charly's purse in the car and what looked like signs of a struggle. I'm afraid I'm going to have to take Charly in to answer some questions."

Liz's heart nearly stopped when he said someone killed Harry with a cane. Then that traitorous organ started thumping all too fast.

Kaeden nodded. "I didn't know about Harry being dead, but I knew there was going to be trouble." He turned to Charly. "Show him your leg."

Charly pulled up her skirt so Ray could see the bandages. "Harry picked me up when my car broke down, then kidnapped me. I fought back and got away. But I left him alive."

Ray bent down to study Charly's injuries. "I'm sure this will all be cleared up quickly, especially with what you've said and from the look of you, but I'm afraid you'll still have to come with me."

Kaeden handed his uncle his phone. "The recording delineates what happened to her, Uncle Ray. And Liz and I can corroborate."

Ray took the phone. "You should have called me as soon as she got here."

"Taking care of her seemed more important."

"Fine, but I still have to take her in."

"Uncle Ray," Kaeden said, but Charly held up a bandaged hand.

"It's okay. I'll call you when I'm done."

Ray spoke up. "I'll make sure she's taken care of and that she gets back here safely." He glanced at Liz and frowned. "According to what I know, we still have time before whatever's coming gets here."

"Soon, but not now," Liz agreed.

Kaeden's uncle nodded once, then turned away with Charly in tow. Liz watched and saw the great care he showed with Charly, helping her down the steps and to his car—the front seat. Seeing the way he took care of her, Liz felt a little more comfortable about Charly going with Ray.

After they left, a huge weight settled on her shoulders. All she wanted to do was curl into a ball and let the world go by. But Kaeden wouldn't let her. He turned to her, his face a mixture of puzzlement, frustration, and worry, his arms crossed over his chest. She could almost see the waves of angst coming off him.

"You and my uncle. What's the history? I mean, I know about the arrest. But why doesn't your file show you lived here?"

She sighed. Kaeden knew most of the story. He should know the rest.

"I lived here for a couple of months before my eighteenth birthday. I guess my time here was short enough that nobody bothered to change the records. Or maybe your uncle did something about them."

"Uncle Ray would never do something like that."

"He would if he was trying to protect someone." She wasn't sure Ray had been trying to protect her, but that was as good an explanation as any.

"So where did you live?"

"Punkin' Center." His eyes widened. Technically, the name was Pumpkin Center, but nobody pronounced pumpkin the proper way, and the site wouldn't show up on any map. The locals used the nickname for the group of low-rent shacks on a back road at the edge of town. To call them houses would be a stretch. "The home I lived in met the minimum requirement for fosters, but barely. The inhabitants, well, let's say some of them didn't meet even the base line for humanity, and I'm not talking about paranormals here. Just the dregs of society."

"I remember," Kaeden said. "No wonder you couldn't find where you lived. The place doesn't exist anymore. There was a bad fire there about…ten…years ago." He eyed her narrowly. "Burned the place out."

"Hey, don't look at me. The house I stayed in—and all the others—were still standing when I left. Your uncle can back me up. But I will say that burning that place down was the best thing that could have happened. I got placed in a lot of homes, but the one there was by far the worst. I won't shed any tears over the destruction. Was anybody hurt?"

"No. The families all moved to other places. Some anonymous donor bought up the land and donated the area to the town for the river park."

"Where we were walking?" He nodded. She'd been there and hadn't even known. "Good riddance." Liz lost herself in memories. *Of escaping that awful place. Of the people who hated her and treated her like dirt…worse than dirt. Of—*

"Earth to Liz." Kaeden waved his hand in front of her face.

"Huh? Oh. Sorry."

About the same time, the back door opened and Charly staggered in.

"Charly!" Liz went to embrace her, then stopped. Hugging didn't come naturally to her. But she did hug Charly. Hard. And Charly returned the gesture. After she finished with Liz, she went to Kaeden and did the same to him. Liz stood back and watched. He did care about her, but in a brother-sister way. Same for her.

That made Liz feel a lot better. She knew Kaeden had told her Charly and him were friends, but sometimes the people involved didn't know how they felt. But these two did. They really were buddies.

"You look like crap," Kaeden said.

"Thanks. I feel that way too. Coffee. Strong." Charly sank into a chair.

Liz handed her a cinnamon bun while Kaeden made a second pot of coffee. "What happened?"

"Uncle Ray grilled me, then decided if I had done anything, I could claim self-defense. The DA agreed, and they let me go."

Charly's hands shook as she took the mug of coffee. The circles under her eyes were from more than lack of sleep. Liz knew that look—the look of sheer exhaustion mingled with despair and fear and a few other emotions Charly needed to deal with. But first, she needed rest. Before she could take more than a sip, Liz took the coffee from her.

"Bed. Now."

"But the diner—"

"The diner is open. Kaeden and I will go down and check on things. You need rest."

"Liz is right." Kaeden steered Charly toward her room. "You sleep. We'll take care of the diner. No arguments."

Liz shoveled piles of clothes off Charly's bed and pulled down the quilt. Kaeden helped her into the bed and tucked the blankets around her while Liz pulled down the shades. Before Liz left, she pushed Charly to sleep. Liz couldn't do a lot of paranormal stuff, but she could do a few things. In Charly's case, she made a strong mental suggestion for the person to relax and go to sleep. She didn't like to do the spell. But Charly needed rest, and she wouldn't get any if she did nothing but dwell on Harry being dead and the diner and everything.

Charly was snoring before they got out of the room.

Kaeden pulled the door shut. "You did something to her, didn't you? Something to make her sleep."

Liz stared at him. How had he known? She led him to the kitchen where she busied herself with cleaning up.

"Don't bother telling me you didn't. I felt something. Like a spark of energy, only not," he said.

She sighed, gripped the counter, and then faced him. "Yes, I did. I gave her a mental suggestion that sleep would be a good thing. Not so much that I put her to sleep, more like her body wanted sleep and I calmed down the frantic parts so she could listen to her needs."

"So, she's in a natural sleep?"

"Delta waves and all. The spell doesn't affect anything, only lets you ignore what's going on around you so you can sleep better."

"Do you want to do some more power work?" Liz asked. She'd been teaching him how to use his elfin skills, though he pretty much already knew how. Instincts counted for a lot in the paranormal world.

"We should probably check on the diner."

Kaeden and Liz went downstairs. The new hires were doing okay but relieved to have their help. Patrons packed the place all day with no let up. The buzz was mostly about Harry's murder and Charly's attack and all the events going on in town. Kaeden fielded questions from behind the counter while Liz and the other waitress kept up with orders and bussed the tables on both sides. Charly joined them around four in the afternoon, and the place went dead silent. Though she'd cleaned up, her injuries were obvious to anyone who could see. Scrapes and bruises mottled her face, bandages covered her hands, and she limped when she walked. Nobody doubted she'd been hurt.

A minute after the silence began, one woman stood and started clapping. Like a bomb went off, everyone joined her, cheering and applauding. Charly bowed her head once, eyes closed, then the Charly Liz knew came back. Her head came up, her shoulders went back, and a grin spread across her face.

"Thank you. I'm having a special on my famous chocolate torte. A free slice for anyone who wants one."

More cheering and clapping sounded, and Liz got busy cutting slices of Charly's torte, the richest, most decadent dessert ever invented. Having several in reserve was a good thing.

By the time they shooed the last customer out and closed the doors that night, all of them were exhausted. After the night shift people left, Kaeden, Charly, and Liz collapsed on chairs, beers in hand, pizza in front of them. They still had the mopping and cleaning to do, but right then, they needed food and drink more.

"Damn, that was one hell of a day," Charly said.

"Been a hell of a couple of days." Kaeden sucked at his beer, then looked at Liz.

A noise by the door startled them, and they turned. Rolling across the floor was a cane. Black with gold-and-silver inlay and a large round crystal on top.

"What the hell?" Kaeden jumped up and dashed to

the door—which was locked from the inside, and nobody else had come into the room. Charly had gone dead white. The cane stopped rolling midway down the aisle. They sat there and stared.

"Is that the cane you used to hit Harry?"

"Maybe. I don't know. I know I grabbed what I thought was a big stick. I didn't have much light, and I wasn't exactly doing a detailed study."

Kaeden pulled out his cell phone and called his uncle. From what Liz heard, the cane used to kill Harry was safely locked up in the local evidence locker. Kaeden even had him check to make sure. Ray confirmed that he had the stick.

"Are there two of these things? Even if there's only one, how did this one get here?" Kaeden asked the room.

Liz gathered up her courage and went over to the cane.

"Liz! What are you doing? Don't touch that thing," Charly yelled.

Instead of doing as ordered, she knelt next to the cane. "This isn't the one used to kill Harry."

She reached for the staff, wrapped her hand around the crystal on top, and the world went cock-eyed.

Chapter Twenty

Liz remained in the diner, but the colors were off—dimmer and no aroma of beer and pizza, no music playing in the background. If not for the fact that she could see everyone and everything, she'd think she had gone to the *nothingness* where she met with her bosses. Charly and Kaeden stood by the counter, horrified looks on their faces. They didn't move, even though Liz did. Holding the cane, she strode over to them.

"Kaeden? Charly?" She waved her hand in front of their faces. Nothing. Then she looked at the clock on the wall above the counter. The second hand was moving, but barely, so time hadn't stopped—just slowed down, but they had stopped. Why?

Okay, this went beyond weird. She glanced outside and froze as shadows flowed down the empty street. They were huge and ugly, and she did not want to see what was making shadows like that. In her shock, she must have dropped the cane because the next thing Liz knew, noise and smells came rushing back.

"Liz! Don't touch that thing," Charly said. "Wait. How did you get over here?"

"Too late. I already did."

"Huh? What are you talking about?" Kaeden asked. So, she told them what had happened.

"And that's how I got over here."

Kaeden strolled over to her. "You grabbed the cane

like this?" Before Liz could stop him, he grabbed the staff, picked it up, and twirled the wood like a baton.

She stood there and stared at him. "Give me that."

He did. Nothing happened.

"You're still here," he said.

Liz grasped the crystal, twisting a little, and the world stopped again. Hmm. Interesting. She needed to remember twisting the crystal activated whatever power this thing had.

She moved over to Charly and sat down on the stool next to her. Then she got up, grabbed a bottle of ketchup and another of mustard and went over to Kaeden. She squirted one on each hand and two bright red spots on his cheeks, then scooted back to Charly and picked up her pizza. Finally, she laid the cane on the counter and the world returned to normal.

Charly choked on her drink and stared at Kaeden who stared at his hands, then at her. "What the hell?"

"Let me try that thing," Charly said. She grabbed the cane. Same as Kaeden. Nothing.

"Try twisting the crystal. Like I did," Liz said. She tried not to smirk at the ketchup and mustard mess.

Charly twisted and turned the crystal, but the ball wouldn't budge. After Kaeden made liberal use of napkins, Charly handed the cane to Kaeden with the same results.

"So, the staff is attuned to you for some reason," Kaeden said. "But what happens to the rest of us? You said the clock didn't stop so not a time thing."

"No. Although you both were stopped." Liz twirled the cane idly through her fingers. The staff was well balanced, not too heavy, and fit her height perfectly, almost as if designed specifically for her.

"How about other things? Did you see any traffic moving?" Kaeden asked.

"No." She didn't tell them about the shadows. They didn't need to know.

"So, we don't know if there is a limit to this," he said. Liz could tell from the gleam in his eyes that the investigator in him wanted answers. Charly, on the other hand, looked like she'd just as soon feed the cane into the garbage disposal.

Liz cocked her head, wondering about limits. "You mean like a bubble?" That would be an interesting idea.

"I guess. We need to test the theory though. Let's try an experiment." The excitement in Kaeden's face drew her in, and in her business finding a little bit of happiness topped everything.

"What?" Liz asked, curious about what he wanted to do.

"First, let's see if you can bring either one of us in with you. What if you hold my hand when you pick up the cane?"

Liz grabbed his hand, picked up the cane, tucked the wood under her arm, and then twisted the crystal. Fortunately, she didn't need much pressure to turn the orb. She covered the crystal with her palm and turned her hand a little.

"Wow. This is weird," Kaeden said. His voice came out muffled, but Liz did hear him. She dropped his hand to hug him, and he went still. She tried touching him again and nothing. She put the cane down.

"Seems like you can join me if I'm touching you before I pick up the cane, but not after."

"Yeah. I kind of noticed," Kaeden said.

"What about distance?" Charly asked. "Go over to the other side of the diner."

Liz grabbed the cane, twisted the top, and strolled over. Kaeden and Charly stayed still until Liz had stepped off about ten paces, then they started moving, acting as if they were looking for her.

"Kaeden? Charly? I'm over here."

Nothing. They continued to look until they were close to her and went still. Liz laid the cane down on a table and returned the world to normal.

"Curiouser and curiouser," Charly said. "You disappeared. Like a light going out. You were standing there, then you weren't."

"The limit seems to be about ten feet," Liz said. "I watched you two looking for me, but when you got close, you went still."

Kaeden studied the cane. "I watched you pick the cane up. You grabbed the top. What if you put your hands around the wood part, lower down?"

Liz grasped the wood below the crystal and waited. Charly and Kaeden stared at her. Nothing changed. "Nothing. Looks like the crystal is the catalyst."

"Makes sense," Kaeden said. "You have an affinity with stones. You need to be careful not to grab there."

"Not exactly. I can grab it there as long as I don't twist. The twist makes the difference."

"Does the direction of the twist change the result?" Charly asked.

Liz tried both ways with the same result both times. "No. Both ways work."

"What do you say we get this place cleaned up and go upstairs?" Charly asked. "And Kae? You're staying."

He raised one eyebrow but smiled and nodded.

Charly chuckled and took a swig of beer. "I'm not comfortable with that thing here, but I do know we need to find out more about what you can do with the power."

The diner had probably never been mopped so quickly. They finished, ran upstairs to Liz's apartment, and started playing with the cane. By one in the morning, they didn't know much more than they'd found out downstairs, and all three of them were yawning. Charly nodded off first, curled up at the bottom of Liz's mattress. Kaeden and Liz snuggled at the top. If they kept up this kind of activity, she'd have to get in more furniture. Three in a bed was one too many.

****

The next morning, Liz woke to thunder. Her room was empty, but the bed was still warm, so she knew Kaeden hadn't left too long ago. A quick glance at the clock told her she'd probably find him and Charly down in the diner. She grabbed the cane and headed downstairs. Thunder rumbled in the distance. When she went out, she glanced up. The clouds all seemed centered over one end of town. Other than that, the sky remained relatively clear.

As Liz reached the landing to Charly's apartment, Kaeden came out. "Hi! I was on my way up to get you. We're in here."

She joined him and Charly and Uncle Ray in Charly's living room. Charly didn't look so good. "You doing okay?"

"She's stiffened up while sleeping and can barely move," Kaeden said. "I found her down in the diner

218

trying to work. I told the others to handle things and brought her up here."

"Forced me up here," she muttered.

"Good for him," Liz said. "You can take a day or two off."

As they talked, Ray kept staring at the cane Liz held. She couldn't hide the piece, so she laid the wood on the table. "This isn't the one used on Harry."

"I know. That cane is secured in my evidence locker. But the similarity is uncanny. The only difference is the color of the crystal on top. The other one has a red ball."

Could there be two of them? And if so, who controlled the second one?

Their discussion led to an explanation of the cane and a demonstration. Ray wanted to take the staff with him, but they all argued against him. He finally agreed to leave the cane with them, but reluctantly. The thunder now rumbled loud enough to rattle the windows.

Liz glanced at the others.

The lights flickered as lightning flashed.

"These storms are really odd," Ray said. "I don't remember the weatherman calling for storms today. The weather is supposed to be clear and sunny."

Liz's stomach clenched. Odd didn't begin to describe what she knew. They hadn't noticed, but she did. The thunder came first. Before the lightning. And no rain. She also noticed something else. The scream that rode the thunder. A sound she'd heard once before.

"I'd wager my car if you look outside, you'll find the sky clear and the sun shining nicely except maybe in one spot."

They did, then they stared at her.

"There's no rain," Kaeden said. "And there isn't a cloud in the sky. How'd the storm clear so fast?"

Liz snorted. "That was an announcement of sorts. And a challenge." She pushed back from the table. "Fortunately, Bannig probably used a lot of his energy with that display."

"Shouldn't we go get him if he's weak?" Ray asked.

"He won't be the one who's weak. That will be one of his minions. He's trying to draw us out and will have traps set. Ones we're not ready to face yet."

"But if he's weak," Kaeden said.

"He's not, like I told you. The poor soul whose life force he used is the weak one if he isn't dead. Our enemy is as strong as ever."

"But you faced him before," Charly said. "You're here. And you got the previous node."

"My last fight with him in DC ended without a winner. He didn't lose, and I didn't beat him. Plus, I nearly died." She rubbed a hand across her ribs.

They all jumped as a huge boom shook the house. Car alarms all along the street blared, and dogs howled from back yards.

"What the hell was that?" Kaeden asked.

Ray ran out the door, the others close behind.

Liz smelled smoke in the air, and the sky to the south of town glowed red. Silently, they scrambled into the car and tore off.

They came to a screeching halt a few blocks away. The entire south end of town was ablaze. Dozens of cars sped toward them, away from the conflagration, but many more headed in the same direction as they did. In addition, people streamed in both directions, some of them injured.

Kaeden jumped out of the car. "Liz, Charly, help who you can."

"Where are you going?" Liz asked.

He nodded toward the center of the blaze. "There."

"Charly?" Liz glanced at her.

Charly nodded. "Go. That's where you need to be."

"Liz? You can't go," Kaeden argued.

"I should more than you. Either come with me or don't, but I'm going there."

Kaeden shook his head, but then nodded, and took off right beside her. A few blocks away, they met with the fire chief and Ray. Fire trucks worked at the blazes, but there were too many and too few trucks to help. "Uncle Ray? Where do you need us?" Kae yelled.

"Help with the injured. I could sure use some of that rain from the other day."

They needed rain? Hmm. Liz had never made rain. But she could make lightning and thunder. And the river flowed less than a block away. And she sensed…a buzz, not a full strength one, but still enough to give her the tingles. This one felt…different than the others had. As if the blast had dispersed the power over a wider area. She followed the buzz to the strongest source point, avoiding the men and trucks where she could. When she'd gotten as close as she could, she bent down and buried her hands in the dirt, absorbing as much of the power as she could. Then she tried to make the sky rain.

Nothing.

Not even a flicker of lightning. But her blood sang with power. Why couldn't she do something?

Every other time she'd brought on thunder and lightning, she'd been pissed off. Maybe she needed to be mad at something. Really mad. Like Mr. Dirty Fingernails mad. She ran over to where Kaeden stood directing ambulances to the injured. "Kae. Hit me!"

He glared at her, a puzzled look on his face. "What?"

"Hit me! I need to get damn mad."

He swept his arm out to encompass their surroundings. "This isn't enough to get you pissed? Because this sure pisses me off."

"Not enough! I need stronger emotions than anger."

"Any strong emotion?"

Liz couldn't figure out the strange look on his face. "I don't know. I just know the power works when I'm good and pissed. Like in a rage."

"So…marry me."

"What!" What the hell? That wasn't even funny. Not funny at all. Not now. Not ever.

"Marry me."

"Are you insane?" He had to be. Maybe the shock from the séance really had done something to him and was just now showing up. Maybe… maybe… Her mind went blank. She couldn't think of any other maybes. How the hell could he think of asking something like that right now?

Thunder rumbled.

"I might be crazy," Kaeden said. "But even if I am, I'd still want you, Elizabeth St. John. You are the most exasperating, beautiful, frustrating, exciting, baffling woman I've ever met. I love you. Will you marry me?"

Clouds moved in. Fat raindrops splashed on the

pavement. Liz's breath stopped in her chest. Lightning flashed in the distance and more thunder rumbled. "You…you think I'm—"

"Hey you two! We need help over here!" Ray called.

"I'll want your answer later," Kaeden said right before he kissed her, then ran to his uncle.

Liz stood there as the clouds opened up and rain poured down. She barely heard the cheer that went up as burning debris smoldered out. She barely heard anything. Or felt anything. Or saw anything.

"Liz?" Charly grabbed her arm, bringing her back into the world. "What's wrong? You look like you're going to pass out."

She shook her head, trying to bring her thoughts back to the needed action. "I…um…later, okay? I…I need…" She blew out a breath and shook her head again. "I need to get to work. You go help with the others. I'll help Ray with the fire."

"Are you sure you're up to doing anything?"

"Yeah. I'm good. Go." She glanced around for Kaeden but didn't see him. The rain tapered to a drizzle, then stopped. But from what Liz could see, the downpour had helped. The smaller fires had died down to ash and smoke. Though the big one still burned. The gas dump! Something didn't make sense here. Something beyond what Kaeden had asked her. "So why the tanks? If there's a node there, why draw people to the power? Bannig can't have wanted this to happen."

She jogged to the edge of town where several trucks and dozens of people fought to contain the conflagration. Dropping rain here wouldn't help, so she didn't even offer, not that she thought she could even get up enough power to do that again. Though she still sensed the buzz from the node, bringing in that much rain in a virtually cloudless sky hadn't been easy. Exhaustion had her fighting to stay upright.

Liz stayed out of the way as much as possible but wove in and out of the crowds that had gathered. She wasn't exactly sure what she was looking for, only that she'd know when she saw—or heard—whatever she needed. In the past, the bad guys stayed under the radar. A few break-ins, deaths, a little mayhem, but nothing big. Nothing that would bring in a lot of notice, like a gas explosion. She wished she'd thought to bring the cane with her. Stopping some of this chaos around her would help.

She put Kaeden's request to the back of her mind and searched. Liz's gaze glossed over the large majority of people—the curiosity seekers and the people trying to work. She was looking for something different. The twitch of nerves or intensity of a face that would give a person away.

Finally, she saw him. A young teen with an extremely pale face standing on the sidelines wringing his hands. "I didn't mean to do this. Honest. Nothing was supposed to happen. Not like this."

His words, barely heard, were out there now. As Liz watched, she saw him drop something on the ground and grind it into the dirt. She burned his image into her mind—around five-seven, lanky, short dark hair with white-blond spikes, letterman jacket with a soccer ball on the back in the local school district colors. She couldn't see his name on the front before he joined a crew hauling equipment out of the way. But she did pick up what he'd dropped.

A pack of cigarettes and matches. This entire mess had been started by a kid smoking. And from the looks of the pack, probably his first. She would have laughed if the situation hadn't been so sad. But his barely breathed comment stuck in her brain. "Nothing was supposed to happen."

What wasn't supposed to happen? And who had put the kid up to his idiocy? Bannig probably had something to do with this, but why? That escaped her. Why would Bannig want this much attention here? And why destroy a node?

Was this all a misdirection? If so, for what? She knew the last node wasn't going to go off tonight. So why the subterfuge? Nothing made any sense. Blowing up the nodes wouldn't make them more accessible. They just…were. You couldn't dig down to find one. Though having them buried under parking lots and buildings did make them harder to absorb. Maybe that was his issue. He wanted easy access to all the power. But blowing the node up wouldn't help. And in blowing this one up, he'd dispersed the energy before the power was at maximum.

A miscalculation? Maybe a sliver of her mentor remained. The demon wouldn't have made a mistake like that. But maybe her Bannig had something to do with this.

Then Liz noticed something else. Something that would have been visible only in the dark. Two faint blue glowing lines going from what would have been the center of the explosion. She climbed to the top of one of the trucks and peered out at them—first one, then the other. She didn't need a map to tell her where they went. Two legs of the pentagram. They were connecting. The nodes were spent, weren't they?

But what if they weren't? What if they were building again?

This did not bode well.

Chapter Twenty-One

Charly arrived with her delivery truck, and Liz put the questions away and went over to help. Then the comments started.

"What's she doing here?"

"Who does she think she is?"

"She doesn't belong here."

"Probably started this."

"Yeah, and poor Harry too. I heard she had something to do with that."

Liz ignored them all and kept unloading supplies from the back of Charly's truck. But Charly slammed a tray of sandwich fixings down on the table she'd finished setting up and glared at the speakers.

"Liz is here to help, which is more than I can say for you lazy twits. She was with Kaeden and me when this happened, on the other side of town. Liz is good people, and I trust her with my life. So shut your stupid traps and either help or get out of the way. And don't think you're getting any free food just because you're here standing around watching everyone work."

Wow. Nobody had ever stood up for her like that. But the grumbling stopped, and although Liz still got a few stares, for the most part, things settled down. And some of them got off their high horses to help.

They served coffee, sodas, and sandwiches until the crews got the fires under control. They were well into the wee hours of the morning before the men from the neighboring towns left. Sunrise rode the horizon before the local fire chief sent most of his people home. Close to mid-morning the chief and Ray declared the area safe.

Charly and Liz collapsed on the tailgate of the truck, washing down cold sandwiches with the last dregs of coffee. Kaeden and his uncle joined them. Dark circles rimmed their eyes. Sweat-streaked soot coated their faces. Their clothes were heavy with mud and water, and their shoulders drooped. Even those with elf blood had their limits, and they'd both reached theirs.

Kaeden glanced at her. "Did Bannig do this?"

"He didn't do the actual deed, but I'd bet my best crystal he was involved." Using a tissue, she pulled out the pack of cigarettes and matches and laid them on the table. "Look for a kid wearing a soccer jacket. Dark hair, white spikes. About fourteen or fifteen." She told them what she'd seen and heard.

"Sounds like Toby Iverson," Ray said. "Damn. This is his dad's place."

"He and his buddies like to come out here and party," Kaeden explained. "I caught them a couple of weeks ago with some bottles. Thought I'd gotten through to them. Told them I wouldn't report them if they stayed away. Guess I was wrong."

"We both were," Ray said. "I caught them out here last week with the same garbage. Thought Toby was smarter than that, though."

"He might be under the influence," Liz said.

"Of drugs?" Ray asked.

"No. Of our nasty friend. Don't be surprised if he's

not sure why he did this. Or how."

Kaeden stood, wavering with fatigue. "Let's get this mess cleaned up and head home."

They all looked up as two cars pulled into the yard. Debra and the other women from the coven stepped out, looking as fresh and clean as Liz and the others weren't.

"Figured you four would still be here. Also figured we'd be needed. I'll be driving you home while the others clean up. Come on."

Charly shook her head. "Debra, you don't—"

"Tut. You hush. And give Sue your keys. She'll drop your truck off at the diner. Come on. You're beyond tired."

Liz, Charly, Ray, and Kaeden looked at one another, grinned through the grime, and went.

Debra dropped Ray off first, then headed for Kaeden's place. He was going to get his truck and some clothes and move in with Liz. Liz wasn't sure how she felt about that, beyond comfortably happy, but she'd deal with her emotions later.

Before they got out, Debra shut off the engine and turned to them. Kaeden sat in the front seat, Charly and Liz in the back. Debra looked at Liz specifically.

"Look, I want you to know you're not to blame for what happened to me and the others during the séance. I insisted on the ritual. I ignored your warnings. I won't make that mistake again. For what it's worth, Liz, I am sorry."

"You're sorry? What happened was not your fault. I wish I could have stopped that thing before you got hurt."

Debra held up her hand. "Stop. Let's just say, a

nine-power is not something we'll enter into lightly ever again. But on the upside, something did happen to me. Something odd that, when you're feeling better, I'd like to talk to you about."

"You think I'm going to sleep after that statement? What happened?"

Debra grinned and raised her eyebrow, then laid her hands on Charly's face. Charly showed shock, then she closed her eyes and smiled. When Debra pulled her hands away, Charly's bruises and cuts disappeared. If Liz's face looked anything close to the way Charly and Kaeden appeared—well, she figured wide-eyed and open-mouthed would be an apt description.

"The others had similar experiences, though mine seems to be the strongest. Go get cleaned up and get some rest. We'll talk later. Call me."

She started the car, and the three of them climbed out but stood there staring as she drove away.

"Damn," Charly said. "That was so cool. Why didn't I get something like that?"

"Because Liz pulled us out," Kaeden said. "And before you say anything, I'm glad she did. I'm not sure I want to know what would have happened otherwise."

"Yeah, I know. But geeze."

"I'll remember that next time and let you stay in." Liz laughed when Charly stuck her tongue out at her.

Kaeden went to unlock his door when Liz tingled.

"Stop!"

Both he and Charly jumped.

"Kaeden, don't unlock the door." The redirection. Here. But why? Kaeden wasn't important to Bannig.

But he was important to her. Damn.

"Liz? I'm too tired—"

"Give me a sec." She checked out the door. Nothing grabbed her, but she knew something was wrong. "Kaeden, wake up that dead brain of yours and look at this door. Is there something wrong?"

He shook his head as if to wake up and bent down to study the door. "Yeah, there is. Someone's jimmied the lock."

"Is there another way into your house?"

"Front door."

"No. There's something wrong with both doors. I mean a way in someone wouldn't think of." Liz didn't know how she knew that, but she did. *Thank you, PTB*.

"Yeah. This way. Haven't used this since I did the porch over."

He stepped to the left of the door and knelt on the porch and pulled up a latch Liz hadn't seen there before—but then, she hadn't been looking. He lifted a section of the porch floor, revealing a set of steep steps that led down to a heavy metal door. He glanced at her before unlocking the door, but the undisturbed dust, cobwebs, and leaf debris on the steps let them know nobody had been down there. They entered the cellar, closing everything behind them.

"This way."

Kaeden led them through the cellar to the steps that led up to the kitchen. They moved quickly and quietly. Liz listened for any sound that there might be someone upstairs, but she heard nothing. Once in the kitchen they all stopped and stared at the back door.

"What is that?" Charly asked, her voice barely above a whisper.

"That is called a pipe bomb," Kaeden said. "Rigged to blow when the door opens."

They found a similar device at the front door.

"So how did they get out?" Charly asked. "I mean, if they rigged both doors, how did they get out when they finished? Or are they still here?"

They moved through the downstairs rooms, checking for anything out of place.

"Here," Liz said. She had found a curtain trapped in a window in Kaeden's office. "They crawled out the window."

While Kaeden worked at disarming the devices, Charly and Liz went through the rest of the house. Nothing else seemed out of place, and she didn't get any more tingles.

They had just finished the last bedroom when they heard a loud bang from downstairs. Charly stared at her. Liz stared at Charly. Then they both ran.

They found Kaeden in the kitchen, sitting on the floor, a surprised look on his face. But at least he had a face. He appeared whole, just dazed. The back door, however, hadn't fared as well, but all the damage landed on the outside. Liz guessed the bad guys hadn't figured on them disarming from inside.

"My knife slipped." He looked up at them.

"Are you hurt?" Liz checked him over pretty thoroughly.

"Yeah." He struggled to stand. "Now I'm mad."

"And tired. You're making mistakes. We all are. We need to go somewhere safe to rest and regroup."

"My place," Charly said. "I did thorough work on protection spells and wards."

****

Rather than go upstairs to Liz's place, they all stayed on Charly's level. For some reason, they didn't want to separate. They took quick showers and crashed. Charly was out almost as soon as she hit the bed. Kaeden lay on the sofa. Liz couldn't hear him moving around so assumed he'd fallen asleep too. She wasn't so lucky.

She lay there, going over everything that had been happening. She had to be missing something. The séance. The incident with Bruce. The fire. The redirection. Bombs at Kaeden's. The nodes. Too many anomalies. Too many oddities. And the oddest thing of all—the cane. And the puzzle. All the events as well as the items had to be tied together, but how? And why?

The puzzle! She sat straight up in bed. The puzzle lay in the trunk of her car—at Kaeden's.

She pulled on a clean shirt from her pack but had to go with the same smoky jeans and boots, though she left the boots off, carrying them as she tiptoed through the outer room.

"Going somewhere?"

She spun around to find a shirtless Kaeden leaning against the doorway to the living room. "Uh, yeah. There's something I need from my car."

"You're not going back there alone."

"You're in no condition to go with me. You're exhausted. And I need to do this now."

"You got as much sleep as I did last night." He grabbed a shirt from the coat rack by the door and jammed his feet into his boots. "Let's go."

He looked so cute with his hair sticking out all over the place, oddly matched clothes, and dark circles under his eyes, how could she say no? Besides, having him at her back was kind of comforting. "Fine. If you're going to be a bear about a little trip. Come on."

She'd let him come, but she wouldn't let him think she was easy.

They drove back to his place and parked on the street in front of the house. Liz wanted whoever was watching to know she had come back. When they got to the door, she pulled Kaeden to the side. "You're sure you got this one disarmed?"

"Yes. You getting any warnings?"

"No."

Still, they stood well out of the way when he unlocked and swung the door open. Smiling at each other, they stepped inside. And stopped as they heard noises from the kitchen.

Liz pulled a knife from each boot and handed one to Kaeden. There were two doors to his kitchen—one from his office, a second from the living room. She motioned for Kaeden to take the left one while she went through the office. Liz made her way through the room and leaned against the wall next to the door, listening to see if she could tell how many they were up against.

"We got the cane," one male voice said. "Let's go."

"Wait. The boss said something about a puzzle."

"Yeah, big deal. He can get one at the store for a few bucks. The cane looks like that's worth more than he's paying us."

Just two of them. Both by the table as far as Liz could tell. Two she could take with her eyes closed. She stepped through the door at the same time as Kaeden. Huh. Good timing.

The two thieves jumped. One, the smaller of the two, ran for the door while the second rounded on Liz, cane in hand.

"Kaeden! Go. I'm good."

Kaeden hesitated only a second before taking off after the runner while Liz faced the second one. He brandished the cane like a formidable weapon. This was going to be too easy. Liz didn't even bother to pull a second knife.

The big guy surprised her though. He showed more talent than she gave him credit for. And obviously had some martial arts training somewhere along the way. But not enough. They were pretty well into trashing the kitchen by the time Kaeden dragged his prey in. Liz couldn't take the time to pay more than glancing attention to him as she fought her own battle.

The fight wasn't as short as she'd figured, but not hugely drawn out as Kaeden cuffed his guy to the handle on the stove and joined the fray. Two against one weren't good odds. Big guy headed for the back door, but Liz took him down with a well-thrown coffee mug she grabbed from the counter. She didn't knock him out exactly but scrambled his brains enough to slow him down. Kaeden took care of tying him up while Liz grabbed the cane. Big-and-Dumb looked like he was going to try something, so she put her hand on the crystal and everyone went still.

Good. Now she had time. She went over to Kaeden's broom closet and found a length of sturdy rope, duct tape, tools, and other handy items. First, she wanted to tape the little guy's feet together so he couldn't be a nuisance. Getting the tape off the roll one-handed wasn't easy while holding onto the top of the cane. She finally figured out she could hold the cane with her palm and three fingers and use her thumb and first finger to hold the tape while she pulled off a length and then tore that with her teeth. But how to wrap it around? She needed more hands.

Liz went over to Kaeden, let go of the cane, grabbed his shirt, and picked up the cane again. She handed him the tape. "Put your hand on top of mine." She nodded toward the one holding the cane. "And pray this works."

He did, and she let go of his shirt. Fortunately, he stayed with her. So that gave each of them one good hand to work with. The task was a little awkward—okay, a lot awkward—but they managed to get both men taped and tied. Then Liz let go of Kaeden and went back to her original position and let go of the cane.

Liz had read about people's eyes bugging out, but never thought about what they looked like until then. They were kind of gross. Their eyes opened so wide, she could see whites all around and almost thought they were going to pop out. Ew. But they had them.

"Who are you working for?" Liz asked the big one.

He glared at her, and she grinned. She loved when they refused to talk. Liz took out her knife and pared her fingernails. "Kaeden, darling, you might want to take a walk."

He frowned at her. "Why?"

"That way, you can't be a witness."

She sniffed, smelled a strong odor, and looked around at the little one. His pants were suspiciously dark. "Maybe I should start with him."

"I don't know nothing. Honest. Mac grabbed me up and told me I'd get some good money for a little job. That's all."

"Shut up, you worm," the big one—Mac?—said.

"That's probably what he told Harry too. And look

at him now." She turned back to Mac. "Seems like anyone who works for your boss has a tendency to get caught—or end up dead."

"I ain't dead yet."

"Ah, yet is the operative word." She sliced a button off his shirt with barely more than a flick. Her blades were sharp as a surgeon's. He bucked and backed up as much as he could.

"Hey! Get her off. You're a cop. Stop her."

Kaeden spread his hands. "You want to stop her? Be my guest. I'm not about to get in her way." He leaned back against the cabinets. If Liz hadn't seen the muscle in his jaw jumping from the way he clenched his teeth, she'd have thought him the most nonchalant person in the world.

She sliced off another button. "Who are you working for?"

Mac had gone from red to white. "I don't know. I get a phone call telling me the job. Half the money is in my mailbox, and I get the rest when the job is done."

"What were you doing here?"

"We were sent to get the cane."

"And the puzzle," the little one said. "Tell her, we was to get the puzzle too."

"Thank you. And do what with them?"

"Deliver them to 501 East Earl Street."

"That's an empty lot," Kaeden said. "Fast food joint burned down a couple of years ago, and nobody ever built anything back up."

"Curious. Anything else? What about the bombs?"

She could tell by the startled look on Mac's face he knew nothing about them, but she asked anyway. If they hadn't planted the explosives, who had?

"Bombs? We don't know nothing 'bout no bombs," Mac said. He glanced at the blown door, and his face went whiter. Liz was half afraid the idiot would pass out. "If we'd a come in that door earlier—"

"You'd be dead. Blown to bits. Front door too. Guess your boss doesn't much care what happens to you." She glanced at Kae. "Kaeden, you got a way to get our guests to a safe place?"

He punched in numbers on the phone, and five minutes later, a black-and-white showed up. Liz let Kaeden handle the cop—someone other than Uncle Ray—while she went after the puzzle, cane in hand. Liz rolled the picture up in a piece of cloth. Though the puzzle was one piece—albeit not complete—the partial picture was pretty flexible. She looked around for something to carry both objects in as they were a bit of a handful.

"Try this." Kaeden handed her a piece of PVC pipe three feet long and four inches across with caps at both ends. "I use this for carrying maps and other large papers."

"Perfect. Thanks."

Outside, once more, she walked into the garage, and stared at her ruined car wishing she could jump in and take off. Everywhere she stayed, someone got hurt, and she wasn't going to let that happen anymore, but where to go.

"Liz?"

She shook her head and backed away from him. "I can't do this. I need…I need to get away. Away from you. Away from Charly. Away from here. This is getting too dangerous. Everyone's getting hurt."

"I didn't take you for a coward."

That brought her up short. "Damn straight I'm not."

"So why run?"

"Who said anything about running? I'm going to go somewhere else and make them bring the fight to me. That way you and Charly will be safe."

"Did I hear my name?" Charly strode into the garage. "Looks like another bomb went off in your kitchen. What happened?" She studied both Kaeden and Liz. "Or don't I want to know? By the way, I'm getting awfully tired of you two ducking out and leaving me behind."

"Sorry." Liz grinned at Kaeden as he apologized at the same time she did.

"We had a couple of unwanted visitors," Kaeden said. "They wanted the cane and some puzzle Liz had hidden in her car, but they had nothing to do with the bombs. And Liz was going to save us from ourselves and leave."

"You were what?"

Uh-oh. If there was one thing Liz knew about Charly, you did not want to get her ire up.

"I thought you would be safer if I got away from you two."

"Safer my ass. We're probably safer with you here than without you. You ever consider that?"

"Uh, no. But, I mean, look at what's happened to you both and this place since I got here."

"I needed to replace that door anyway," Kaeden said.

"I suggest we pack up and head back to the diner," Charly said. "My place is more defensible. Kaeden, you've got too many windows. Too many ways in."

"Agreed. Let me board up the doors, and we'll go."

And just like that, they'd decided Liz's destination.

Chapter Twenty-Two

Liz would have been upset at their ordering her around, but their concern made her feel kind of good. Charly and Liz helped Kaeden with boarding the windows and door, and then they all piled into his car for the drive back to the diner.

When they got back, they trudged upstairs to Charly's apartment and locked everything up.

"What's this puzzle they were so interested in?" Kaeden asked around a huge yawn.

Liz blew out her breath as she unrolled the picture. "I know there's something important about this, but right now, I can't think straight. I can't even see straight. I think we've got a little bit of time. Can we get some shuteye first and then look at the puzzle?"

Kaeden and Charly both nodded. Liz could almost see the waves of exhaustion coming off both. She shooed Charly off to her room and turned toward the guest room. Before he settled down on the sofa, Kaeden caught her against the wall, his arms on either side of her, his face far too close. Her heart started to ping a little too fast. She caught her breath, knowing exactly what she wanted, but she shook her head. Yes, she'd absorbed some power from the node, but she'd also spent a lot of the energy on the rain.

"Kaeden, much as I'd love to have a roll, I'm too tired."

He grinned that lopsided grin of his, and Liz nearly capitulated. "I agree. We both are. But I'll keep your interest in mind for later. But what I want to know is if you're going to stay here this time."

"Might as well. You sleep far too lightly. I can't seem to get past you."

He gave her a quick peck that turned much deeper, and Liz nearly hauled him into her bedroom anyway. But he pulled back before she could and sauntered back toward the couch. Liz kind of floated into her room. And finally with the cane and puzzle on the bed with her, she fell asleep.

****

The aroma of fresh coffee teased her nose, but her eyes weren't ready to open yet. Then a finger smoothed warm icing laced with cinnamon over her lips. On its own, her mouth opened and drew that delicious finger in, licking off warm butter and icing and spices. One eye opened.

"She lives."

Kaeden waved a plate filled with French toast, sausages, and scrambled eggs under her nose. What a wonderful way to wake up. A girl could get ideas. She hadn't yet let go of his finger and circled the digit with her tongue, sucking and letting go a little. Her other eye opened when he raised his right eyebrow.

"'Bout time." Charly appeared in the doorway.

Drat. Liz let go of his finger and struggled to sit up. "How long have you two been up?" She snatched the plate from Kaeden. Liz figured as long as she had to be awake and not occupied with something else, she might as well fill her stomach. Besides, the food smelled amazing.

"Not long." Charly perched on the end of the bed, a plate in her hand. Kaeden sat in a chair by the window.

Liz glanced outside. Dim light shone in the sky, but from dusk—or dawn? "What day is it?"

"Tomorrow. Morning. We all slept the day and night through," Charly said.

"Nothing happened last night?"

"Not that we know of," Kaeden said.

"Not even another node?"

"Nope."

They all got quiet as they ate. Liz finished her meal off, as did the others, but she still wanted more.

Without saying anything, they all gravitated to the kitchen where Charly poured coffee and they had slightly stale Danishes. Kaeden softened the pastries in the microwave while Liz peeled an orange and separated the sections onto their plates.

Once they sated their hunger, they leaned back in the chairs and stared at one another. "What do we do now?" Charly asked.

"We figure out what the hell is going on," Liz said. "But first, I want a shower and clean clothes."

"And I should check in with Uncle Ray," Kaeden said.

"I need to take care of some things downstairs," Charly put in.

Liz laughed. "How 'bout if we meet back here in an hour?"

They agreed and went their separate ways. Twenty minutes later, after a really fast shower, Liz sat in the middle of her bed surrounded by candles and several of her stones she'd been able to salvage from her car. She closed her eyes and centered herself. She wanted more info. And to get it, she set protection wards, centered, and went deep.

And deeper.

And felt power surrounding her. Infusing her. Pinging through her blood, settling into her bones.

"We are here, Elizabeth."

She opened her eyes to find the woman and the Santa Claus look-a-like standing in front of her.

"Thank you for coming." She rose to her feet and bowed to both. She didn't know their names so never addressed them directly. "I need your help."

"We've heard." The man chuckled. "You've gotten yourself in a real quagmire this time."

To say his words astonished her would have been the understatement of the millennium. "I got myself into? I'm here because this is where O.W.L. directed me. Aren't you the leaders?"

"Us?" The woman's eyes widened. "No. We are merely messengers."

Curiouser and curiouser. "But you know who runs the organization."

"That is not why you're here. What do you need from us?" the woman asked.

"What about the cane and the puzzle? How do they play into this?"

Both of them frowned. "This is the first we've heard of any artifacts being involved. Show us."

She closed her eyes, and the woman touched her head. A flash of light brighter than the brightest sun burned her brain. The touch was briefer than a second, and longer than a lifetime. But when Liz opened her eyes, she knew they had seen everything from Florida to now.

"We will need to speak to the council," Nick said. "There is much going on here that we were unaware of." The look that passed between the two of them did not give Liz a good vibe. More like a pound of lead in her stomach.

"What council? Who are they?" Ray had mentioned a council when he'd almost revealed her background.

"We will contact you," the woman said. "Take care, Elizabeth. You are…a good person. We would not like to see you hurt."

They wouldn't? "Yeah, me either. Look, I can use all the help you can get me. You know where I'll be."

"Go in peace, Elizabeth. We will be in touch. And remember the limestone."

And just that fast, Liz woke back in her room, in her bed with a drum corps beating in her head. That had happened only once before when she'd contacted O.W.L. The last time she'd faced Bannig—and almost died. The pain was so intense she couldn't even open her eyes. "Thanks a lot, Spirits."

"Here. Take these. Drink." Kaeden's voice was soft and full of concern. His hands strong and gentle as he gave her two tablets and helped hold the glass of water to her lips.

She curled up on the bed, praying for an end to the pain, shivering in reaction. A warm quilt covered her, and a strong body enveloped her.

"Sleep, love. I'll watch over you."

****

When Liz came around, she thought several hours had passed. A mug of hot tea and a bowl of nuts and dried fruit sat on the table. She glanced at the clock, then stared at the numbers. Either she had slept the day—and night—through, or she'd been asleep less than an hour.

"Ah, she's awake." Kaeden pushed open the door and smiled at her.

"What day is it?"

"Same as an hour ago. How do you feel?"

"Oddly good." She stretched and took inventory. She really did feel good. Rested. Whole. Not bruised or in pain or tired or anything. "How?"

Charly came in, followed by Debra, and Liz relaxed. "You?"

She smiled at her. "Yes."

"Thank you. You don't know how much I thank you." She tossed back the blanket and stretched.

"You are most welcome."

"You want to tell us what you were doing? Charly and I tried several times to rouse you but couldn't," Kaeden said.

"Yeah. I was getting ready to give you back some of your own." Charly laughed, then she glanced at Kaeden who nodded back at her. "Then we heard this voice. Actually, several voices, including yours. Having a rather strange conversation."

"I was talking with the bosses. If you heard us, then you know as much as I do about what's going on."

"Which is nothing," Kaeden said.

"Not exactly." Liz picked up her piece of quartz and swung the pendulum idly back and forth. "They said 'Remember the limestone.' "

"What does that mean?" Charly asked.

"This part of the state is a heavy limestone area, right?"

"Yeah. All you have to do is look at the rock field on the south slope of the mountain to see that," Charly said. "Why?"

"You can find quartz in limestone. Though they don't conduct electricity, quartz is used in electrical circuits or energy, including spiritual energy."

"Most of the state has large amounts of limestone and quartz. Why here?" Debra asked.

She shrugged. "Who knows? Maybe for a lot of reasons. The open rock face gives easy access, the river flowing nearby, the seclusion. Maybe something as simple as *just because*."

The others chuckled.

"What do we do?" Charly asked.

Why was she always the boss? Just once, Liz would like to be the flunky. "Okay, I officially call this committee to order. First, we cordon this place off spiritually, and we figure out that cane and puzzle. I think they're the keys. Charly, how much salt do you have?"

"A lot. And if I don't have enough, I'll get more."

"Good. Debra, we need herbs. You know which ones. And you might want to contact the others to let them know they need to protect themselves too. The best protection would be for all of them to get out of town, but if they won't, they need to prepare."

"Okay."

"Kaeden, call your uncle and let him in on what's going on and to take precautions." She felt like a general marshaling her troops. And, in a way, she figured they were an army of sorts, which put her in charge.

Chapter Twenty-Three

They got to work. Charly got boxes of salt from the diner and poured barriers around the building. Debra left, returning later with bundles of protective herbs she tacked at the windows and doors, enhancing them with spells. She also brought a cot that she set up in the diner and a suitcase.

"You plan on staying?" Charly asked.

"Yep. And the others will be here shortly."

Charly glanced around the diner, then nodded and flipped the sign to closed on the front door.

"You're closing?" Liz asked.

"If this is going to be war central, makes sense to me. Besides, sounds like we're going to have more guests, and I don't mean the paying kind."

Damn. Bannig had a lot to answer for. Liz needed to end this soon. She'd always been a loner. Never depended on anyone else or had anyone else depend on her. Never really had a good friend either. But now, with Charly, she felt responsible. She knew none of this was her fault, but still…

"Stop that," Charly said.

"Stop what?" Liz asked, completely at a loss as to what she should stop.

"Blaming yourself. I can see what you're thinking on your face. This is so not your fault. Besides, I've never taken a vacation. Time I did."

"Go find some of those cabana boys I was talking about earlier."

"Nope. Prefer some place with a little excitement."

"A little?" Liz snorted. "Got that in spades."

Debra chuckled. "Plus, this is going to be the safest place to be with all the protection we put around."

"Or this could be the center of danger," Liz corrected. "The safest place for you all to be would be another town. Preferably as far away as you can get."

"Not going to happen," Debra said.

"What about your families?" Liz asked.

She cocked her head. "We'll make arrangements either for them to leave or for safety. We figure they'll be safe as long as we aren't there. Is that right?"

How could Liz tell her what she didn't know? "Possibly. The best thing is for them to go away."

Debra left to take care of the others and their families. She would also get the word out to everyone she could. The time had come for the town to prepare for war. In reality, they should have prepared months ago.

Liz ran upstairs to get the puzzle and cane. As she opened the container, she noticed something strange. A blue light of sorts. The puzzle was glowing. She unrolled the scene and to her surprise the puzzle was nearly finished. When she'd added the last piece she'd gotten in Florida, the scene had been less than half done. Squiggly lines Liz thought were designs glowed gold in the dark background. She laid the cane down on the table, and the designs along the length of the wood started to glow too. Liz stared at them. She could almost read something in the designs. Like letters. Like if she looked long enough, they'd make sense.

She shook her head and rolled the puzzle back up and dashed back downstairs where she opened the puzzle back up again on a table in a protected corner. Charly and Kaeden came over to look. She told them about the puzzle and about how she got the pieces.

"You said when you added your last piece, you'd finished less than half of this."

"Yeah, Charly. And now, I think there are only six pieces missing. But look at this." She pointed to two spots near the center of the puzzle. Embedded in a part of the pattern laid out in gold were Charly's and Kaeden's names.

"Our names? How? And why?" Charly asked.

"Your guess is as good as mine. There's more. Kaeden, close the blinds." She waited until the only light came from the other side of the diner. She picked up the cane and brought the wood close to the puzzle. Like in her room, both started to glow, almost as though the symbols floated above the puzzle.

"What the hell?" Kaeden bent over the puzzle.

"I first noticed the glow upstairs. The puzzle has always had a tiny spark when I add a piece, but this is the first this has happened. If you look at the design that's glowing and the design on the cane, they match. But I've never seen symbols like these."

"I have," Charly said. "Kaeden, upstairs in my apartment on the shelves. Norse Mythology." He took off at a run as Charly flipped the lights on and came back to Liz, a big grin on her face. "The symbols look like ancient runes—"

Kaeden returned with a book in his hand that he'd opened to the back.

"Here."

Liz looked at the page he showed her and swallowed in a mouth gone dry. There, staring at her in black and white, were the symbols. "But how? Why?"

"Don't know. But what do you say we see what they say?" He handed Liz a legal pad and pencil. "You're the best artist."

Charly turned the lights off again. The letters floated above the puzzle.

"Where should I start?" Liz asked. The design lay in a circle with no real beginning or end.

"Which one did you receive first? Do you remember?" Kaeden asked.

"Top center."

"Then I suggest you start there."

Liz drew as quickly as she could, with Charly and Kaeden helping her figure out where one letter ended and another began. Once they had them all down on paper, they started on the cane, marking down the ones in gold first, then the silver ones.

Then Charly turned the overhead light back on and they got to work translating.

Two pots of coffee later, they finished. All three of them sat there and stared at the message. Then at one another, shock on each of their faces. Liz read the lines out loud, as if that would explain everything, "Clear waters run deep. Gather the armies in the keep. Here the final battle is fought. Three are two and one is not."

They all looked up as someone knocked at the door to the diner. Charly unlocked the door and let the others in. All carried air mattresses or camp beds, suitcases, and boxes of paraphernalia. Outside a gentle shower came down—a regular rainstorm. Unfortunately, the temperatures were getting colder as well, and Liz was concerned the rain would turn to ice before long. That would make searching for the nodes even more treacherous.

They moved all the tables and chairs to one side of the diner and set up areas for each of the new arrivals.

"I wish you had inside access to the apartment," Liz said after they'd gotten everyone settled. Climbing the steps in the rain and ice on metal steps could be dangerous. And she wasn't comfortable leaving the cane and puzzle out in the open. She trusted Debra, especially after what she'd done for her. But what about the others? She didn't know them at all.

Charly gaped, then grinned. "Who says I don't? I don't know why I didn't think of this sooner!"

Kaeden and Liz stared at her, then followed as she led them back to the kitchen. She went to the closet where they kept the mops and other cleaning supplies and pulled them all out, then grabbed one of the hooks the mops hung on, and the back wall of the closet slid out of sight. Liz knew her mouth was open as she looked at a set of dark, narrow steps.

"It's not a great way to get up and down—the steps are rather steep and narrow—but there you go."

"How come I never knew about this?" Kaeden stuck his head in and twisted to look up. "Where do these come out?"

"I found the stairs by accident when I remodeled the kitchen. I planned on taking them out, then decided to keep them there in case I needed an escape route for something. They open in the closet in my room, the basement, and the attic."

Liz started laughing. She couldn't help herself. Everyone looked at her like she'd gone mad, and maybe she had a little. "I've been to a lot of places, seen a lot of things, but this town—you all take the prize. Secret staircases, covens, witches with real powers, elves, vampires, shape-shifters, and more. There is so much going on here, you'd never know this town was a sleepy little bump in the road."

Kaeden grinned, then chuckled. "I guess we do have more than our share of oddities. What do you say we get to work?"

Liz figured out the timetable and guessed they had a few hours before the final node built to strength, although she didn't sense a strong buzz yet. Maybe the last one would take more time to build. But at least she knew exactly where this one would be. Liz also figured Bannig and she were about even. They'd both absorbed two nodes. Okay, one and a half for her, but still…

They laid the puzzle out on the table in the upstairs kitchen. Liz kept the cane with her rather than leave it lying around. She rigged a holder from a thin scarf that she looped her belt through. The getup kept the cane at her side, sort of like an old-fashioned sword.

Back down in the diner, they spent the next hour learning what powers the six who'd been hit had, figuring out ways to give them all some privacy and schedules. Fortunately, Charly had fold-out walls for when she had parties in, so they put them to use. All traffic to other parts of the building would be via the inside stairs. Kaeden and Chris strung wires and added lighting so they wouldn't kill themselves going up or down. Then they went exploring. Or rather Kaeden and Charly and Liz did. They started with the basement.

As soon as Liz got to the bottom of those steps, she knew exactly where the power source lay, and she made a beeline for the spot. Her instincts drew her to the back wall.

Like most of the buildings in this area of town, Charly's place had been built over a hundred years ago. The basement was little more than a dug out cellar. The walls were old limestone rocks. Most of the original chinking was gone and they'd been plastered over, but they were still nothing more than rocks. Limestone rocks. With lots of quartz embedded throughout resonating with all that energy. Liz was so buzzed with the power in that place, but she could tell the node hadn't reached full bore yet. She tried absorbing the energy but couldn't. She guessed the nodes only let you have the power when they wanted to.

Okay, she knew the nodes were not living things with intelligence, but sometimes they sure seemed like they were. She could sense the power, but not use any.

Liz shoved at the shelves lining the back wall, trying to get to the source. Kaeden and Charly joined in.

"Can you feel the energy?" Liz asked.

"I feel something," Kaeden said. "Like an itch or static."

"I'm not sure I do," Charly said with a pout.

Liz pulled away the last shelf and ran her hand along the rock wall, stopping at a spot near the right corner. "Here. The pull is strongest here."

She leaned against that wall, drinking in the power. The sensation felt like having the best orgasm ever—multiple times. From sensing the energy and not even absorbing anything.

Kaeden marked the spot with a spray of paint from the shelf they'd emptied.

"What do we do, now that we know where the

node is?" Charly asked.

Liz dragged her befuddled brain back to the task at hand. "What's above us, especially beyond this wall?"

"The front edge of the kitchen. The new part extends past this."

"Good. That means they can't dig down. The more we can protect this spot, the better."

Liz's stomach rumbled, and Charly raised an eyebrow at her. "When's the last time you ate?"

"Um…breakfast with you and Kaeden?"

Charly nodded, then sighed, and shook her head. "I don't care if Bannig himself shows up here. Right now, you're not going to do anything else until you eat a full meal. Along with Kae and me."

"Charly, we don't have time—"

"We're going to eat. End of discussion." She stomped up the steps, and Kaeden stood there laughing.

"I hope you're not going to try to argue with her," he said through chortles.

"Wouldn't do me any good, I guess." A giggle broke through her lips.

"Nope. Not when she's in someone-needs-fed mode. Come on, we might as well help her." He paused and grinned at her. "Well, I'll help cook. You can set things up."

****

A short time later, Liz sat in the chair Kaeden held out for her. He grabbed a chair on her right, Charly on her left, at the head of the table, Debra across from her. The other witches joined them.

They chowed down on fried chicken, potato salad, buttermilk biscuits, and cole slaw.

"Fried chicken and not grilled?" Liz bit into a

piece, licking the juices from her chin and hands.

"Times like this call for food that's good for the soul," Charly said. "We'll go back to healthy after we win the fight."

Her use of *we* both gave Liz a sense of comfort and freaked her out. All this togetherness wrenched her off balance. Her life—her job—up until now meant being alone. Winning or losing depended on her and what she did. But this war had turned into a group effort. And that made her more than a little nervous.

Though the power buzzing through her might have a little to do with that too, she thought as she grabbed another piece of chicken.

Chapter Twenty-Four

They chatted about anything and everything while they ate—or at least anything and everything except the reason they were there. And if the laughter sounded a bit forced, Liz guessed they could be forgiven. But eventually, they'd finished the food and drinks, and they were left staring at one another.

"My turn." Everyone stared at Liz as she rose, then they started laughing when she grabbed a tub and started busing the table. When they went to help her, she waved them off. "You all cooked and set things up. This is the one thing I know how to do. Relax a few."

They helped anyway. She bussed while they wiped spills and put away condiments. Too soon they were done. They sat back down at the table, but this time, Liz sat at the head.

She blew out a breath and took a deep one in. "You still have time to get out of here before this all goes down."

"How long do we have?" Debra asked.

"I figure a day."

"How do you know?" Charly asked.

"An educated guess? Experience? A hunch? I don't know. But I sensed that energy downstairs, and I know the node isn't ready yet. The power is still building. But how long until full intensity is reached is anyone's guess."

"Works for me." Charly grinned at her. "What about Bannig? And what was that thing you saw during the séance?"

Liz closed her eyes and tried to remember the passages she'd read from the old leather book she'd seen at Kaeden's. "The Nameless One. An entity that controls dark powers. He can take on the aspect of many beings and take over the wills of others. No one knows whether he can be defeated since none who have met him have ever lived."

"Except you," Kaeden said.

"Maybe except me. I don't know if I met the Nameless One, or merely a run-of-the-mill demon."

"If he's run-of-the-mill, I don't want to meet the other," Debra said. And the others all agreed.

"Anyway, the Nameless One is older than you can imagine and has been around since the beginning."

"The beginning of what?" Kaeden asked. "The world?"

"Time."

The others shifted around in their seats, looking everywhere but at her and one another. Liz could almost touch their emotions—fear, disbelief, acceptance. This last came from Kaeden. That surprised her a little. After all, he'd had to accept a lot over the last few days. Not the least of which, his partial elfism.

He ticked things off on his fingers. "Okay, to sum up, we're up against at least one bad guy who's absorbed powers from the nodes, an uber-bad guy who is powerful in the extreme, who has anyone he wants at his mercy. We're sitting in the middle of a cauldron of power nodes that seems to be getting larger."

"You noticed?"

"Are you talking about the lines I saw at the fire? Yeah, I noticed. So did others. Uncle Ray sent some people out. The lines aren't everywhere, but they seem to be growing."

How did she not know this? He'd kept this from her? She was supposed to be in charge here. Then she stopped. She could no longer afford that kind of thinking. The fight belonged to all of them, not just Liz.

"If the power keeps growing and connecting, this will be the biggest energy source ever. Anyone who taps into that will have power beyond imagination."

"So why don't you tap into that energy and stop him?" Mandy asked. She studied her black-tipped fingernails and drew designs on the backs of her hands. Liz wondered if she had ever been that young? Not in her memory. She tried to be nice.

"Do you remember a few days ago when we tried to have a séance? Do you remember what happened?"

"Uh, yeah. Sort of."

"Our experience came from just one node, one that hadn't even reached full power yet. And I wasn't even truly tapped in. Think of that effect like a little firecracker. This will be several atomic bombs. The results are cumulative." Liz bet the others didn't believe she knew a word like that. But the explanation had the desired effect. Mandy's mouth opened in a little *O*, and her eyes widened and centered on Liz now instead of her fingers.

"Not good," Charly said.

"You think?"

"So how do we stop them?" Charly asked.

"What about a spell to show them to us?" Mandy asked.

"Too dangerous."

"But we have all these protections up and know what to expect—"

"Only as a last resort," Kaeden said. "We'll patrol the streets before we do that."

Hmmmm. "That might not be such a bad idea," Liz said. Everyone stared at her. "Think. You know these people and this town. What if you just wander around? Go to their places. Talk to people. Find out if anything strange is happening where they are."

That brought a loud round of chuckles that turned to outright laughter.

"Anything strange?" Charly managed to gasp out.

At least Liz managed to get them smiling. All their angst got to her—

They all jumped as something thudded against the front door. Kaeden reacted first. "Stay here."

He headed for the door, and of course, Liz went with him. He glared at her, and she grinned back. The others crowded behind them.

A blob of bright orange neon paint dripped down the glass. They scanned the street, but nothing moved. While Kaeden checked the alley beside the diner, Liz studied the one across from them. Something crouched in the shadows. She glanced around, picked up a fist-sized rock from the flowerbed, and hurled the stone at whatever was there.

The howl that came back didn't come from any animal you'd find in a pet store. Kaeden rejoined her in a hurry, gun drawn.

"What the hell was that?"

"Probably a watcher. You find anything?"

"No. Should I go after him? Her? It?"

260

"Don't bother. It's gone. Those things never stay around once they've been spotted."

"What did you call it? A watcher?"

"Yeah. You can kind of think of them as pit bulls on steroids. They're big, ugly, and powerful. They can be mean bastards when cornered, but they're basically cowards unless in a pack." He held the door open for her to go back in. A gentleman. Gee. A girl could get used to this in different circumstances.

"What happened?" Everyone asked at about the same time.

"Nothing," Liz said. "Just someone trying to get our attention." Which got her thinking. Why? Why did someone want them out front?

"Damn!" Liz ran out back, followed closely by Kaeden. But they found nothing. She prowled around the entire perimeter of the parking lot, which didn't take long since the space was mostly empty. And nothing. Had the paint attack been someone doing a stupid stunt? After another circuit, Kaeden and Liz went back inside.

Charly motioned with her hand for Liz to sit. "While you were out back, we had a chat and think we might have come up with an idea."

"What?" She settled back into her seat, more than a little leery. The last idea they'd all come up with had led to the séance attack.

"We've spent a lot of time playing defense. We believe now is the time to go on the offense."

"You want to play football?"

Charly stuck her tongue out at Liz. "I want to bring the fight to us."

She glanced at the paint dripping down the door. "I

think that's already happened."

Charly grasped her hand and squeezed, then let go. "Yes. But that was on their terms. We want to do this on our terms."

"How do you propose to do that?"

"First, we need to figure out exactly how much time we have before this whole place becomes a node. You said a day. Chris is going to try to pinpoint the time a little closer." Charly nodded at him. He already had his laptop open and was typing away, a plate of cookies at one side, and several bottles of cola on the other.

"Ray has people watching the other nodes in case they are building again. We'll add protection spells and wards around them. With the new powers some of the others have, we should be able to make them stronger."

"Okay. I'm with you so far."

"Then we take the protections away from here." Charly's voice went almost silent, but the words she said rang through the room as if she held a megaphone.

Liz was glad she was already sitting down because if she'd been standing, that would have dropped her to the floor. "Excuse me?"

"Think. If we've put protections around everything else, but not here, where else will they go but here? That's like dangling a carrot in front of a horse or something like that."

"That's insane! This is your home. Your place of business. If you bring them here, there's no telling what will happen. Look what happened to my car! And Kaeden's place. And the gas repository. You want that to happen here? No. I won't let you do that."

Kaeden reached out to her, but she shook him off.

She couldn't let these people get hurt. She'd figure something out by herself. "No."

The others argued with her for longer than she wanted—which went five minutes beyond forever. Liz finally got up and left. She couldn't go to her car, so she stomped upstairs to her room and sat there, in the middle of the bed, doing nothing. Not even thinking. She was so tired she couldn't see straight, but her exhaustion went beyond physical exhaustion. This was mental. Emotional. Spiritual. She had nothing left.

When Kaeden came in, she nearly sent him out again, but he came to her anyway. Then he started rubbing. Feet. Hands. Head. Other parts. And she melted.

The sex was incredible. The man knew how to make a girl feel good. But after, while he lay there sleeping, she lay awake thinking.

Which was a dangerous thing.

She didn't like to make people sleep but had on occasion. Charly forgave her. Would Kaeden?

She kissed him on the cheek. Then pushed.

Liz waited a minute, then as quietly as she could, she got up, got dressed, and tiptoed out. Though she didn't use the skill regularly, she could get past most wards without setting them off, especially if she knew how they'd been built—which she did. And melting into the shadows came as naturally to her as the watchers.

These people were her responsibility. Liz needed to deal with this mess. She needed to make sure they stayed safe. Her breath puffed white outside, so she hid the telltale by wrapping a scarf over her mouth and nose.

The first place Liz went was Kaeden's garage and her car. The damage gave her strength. Her shoulders straightened, and her chin went up. What they'd done was an insult that would be repaid with interest. She loaded up with blades and holy water and grabbed her long coat, then she went out.

Liz slipped into the shadows and started walking, following the streets that connected the dots. Or nodes. Most towns are laid out more-or-less in a square grid pattern, but not Clear Water. The town was laid out based on triangles. Thus, a perfect pentagram was not only possible, but inevitable.

That made her wonder about the people who founded the town. A town based on pentagrams and set in a cauldron of quartz and with power nodes. There was more going on here than anybody probably knew. If she lived through this, she wanted to do some serious checking into the history of this town.

Liz walked to each node, noting where the power seemed the strongest. She kept out of sight of the guards. At each node, she sensed the power growing again. Liz buzzed with energy when she got to the last one. She blew on her hands. The walk had warmed her, but now that she'd stopped, the chilly wind stung her face and hands. Liz studied the area. Though a lot of the surrounding buildings had been scarred by the blast, one seemed particularly undamaged—a huge, old brick Victorian with wide porches and rounded rooms, almost like turrets, at two corners. A large, two-story four-bay brick garage sat in the back. An eight-foot-high privacy fence enclosed the yard. They didn't need the signs she saw on the fence. The whole place said, "Keep Out."

Of course, she went in. A gate next to the garage

had a nice heavy-duty lock that took her all of ten seconds to pick. The well-oiled hinges didn't make a sound when she pushed the gate open. But she did when she saw what that fence kept in.

Watchers. A whole bunch of them. And behind them, Bannig stood, an evil grin on his face.

"You will be safe if you join me, Elizabeth. If not…" He shrugged.

Damn.

She reached for the cane.

Double damn.

The cane was back in her apartment. Liz couldn't take the time to shut the gate as she took off with the hellhounds on her heels. She knew they were faster, bigger, and stronger than her, but she ran anyway. Her coattails flapping behind her, she searched desperately for a place to take a stand. One got close enough to grab her coat, and she had no choice but to stop, her knives at the ready. She stabbed and swiped at those slavering jaws, all the while knowing she was in a bad fix.

One got hold of her arm, and she stabbed him until he dropped off, but that had given the others a chance to close in. All she could see were gleaming teeth. All she could hear were snarls and growls. Liz fought as hard as she ever had, but watchers don't get tired. Unfortunately, she did. She went down to her knees and was really afraid she'd seen her last sunrise.

Chapter Twenty-Five

When Kaeden woke up and rolled over to find Liz's side of the bed empty, he knew what she'd done. He wouldn't have slept through her leaving unless she'd put a sleep spell on him. He grabbed his clothes and dashed downstairs to the diner.

He ran up to Charly's and woke her. "Liz is gone."

Charly never woke easily, he knew, but this time, she instantly became alert. "You're sure?" She grabbed a robe to pull over her sleep shorts and tank.

"Yeah. She sleep-spelled me. And I already checked downstairs." He watched as Charly pulled out a pendulum and map, then paced while she searched.

"South end of town. Maple Street. Middle of the block." She closed her eyes for a moment, then opened them wide. "She's in bad trouble."

Kaeden flew out the door before she finished talking. He jumped in his car and sped off. Fortunately, that time of night, he didn't need to worry about traffic. In less than five minutes, he reached the spot. From what he saw, nearly a dozen huge, slavering dogs were going after something in the middle of the road. He was certain he knew what that something was, and that scared him more than anything. *Please, let her be okay.*

Kaeden grabbed his gun, got out, and started shooting. He didn't know if his plain bullets would do anything, but after one of the beasts went running, he kept shooting until they all took off.

And there, sitting in the middle of the road, he saw Liz. Looking much worse for wear but breathing.

He was glad she was alive, but also pissed at what she'd done, and almost ready to shoot her himself. Once again, she'd taken off without a thought as to the rest of them. Yes, she was some kind of uber-agent, but she could be killed. The attack by the beasts proved that. He let his anger take over. Let her see how she'd hurt him. How she'd betrayed him by her actions. Did she even care about anyone other than herself?

"I can explain," she said to Kaeden.

"I don't want to hear your excuses. Come on."

He didn't even help her up. Just turned and stomped to his car sitting not ten feet away. Liz had barely slid into the seat before he took off. Since boards still covered the doors and windows at his place, Kaeden drove to the diner. He shut off the car and got out without a word, not really caring if she followed—though she did.

They went into the kitchen of the diner where he pulled out a chair. "Sit."

"Kaeden—"

"Stop. Not a word." He turned his back on her and yanked out the first aid kit from a cabinet. Liz pulled off her coat, and he glanced at the leather. The material looked worse for the wear. Several tears and holes marred the dark covering, two serious ones that he wasn't sure could be fixed, but she'd been lucky the coat had sustained the only real damage. If she hadn't been wearing that, those rips would be in her flesh. Her arm had some nasty scratches and bruises. Kaeden dumped antiseptic over her cuts, snorting when she refused to even wince. Two could play the silent game. Then he hit the worst injury on her arm, and he caught the tightening of her lips and narrowed eyes. Served her right. Finally, though, he finished cleaning and bandaging her injuries. He stood facing the cabinet, and she sat still.

"You really don't understand, do you?" he said to the cabinet.

"Sorry?"

He spun around and glared at her. "Have you ever cared about anyone other than yourself?"

"Yes! I care about you! And Charly!"

"No. You don't. If you did, you'd know how much you hurt us. How much you hurt me. I thought we had something, Liz. But I guess I was wrong."

Liz rose, slowly, and went to him. She reached out to touch his face, but he backed away. This time, a simple apology wouldn't work. Her actions hurt him deeply. After everything they'd been through, she still didn't trust him.

"Kaeden, I do care. Honest. But you have to understand. This is all new to me. I don't know how to handle this. Us."

"You don't handle this by putting us to sleep and sneaking off on your own. You could have been killed out there tonight." He let his frustration show in his voice.

She sighed. "Yeah. I know. And I'm sorry. But—"

"No. No 'buts,' Liz. Either you trust me, or you don't. As we've found out, I'm not without my own resources. And this is my home. Like it or not, I'm part of this fight. We all are." Kaeden knew the moment she gave up. He could see the sorrow in her face, but that didn't mean he'd given up his anger.

"I know my apology doesn't mean much, but I am sorry."

He went over to her and held her face between his hands. "Liz, I know you've had a rough life. That you've had to rely only on yourself. But you've got friends now. And you've got me. You know we trust you. All we ask is that you trust us in return. Can you do that?"

"I can try."

"That's all I can ask. But one more thing." He glared at her. "If you ever push me to sleep again, I will be worse than those beasts. Understood?"

"Loud and clear."

"Fine." He hugged her, but the restraint still remained. She'd hurt him. A lot. Love was easy, but trust? That came hard—on both sides.

Charly pushed through the swinging door and faced them. "You two done?"

Kaeden backed away and studied Liz. "I'm not sure. You'd have to ask her, but at this point, I can't say I trust much of anything she says or does."

"I'm sorry." This time Liz aimed her apology at her best friend.

"Not gonna work. You have some serious atonement to do." Charly frowned at her.

"I know." And she did know. These two people meant more to her than anyone in her entire life. Liz thought going out would save them, but that just caused more problems. She needed to change. To stop shutting them out.

"Go get some sleep." Kaeden pushed Liz toward the stairs.

"What about you?"

"I'm good. I got plenty of sleep. Remember? Go."

She did. And she slept, though not well. She kept having dreams about big animals with lots of teeth.

Later, Liz apologized again. This time to everyone. She could see the hurt in their faces, and that bothered her more than her bites. Debra wanted to heal her, but Kaeden stopped her.

"Let her feel these, Deb. I think she needs the reminder." He stared at her while he talked. She swallowed hard. Because of her actions, he'd changed toward her. And that hurt more than a few bruises and cuts. Especially since she knew the change was all her fault. She hoped she could bring him back, but feared she couldn't.

"He's right. I'll be okay." The next part was harder for her, but she managed. "And you all were right about your plan. If we put wards around the other nodes and take them off this place, we'll have a better chance. We know this place and can mount a defense here. But we need to do a lot of work first. Chris, do you have an idea of how much time we have?"

He gulped down the last of his cinnamon roll and wiped his hands on a napkin before opening his computer. "From what I could figure out, this one's taking longer to build. We have another forty hours, give or take a few minutes. I couldn't be exact on when this all started."

"That's fine." Almost two days from now. Liz had figured less than that, but she let him have his minute. "The first thing we need to do is fortify this place. I assume there's a good building supply store around here?"

"Yes," Kaeden said. "Tell me what we'll need, and I'll get the supplies."

"You, Charly, and I will work on that. The rest of you, please concentrate on setting wards around the other places. And don't go alone. Be sure there are at least two or three of you together at all times."

While the other six figured out who would go where and do what, Charly, Kaeden, and Liz went around the building figuring out what they needed to do.

"Plywood and shatterproof acrylic for the windows," Kaeden said. "What about a generator?"

They finished figuring out what they needed and went shopping. Thank goodness, everyone who left town complied with Ray's request to leave the keys to their stores with him in case they needed supplies. They filled up Charly's van and the back of Kaeden's SUV by the time they finished.

The others were gone when they got back. They unloaded the supplies and took a break for lunch.

"Kaeden, I'd like to talk to your uncle. Think you can arrange that?" Liz needed to know what kind of troops they could muster. The odds of nine people conquering an unknown evil army weren't good. Especially if they used beasts like watchers.

He had his cell phone out before Liz finished speaking. She listened as he asked his uncle to come to the diner. A minute later, he shut the phone. "Ray will be here shortly. And he's got several pints of holy water with him."

Pints? She wanted gallons, but some was better than none. "Why don't you two start on lunch while I tackle this stuff?"

"We can help," Charly said.

Liz shook her head. "Your talent is cooking. Mine is traps. Besides, I need to draw some of this up before I do anything physical. Got any paper around I can use?"

Charly pulled off a length of butcher paper and handed Liz a pencil. While Charly and Kaeden disappeared into the kitchen, Liz got to work. By the time she finished, the others had returned, and soup, salad, and sandwiches lined the table.

The witches detailed what they'd done while everyone ate. "Any problems?" Liz asked.

"Nah. The guards said everything's been quiet."

They all looked around as someone rapped on the front door. Kaeden rose to answer with Liz standing at one side with her knives, Charly on the other with a heavy skillet. Liz grinned at Charly who smirked back at her. Bad guys never knocked, but there they stood ready to take on whatever came through the door.

They relaxed when Ray stepped inside and put away their weapons when he snorted at them. Then he saw the piles of hardware and other supplies.

"Kaeden?"

"Let's go upstairs, Uncle Ray. We need to talk."

Debra nodded at the four of them. "We'll clean up down here."

Charly handed her the skillet. Liz bit back the smile at the thought of sweet little Debra conking someone over the head with that thing. She could barely lift the cast iron. But Liz also thought that, if needed, Debra would find the strength.

Liz followed Kaeden and Ray upstairs with Charly close behind her. They sat at the kitchen table. Charly poured coffee. All so bland. All so normal. All so wrong. What they faced was neither bland nor normal.

"And how long have those inside stairs been here?" Ray asked.

"It's not important at the moment." Kaeden pointed out.

"Well, what I've found out is. People are leaving. A lot of them. And when I ask, nobody can give me a good reason. Like they're running scared." Ray pulled a piece of paper from his pocket and smoothed the page out on the table. "One of them gave me this."

The sheet held a badly photocopied warning. That the time of choice had come. They could choose to stay and die. Or choose to leave.

"Interesting," Liz said. She touched the paper and got a mild shock.

"*Interesting*? That's all you can say about this?" Ray said. "That thing even makes me want to pack up and go."

"That's because the paper contains a spell. What I find interesting is that our opposition is trying to get rid of either innocents or our possible allies. Normally the bad guys don't care about collateral damage. How many people got these?"

"Near as we can tell, everyone. They were stuck in doors all over town."

"When did that happen?"

"Weren't there at midnight, some said, but were by dawn."

"Funny, I didn't see anyone out when I was—" Oops. Too late, Liz realized she should have kept her mouth shut. Kaeden glared at her. Ray glanced from him to her and back. "Okay, I went out out. Alone. Big nasties attacked me. Kaeden saved my ass. I am more sorry than any of you can understand. End of story."

"Fine." Ray tossed the paper in the sink, dumped in salt, and then ran water. The paper sizzled and burst into flames. He washed the ashes down the drain. "Putting this together with what you have downstairs. I assume the battle is getting closer."

"Yes." She wanted more from him. "What I want to know is, how many more people can we get to help us?"

Ray glared at her until Liz began to sweat. She didn't often give into nerves, but that man had the intimidation stare down pat.

He turned to Kaeden. "She doesn't want much, does she?"

"Just what's needed."

Liz really hated when people talked around her, but she held her tongue. She was in deep enough with Kaeden already.

"Is she worth all this trouble?" Ray asked.

"Yep."

Damn. Just when Liz was about ready to pop, he came up with sweet words. Her temper chilled, and that pleasurable feeling she was learning about turned on.

Ray nodded. "Okay. I've already talked to the Elven community. Boreon put the word out. We should know by later today who and how many we have. I guess we're gathering here?"

"The fight will center here," Liz said. "Kaeden can tell you the whys and wherefores later, but as long as I know we've got help coming, I can come up with a plan."

Ray looked down at the puzzle covering the table. "I thought you said there were more pieces missing than this."

They all picked up their coffee cups and pieces of paper and other stuff and studied the puzzle. All the pieces were there except one. The center piece.

Chapter Twenty-Six

"How? When?" Charly sputtered. "Nobody could get in. Nobody."

Liz sighed. "Don't bother trying to figure this out. You'll give yourself a headache." The picture had changed once again. Instead of the symbols, there were now scenes from around town. She saw her fight with Bruce, the séance, her dancing with the cane, and the fight with the watchers.

"Well, at least we know nothing else is going to happen until the final fight," Liz said.

"What? How do you know that?" Charly asked.

"Only one more piece. Each piece is a part of something I did. There's only room left for one more. The final one. The final challenge."

"There's always the chance something will happen to you before we have to fight the battle," Ray said.

She shook her head. "No. Not going to happen."

"It almost did last night," Kaeden said. "Liz, you can't take any more chances like that."

"I know. Okay? I know."

Kaeden stared at the puzzle. "I can't figure this piece out."

"What do you mean?"

"Well, you know how in most puzzles, if you're missing a piece, you can sort of figure out what the shape and color are like from the ones surrounding that spot. But I can't figure this one out. This one doesn't make any sense."

"None of this makes sense." Liz bent over the puzzle. She knew if she concentrated, she'd be able to see what she needed to see.

And the next thing she knew, the nothingness surrounded her. The sudden change surprised the heck out of her, but she settled down. She figured her bosses brought her there for a reason. So, she waited.

And waited.

And waited.

An eternity later, Nick showed up. He didn't look so good. Kind of rough around the edges. Like he'd been down one too many chimneys.

"Elizabeth. We weren't expecting you."

"I wasn't expecting to be here. Just happened. What's going on? And where's your partner?"

"The battle goes badly, and I'm afraid she became one of the latest casualties."

Huh? Somebody had hurt her spirits? Liz didn't know that could happen. "I'm sorry. Wait, you said the battle? I thought I was the one fighting. That you all were sitting up here safe and clean and all-knowing."

"We each have our own campaigns to fight. The fallen ones have encroached into areas previously forbidden to them."

"So why am I here?"

"I'm not sure I know. Perhaps—" He closed his eyes for a moment, then opened them and reached into his sleeve. He pulled out a piece of paper and handed the sheet to her. "Use this when all is darkest."

Liz took the paper and glanced at the sheet, flipping the blank page from one side to the other. And when she looked up, Nick had disappeared.

And a second later, Liz awoke back in the kitchen and Kaeden and the others were staring at her. Oddly enough, her head didn't hurt as much as the last time.

"Liz? What happened? We tried calling you, but you didn't answer, like you weren't here," Charly said. "Were you back in your spirit world?"

"Yes." She told them what had happened and showed them the paper. "This is the first time they've ever given me something concrete to bring back with me."

Kaeden studied the blank piece of paper. "There's nothing on this."

"I know. But Nick told me to use this when things got bad."

"Nick?" Though Kaeden said the name, the other two stared at her with the same question.

"That's what I call the one spirit. Mostly because he looks like Santa. He's kind of short, round, has a white beard, a happy face—though he wasn't looking so happy this time."

Liz took the paper back from Kaeden and tucked the page in her jeans pocket. She wasn't sure what good a blank sheet of paper would be, but she did not question the spirits.

"So where were we?"

"You mean before you went missing?" Kaeden grinned at her. "Uncle Ray is going to get in touch with the others and will get back to us with numbers and types of help. He's also going to bring in more supplies. We might have to house a lot of people. The basement of the municipal building has stacks of cots and other emergency supplies."

"Do you need help?" Liz asked.

"No. I'll get some of the others to help. What about you all?"

"We're going to barricade. We have a little less than a day."

"But Chris said we have almost two," Kaeden said.

Liz blew out a sigh. "I'm not sure I trust his calculations. Besides, doesn't hurt to be ready early, right?"

"No problem."

"What about the cane?" Charly asked.

"What about it?"

"Can we use that somehow?"

About that time, they heard a thud and yells from downstairs. They all headed for the inside steps and slipped and slid down them as fast as they could, Kaeden in the lead, her next, followed by Ray and Charly.

Debra and the others were there, staring at the kitchen area. "What happened?"

Another thud from the back. "Ray, stay with Charly and the others. Kaeden, with me." Liz pulled her knives and headed for the kitchen area. The heavy fire door sported a dent the size of her head.

"I thought we had protection around here." Like most industrial kitchens, there were no windows, so she couldn't look outside.

"Probably got messed up when we were bringing in the wood."

"Or when someone came in or went out." Another thud and the whole wall shook. And the hinges pinged. She did not want to know what could do that kind of damage and keep coming. But how to get rid of whatever was out there?

Liz closed her eyes and centered herself. She wasn't great at casting spells but could when needed. But what kind of spell? Protection? Yes, but also something to repel the intruder.

Thud. So much for centering. Her eyes opened, and she saw the door bent in, leaving a gap of daylight. One more good hit and they'd have a real problem.

Liz tried centering again. Then she felt Kaeden's hands on her shoulders. Calming her. Giving her strength. Then Charly joined her, holding her hand. And Liz found the words.

An inhuman howl from outside and no more thuds let her know her spell had worked. Now if she could remember what she said. Sure would be nice if she ever had to do that again.

She turned around into Kaeden's arms, and he pulled her in close. Charly wrapped her arms around both of them. Nobody had ever hugged her after a fight. She needed to do that more often.

"I assume whatever did that is gone." Ray's voice pushed them apart, but Kaeden kept her hand in his. That felt even better. The others stood at the door and outside the serving ledge staring at them, some with worry, others with knowing grins.

"Yes. For now. But we need to rebuild our protections," Liz said.

"I thought we were going to drop them," Mandy pointed out.

"We will, but not yet. Not until we're ready. Charly, where's the salt?"

"Here." She handed Liz a bucket.

"Kaeden, you and your uncle go to work on that

door. I'm going to make sure our perimeter is secure."

"You don't want backup?"

"No. Whatever was out there is gone for now. But I don't know how long my spell will last. I'll be back quick." She really didn't know, mostly because she'd never cast one like that before.

While the others cleaned up and worked, Liz went outside. She had two reasons for going out there. She really did want to shore up their defenses. But she also wanted to see if she could get a sense of what had attacked them.

By the time Liz got to the back of the building, the others had the damaged door nearly off. Hammering out the dents would go much faster if they lay the material flat, plus they could reinforce it with more metal. Kaeden smiled at her, and she smiled back but kept to her task.

She took note of the building next door to Charly's. In the main business area, buildings were built right up against each other, often sharing a common wall. In Charly's case, the attached building sat empty and ended at a narrow walkway before the next one. That meant they had an alley on one side, empty building and walkway on the other. Liz extended her circle of salt to include the adjoining space, an idea forming in her mind.

When she finished the circle, she went back to where the others worked on the door, but she stayed out of sight. Liz held out her hands and let her senses take over.

Liz picked up on the darkness left by the animal. The beast was a watcher. And yet not. Something more. Something bigger. And more powerful. She didn't like that at all. The bad guys were bringing in the big guns. Liz hoped her group had some of their own around.

She went back in. Kaeden and the others had blocked the doorway with metal sheeting and then backed that with the damaged metal door held in place by more sheeting. Nothing was coming in that way.

Finished with their immediate tasks, they waved Ray off and got back to work. The first thing they did was rearrange the dining areas for a possible arrival of guests. Liz hoped they got an influx. While the others worked, she studied the wall that served as the barrier between them and the empty building next door.

"What's up, Liz?" Kaeden asked.

"How thick is the wall between here and the space next door?"

"Anywhere between six inches and two feet, I guess. Hard to tell with some of these old buildings."

"Twelve inches tops." Charly joined them. "I planned to buy the building and expand my place, so I had some studies done. Why?"

"Think we can break through? If we're going to get more people in, using that empty space would give us more room for bunking."

"Not a bad idea. Let me get the plans." Charly dashed upstairs.

"We're going to need a sledgehammer. I think I saw one downstairs," Kaeden said.

While he headed for the basement, Liz ran her hands over the wall. She didn't know what she searched for, but her senses kept bringing her back to one spot about four feet from the front. Liz took out her pencil and marked an X there. Then she started taking down the pictures Charly had hung. She handed them off to the others who stacked them on an empty table.

Charly and Kaeden returned at the same time—Charly with rolls of blueprints, Kaeden with a sledgehammer and crowbar. Charly laid out the plans and pointed at a spot. "This is where the engineer said we should put the walkthrough. He said this is the safest spot."

Liz compared the plan to the wall. The same place as her X. Huh. She didn't know she could do that.

Kaeden stripped out of his tee, spit on his hands, and got to work. Damn, that man looked delicious. Liz reined in her raging hormones and got to work with the crowbar. They made one heck of a mess, but they got an opening big enough for two people to walk through. They shored up the space with wood, making a safe pass-through.

The other side had as much space as Charly's and was divided into two large rooms with a wide staircase leading up to Liz assumed more rooms.

"This will be great. We can use this side for sleeping, Charly's for eating and meeting."

They boarded up all the windows, making the rooms rather dark, but the sun wasn't exactly shining anyway. The possibility of rain or snow bothered Liz as that would also wash away the salt. She took up the bucket and started going around the interior walls and windows of both buildings.

Less than a quarter of the way around the first room, Ann and Sue came up to her and took the bucket. "Let us do this. This is our specialty," Ann said.

Liz didn't argue. Ann was right. They specialized in protection, she didn't. Well, not that kind of protection. Hers tended more toward the physical, destructive type.

She went back to the diner area in time to see Ray come through the front door. They hadn't boarded that door up, but they had reinforced the opening with a heavy sheet of clear, shatter-proof acrylic.

"Hey, Ray."

"Hey. Looks like you've been busy."

"Yeah. What have you got for me?"

"Help. As much as I could come up with." He opened the door wide, and people started coming in. Dozens of them. Though they all looked perfectly human, Liz detected lycan, elf, vamp, and a few hybrids she couldn't categorize. Liz directed them to the other building, more than a little nervous about such a gathering.

On the surface, most groups could get along, but the briefer the meeting, the better. But here, they'd be closed up in cramped quarters for an extended time. Even under the best of circumstances, Liz knew tempers could get short. And this was most assuredly not the best of circumstances. At least they had one thing in their favor—the full moon had been the previous week, so the lycans wouldn't be hungry, but what about the vamps?

While Liz paced, they moved in. When she finally got around to looking at things, she could see she had been worrying over nothing. Each group had taken over a separate part of the building and had set up public and private areas. The vampire contingent had even brought in small fridges and coolers for their specific needs. She did not want to know.

She lost count of how many there were, but the numbers didn't seem like enough for a town this size.

And she wondered where the kids were. Hopefully, somewhere far away and safe.

While everyone moved things in, Charly and Kaeden got to cooking. Liz figured there wasn't much she could do in that department, so she started setting up tables. After all, they'd need places to eat, and this was something she could do. She also dragged four tables together in the center of the room, planning on making that their center of operations.

Rather than waiting tables, they set things up like a buffet for everyone to get their own stuff. Well after sunset, people started gathering in the diner. The noise was subdued, and Liz noted that each group stayed together, eyeing one another. If they couldn't even eat together, how would they work together?

Liz gave everyone plenty of time to eat, then she started cleaning up. She went to the vampires first. Even though she'd worked with their kind before, they gave her the worst creeps. She got more than a few weird stares as she started bussing tables.

"Liz? What are you doing?" Charly asked.

"Cleaning up. I refuse to work in a mess. And I don't see anyone else doing the job."

Charly grinned at her and grabbed another tub, but instead of filling the tub herself, she went to the leader of the lycans, a well-dressed woman who oozed money. "Give us a hand."

Liz bit back a chuckle as the woman's eyes went wide and she came up out of her chair. The man next to her, as well dressed as she, picked up the tub. "I'll take care of the job this time, my dear. Relax."

He started clearing tables. As he did, one of the elves and a vampire also rose and went to work. Several others grabbed rags and started wiping things down while others asked for the brooms and cleaned the floors. In less than a half hour, they had the place cleaned up and people were laughing with one another. If some still stood in the shadows, that was okay. Liz didn't expect everyone to become best friends. But she had enough of a war to fight without skirmishes here.

Liz drifted to the center table and stood at the head. She felt rather conspicuous, but Kaeden, Charly, Debra, and Ray joined her, fanning out to either side. She appreciated their support.

"I'd like everyone's attention please."

Liz didn't need a gavel or whistle or anything. In an instant, the place got deadly quiet, and every eye centered on her. She really hated this kind of thing. Being the center of attention did not come easily to her, but she didn't have a whole lot of choice.

"I don't know how much you all know about what's going on here in town, so I'm going to give you the condensed version." And she did. Liz expected argument or disbelief. She got none of that. Then she realized, these people were uber-human. They could sense the nodes. Sense the power building. They knew something was going on.

"Ray called you all here to ask for your help. We are going up against a big nasty. Something so dark, so old, he goes back to the beginning of time itself."

"So why here? Why now?" one of the lycans asked.

"Come on, Tony," the head of the vampires said. "Even you have to be able to sense the power building."

Tony jumped up and would have gone for the other guy if Ray hadn't stepped in.

"That's enough, Tony. You too, Marcus. All of you, listen up and listen good. You've managed to keep the peace for a lot of years. Don't let all that work go to waste. This is not the time or place for airing our differences. This is a problem for the entire populace, especially us others."

He came back to where Liz stood. "Liz here knows what she's talking about. She's our best hope of coming out of this thing alive."

Gee, thanks. No pressure there. But his support helped her nerves. "Okay, we have approximately a day to get things together. First, for those of you with families, I suggest you get them out of town fast."

"Already done," Tony said. "Most of our people started leaving a few weeks ago."

"Ours too," the leader of the elves said. The vampires didn't bother to say anything. They didn't need to. No kids there to worry about.

"Fine. Now we need—"

Liz never got to finish her sentence as a loud explosion from out back shook the building, raining dust on their heads, and the lights went out.

Chapter Twenty-Seven

There was a moment's confusion, the noise of many voices raised. Liz stayed still and shouted, "Quiet!"

They eventually settled down. "Mandy!"

A flicker of light appeared at her elbow at about the same time the emergency lights kicked on. The flicker grew into a ball that floated above their heads. Mandy stood there, hands outstretched, grinning. Between that and the emergency lights, they had enough to see by.

"Cool." She turned her attention to Chris. "Can you give me a look see outside?" Thank goodness for batteries and generators.

He opened his computer, the glow adding to the ambient light. He tapped a few keys and turned the screen so they could see. One camera in front, another out back, one to each side. The one in back was the one that interested her most. There was a rather large hole in the parking lot—about where what was left of her car would have been if she'd parked there.

"They're going to try to blast their way in."

"How? With what? Who?" The questions came from every side, stopping only when Liz held up her hand.

"How? I'd say with what they got from old Bruce the other night. He had a farm supply store, so I assume

288

fertilizer, wires, batteries, and so on."

"Probably TNT too," Ray said. "He kept some on hand for taking care of field rocks."

"All that stuff can make a sizable bang. I'm surprised they didn't do more damage than a big hole," one of the lycan's stated.

"They're being careful because of the power node. They don't want to destroy the node, and they don't know what blasting will do with one that large." She glanced around at who she had there, and an idea came to her. Liz noticed that nobody else was around outside. A bang that big would normally draw the curious. Nothing.

That could only mean that those still in town knew about the fight. Okay, so she didn't have to worry about innocents getting caught in the crossfire. She glanced at the vampire contingent.

"You all have the best night vision. Think you can set up patrols for us?"

The snooty woman nodded, no longer quite so snooty. "How far out do you want the perimeter?"

"Doesn't have to be big. One block maybe? Just enough to give us some forewarning."

"Done. What about the other nodes?"

"We have protection spells around them," Charly said.

Liz nodded. "We pulled in the teams from them. But do yourselves a favor for those going out. The bad guys are using watchers. Look out for them."

"Are those the uber-dogs?" one of the lycans asked.

"Yeah." She rubbed her arm where the bruises still ached.

"We'll take care of them. Some of us can shift at will."

Liz nodded. Werewolves were at their strongest when they were in wolf form, but they weren't so bad in human form. All lean muscle, fast, enhanced senses. And if they had regular shape-shifters, that was even better. "You and the vampires can work things out. Those of you who can handle the liquid, there are bottles of holy water by the door."

"What about us?" The leader of the elves came to her.

"Debra and the other witches have set some protection spells, but if you could strengthen them?"

He nodded. "That and we'll set snipers on the roof here and next door."

"Good idea."

Everyone cleared out except the original group. Liz sat down in her chair, exhaustion setting in. But she didn't have time to be tired. Charly set a huge mug of coffee in front of her.

Liz grinned at her. "Thanks."

"Figured you'd need this."

"She does, but she's also going to need some real sleep," Kaeden said. "We all will. Tired people make mistakes."

"Once everything's set up, we'll get some shut eye." Liz took a swig of her coffee.

And everything went gray.

"Elizabeth."

Nick stood there in front of her. He looked worse than Liz felt—not a good feeling.

"Hey. How goes the fight?"

"Not well, I'm afraid. You mentioned earlier

something about some artifacts."

"Yeah. My puzzle and the cane." She pointed to the fancy stick hanging from her belt. Nick stared at the cane.

"May I see that?"

"Um…"

Liz's reluctance brought out a glimmer of the smile she knew so well. "Ah. Yes. What if you hold the cane and I just look?"

She couldn't see any problem with that. She unhooked and held the cane out in front of her. He bent over, studying the staff, hands locked behind his back.

"Interesting. And you say this has odd properties?"

"Only one that I've found. If I twist the crystal on top, everyone in about ten feet goes still. I can still move around, but they're like in a time warp or something."

"I'd heard of this. The cane disappeared a long time ago along with its twin." He stood straight and peered at her. "You are a special person, Elizabeth. We always knew that, but not exactly how special you were."

"Um, thanks. I think. But, if I may, why do you say that?"

"Because this cane will only work for people with unique and specific qualities. I've only known one other person for whom this worked, and he's been gone from our ranks for years."

Uh-oh. Why did she have a strange feeling she knew who he was talking about? "Can you describe him to me?"

"Tall, lanky gentleman with a shock of white hair, liked to sport a goatee, pale blue eyes."

That took her back. His description didn't sound at all like the man she thought of. "He wasn't a tall, black man with graying hair?"

"No."

Dang. "Is stopping time all this thing can do?"

"No, but I am not at liberty to tell you the other properties."

"But—"

He held up his hand to stop her. "I am not at liberty to tell you, but that doesn't mean you can't find out. Do yourself a favor and try twisting a different way."

Her hand itched to do just that, but she waited. "Can you give us any help down below? The bad guys tried to blow us up."

"I know. I cannot interfere, but I can tell you this much. You are on the right track in what you do. Use the strengths of those with you. And remember, not all friends are friends and not all enemies are enemies."

Before Liz could ask him what the heck he meant, he disappeared, and she woke up back in the diner. Kaeden stood to one side, Charly on the other, and her head somewhere in the stratosphere.

"I assume you were in the spirit world?" Kaeden asked.

"Yeah."

"Debra!" Kaeden called to her.

"No, I'm fine."

"Be quiet." He turned as Debra arrived. "She had another session with the spirits."

"Understood." She came to Liz and placed her hands on Liz's temples.

"You really don't—"

"Quiet," Debra, Kaeden, and Charly all said at the

same time.

She shut up. The heat from Debra's hands spread from her temples throughout her body. A minute later, Debra took her hands away, and Liz nodded her thanks. Not only did her head not hurt, neither did the bruises and bites from the watchers. And she had more energy.

Unfortunately, she couldn't say the same for Debra. Dark circles accentuated her eyes, and deep lines etched canyons in her face.

"Kaeden, get her next door and to a bed. And no arguments. She's overstretched herself."

"I'm fine," Debra said.

"Uh-huh. And I could have taken some aspirin. Go. No arguments."

She smiled tiredly but went.

Liz wanted someplace private to play with the cane, but with people milling around the diner, she didn't see anywhere. She grabbed one of the people. "When Kaeden comes back in, tell him to meet me upstairs." The man nodded, and Liz went into the kitchen after Charly. "Charly, come with me."

Liz headed up the inside stairs dragging Charly behind her. Kaeden joined them before they'd gotten to the top. Ever since Charly had opened the inside ones up, they didn't use the exterior ones anymore. This way, they couldn't be targets.

"What's up?" he asked.

"Us. To Charly's." Liz shut the door behind them once they were in the apartment and set the lock, then unhooked the cane.

"Want to tell us what's going on?" Charly asked.

"This. Nick told me there's more to this than meets the eye. Or hand. Or whatever. He told me I needed to try different things. Figured since you two knew about this, you were the most logical ones to help me."

"But you're the only one who can make the magic work," Charly said from the middle of the bed in the guest room. Kaeden sat on the chair by the window. Liz stood between him and the bed.

"Doesn't mean I can't use your input." Liz held the cane out. "We know that if I turn the crystal to the right, I stop things in my general area, but the left did nothing. Wonder what happens if I twist the tip of the cane." The tip refused to turn. And so did the claw when she tried that solution.

Liz was about ready to give up, figuring Nick had goofed. After all, he wasn't exactly himself, so maybe he'd mistaken this cane for another one. He had said there was a twin.

She sat there, fiddling with the staff, twirling it, faster and faster. As she did, the cane took on a life of its own, floating away from her hands. And sliced off the high post at the foot of Charly's bed like a piece of butter.

Charly scrambled back against the headboard, making herself as small as she could, and Kaeden rose and backed away too.

"How the hell did you do that?" he asked.

"I…I don't know!"

"Make it stop!" Charly yelled.

"I don't know how!" Truth to tell, Liz felt a little nervous about getting any closer to that whirling weapon herself. She held out her hands and concentrated on the cane. Nothing.

She moved closer, and the second bedpost fell to the ground. Liz backed off and the cane hung there, spinning like a buzz saw. Charly had scrambled off the bed and inched toward the door. As she moved, so did the cane. Toward her!

"Charly! Stop!" She did and so did the cane. "Whatever you do, don't move."

"This is me not moving. Nope. Not gonna budge. So not moving."

"Charly. Shut up."

There had to be a way to make this thing stop. Liz closed her eyes and centered herself, then opened her mind to the power of the crystal. She held out her right hand. A moment later, she felt something in her hand. She opened her eyes and the smooth, black piece of wood with fancy decorations rested on her palm. No sharp edges, no places for knives to come shooting out. She tapped the cane on the floor, then held it straight out and let go. The staff dropped to the floor like a cane.

"Are we safe?" Charly asked.

"I think so."

Kaeden picked up the pieces of the posts and examined them. "They're perfectly smooth cuts—like a laser."

"But a laser would have cut other things in the room. This only cut what it touched. And followed motion."

"We noticed. Liz, as far as we know, you're the only one who can control that thing. I suggest we don't let anyone else even close. If someone else can handle the power, there's no telling what they'll do," Kaeden said.

Liz secured the cane back to her belt, but keeping the artifact with her made her more than a little nervous. And Charly didn't stick around long. As soon as she could, she made a beeline for the door, her eyes on the cane the entire time.

Kaeden shook his head and settled on the bed. He patted the spot next to him, and Liz sat down. "One hell of a mess we're in, aren't we?"

"You think?"

"I never thought when you breezed in here that we'd end up here."

"In bed?"

He laughed. God, she loved the way he laughed. His whole face lit up and sounded like pure joy. She wanted more and hoped they survived the battle so she could hear it again.

"That's not exactly what I meant but is a good idea." He undid her belt and carefully laid the cane on the floor. Kaeden ran his hands down her sides, making her shiver in anticipation. "I would rather not have that in my way."

Liz grinned at him as she undid his belt and ran her hands over his taut stomach. Then she let him have his way.

And a very good way he had.

****

Later, after the fun and sleep, Liz woke. Even without being able to see outside, she sensed daylight hadn't broken yet.

"Liz?" Kaeden rolled over and reached for her. He really was a light sleeper. "What's wrong?"

"Not sure. Just can't sleep."

He sat up, leaned against the headboard, and pulled her to him. She rested against him, loving the warmth and solid muscles. His heart beat a steady pattern under her hand. He had her heart—something she thought would never happen to her. Liz wished they could stay like this forever, but she also knew there were more important situations to take care of.

"Something's really bothering you." He stroked one finger down her jawline.

"Yes. I think I need to be someplace."

"Besides here in Clear Water? Right now, I wish we all were someplace else."

She sighed and shook her head. He smoothed her hair back. How could such a small gesture mean so much? "No, that's not what I mean—although I do agree with the sentiment. And if you recall, I did try to get you all to leave. No, I think I need to go for a walk."

"That's a change."

"What do you mean?"

"That you're telling me instead of leaving. You do know I'm going with you, right?"

"I was kind of counting on that."

She climbed out of the bed and found her clothes, while Kaeden did the same. Liz took a minute to watch him, wanting nothing more than to crawl back under the covers and let him have his way with her. Again. And again. The man did know how to satisfy a woman. She didn't know who taught him or where he learned, but rather than being jealous, Liz thanked whoever the woman, or women, were. He'd learned his lessons well.

Downstairs, there were a few people lounging around, mostly vampires and a couple of lycans. They glanced at them as Kaeden and Liz came in, several giving them knowing grins. Funny how their grins didn't embarrass her or that anyone knew she and Kaeden slept together.

Liz stopped by the two guards at the front door. Tall, heavily muscled shape-shifters armed with knives, guns, and staffs. "Everything quiet?"

"Yes, ma'am. You going out?"

"Yeah. Just going to check on everyone."

The one on the right raised a cell phone and clicked the button. "Boss lady and her man are coming out." He grinned at her, and Liz shook her head but had a grin on her face.

"There are sentinels on the roofs. Didn't want them shooting you by mistake."

"Gee, thanks."

He opened the door for them, and they went out into a dark street. No streetlights lit the sidewalks. No shop lights shone from doorways and windows. No traffic moved on the streets. Clear Water had become a ghost town.

"Which way?" Kaeden asked. Even though soft, his voice sounded unnaturally loud in the silence.

"This way." Liz started off, not knowing exactly why she needed to go in that direction, just knowing she had to. She pulled up the collar on her coat. Her old coat wouldn't win any prizes for looks, but duct tape worked fine when you needed something patched. Two blocks later, she knew exactly where they were going. She stopped at a corner.

"You're heading for that old Victorian on Maple," Kaeden said.

"Sure seems that way."

"Do you know why yet?"

"Nope."

"Know what we're going to find there?"

"Nope."

"Still want to do this?"

"Nope."

They continued on. Even though Debra had healed her, Liz's arm twinged where the watchers had grabbed her. She checked her pockets for blades and made sure the cane hung securely at her side. She heard a click and glanced over at Kaeden to find him checking the load on his gun. They didn't say a word as they walked. There didn't seem to be any reason to talk.

"Now what?" Kaeden asked when they reached the house.

"I don't know."

"Perhaps I can be of assistance."

Liz swung around, knives at the ready, at the same time Kaeden pulled his gun. She'd been half-expecting Bannig, but instead, Jacob Smith stood there. He held his arms out from his sides.

"I am unarmed. You can put your weapons away."

They didn't.

"Out for an early morning stroll?" Liz asked. He had given her the cane and appeared to be one of her bosses, but she didn't quite trust him. Why had he shown up here? And why now?

"I enjoy this time of day when there is nothing but quiet. The streets are usually devoid of traffic and the rush that defines the daylight hours."

Liz could keep making small talk or get to the root of the problem. She did not do small talk. "What do you know about what's happening around here?"

He tilted his head toward the house. "Would you care to share a cup of tea with me?"

She glanced at Kaeden who shrugged. Did she want to go in to where Bannig probably lived? Kind of.

Doing so would give her a chance to confront him and, maybe, stop what was coming.

Yeah, and the sun would rise in the west tomorrow. But if she had even a slight chance, she had to try. "Sure. I mean, yes. Thank you."

He strolled toward the gate that held back the watchers. Liz hung back. "Wait."

Hand on the lock, Jacob glanced at her. "Is there a problem?"

"Um, the dogs. I'm not comfortable with them."

"I'm sorry? Dogs? I do not know about any dogs being here at this moment." He pushed the gate wide, and Liz cringed back.

But nothing happened. Nothing came out. Nothing waited in the shadows. They crossed the yard and climbed the rear steps. He paused in front of the back door. "No. We'll go another way."

Curious. They followed as he led them around the porch and down steps to an exposed basement door. "Give me a moment to find a candle. We seem to have lost power. And, as we know, you cannot find the light without power."

They waited outside until Jacob returned with a candle. "I must apologize. I forgot that with no power, I cannot heat water for the tea."

"Thank you, anyway. I guess we should be heading back." Liz really wanted to get out of there. She was getting some serious vibes that they needed to be going. Now.

Liz pulled at Kaeden and went back to the yard. "I enjoyed seeing you again, Jacob. Good night."

They got to the end of the yard, nearly at the gate, when Jacob called to them. "Elizabeth? A moment?"

They stopped and waited as he hurried up to them. "Please. Take this."

He thrust a piece of heavy paper into her hand. "And take care whom you trust."

They heard a noise from the garage, like a hound baying. Both Kaeden and Liz jumped. When she looked around, Jacob had disappeared, and a light shone in the upstairs window.

A light? "I'd like to get out of here," Liz said.

"Yeah, I think that's an excellent idea."

As they rushed back, Liz thought about Jacob. "I'm not sure exactly what happened here, but…I almost have a feeling he stopped time."

"Why do you say that?"

"His words. He said the dogs weren't there at that moment. So…were we in a moment out of time? Like maybe with the cane, but more powerful? And what about his words about not finding the light without the power?" She shook her head. "I don't get any of this."

"You don't?" Kaeden snorted. "A week ago, I didn't even know about any of this. But you've been dealing with this sort of thing all of your adult life."

They took a lot less time to return to their base than to get to the mansion. By the time they got back, false dawn lightened the sky in the east. More people milled about, but not as many as she felt they needed. Kaeden and Liz went upstairs to her room. The paper weighed heavily in her pocket. After she closed the door, Liz took the paper out and nearly dropped the page on the floor.

He had given her a heavy envelope with fancy calligraphy writing on the outside.

"This is from my bosses."

"We don't know that," Kaeden argued. "Where are some of your other envelopes? We can compare the writing."

She got two of the ones she'd kept out. The writing appeared to be a perfect match.

"Should I open this?"

"I'd say you have to."

Liz slit the envelope, pulled the heavy piece of fancy paper out, and smoothed the page on the bed. "All is not as it seems. Trust your instincts. Trust your companion."

"What does that mean?" Liz asked. "Or his comment about the light and power?"

Kaeden leered at her, wagging his eyebrows. "Don't know, but he must like me. I mean, I am your companion, aren't I?"

She punched him lightly on the arm. "Yeah, right. He doesn't even know you."

Kaeden grabbed her and flung her onto the bed. "But you do. Trust me?"

"Never!"

He started tickling her, and she fought back but only half-heartedly. Her giggles turned to laughter. "Shhh. We'll wake up Charly," he said.

"And she's such a bear if she's awakened before ten." Liz struggled to stifle her laughter, but the harder she tried, the worse she got.

Somehow their clothes disappeared, and Kaeden and Liz continued their exploration of the lighter side of their relationship. All Liz knew was that she'd had the best sex she'd ever had.

Later, after a nice hot shower, she went back downstairs. Kaeden stood behind the counter setting up urns for coffee and tea and boiling water on one of the gas stoves. She went to the basement and laid her hands on the blocks. Still building but getting stronger. Reluctantly, Liz pulled away from the power and went back upstairs.

Kaeden raised an eyebrow at her, and she shook her head. They still had time.

She went into the walk-in freezer and pulled out a couple of boxes of frozen sweet rolls. Unfortunately, without the power, the frozen stuff would start thawing soon. But so far, the chiller was still cold enough to keep things safe.

She set out trays of rolls, covering them with plastic wrap to keep them from drying out. One of the lycans—she thought his name was George—threw slabs of bacon on the grill while Uncle Ray scrambled eggs.

She looked around as there was a commotion at the front door. The guard opened up, and two vampires straggled in helping a severely injured lycan. Behind them came others in no better shape. They got them to seats and sent for Debra. Kaeden came out with the first aid box and went to work where he could.

"What happened?" She cut the pant leg off the lycan and winced at the wound there. The gash ran from ankle to knee and was bone deep. She did the best she could until Debra came down.

"What happened?"

"We were checking out the other nodes," the vampire said. "First two were no problem. The third and fourth had watchers and shades. We barely got away. Good thing the lycans had that holy water."

"Good thing you vamps sensed them before we got

any closer," the lycan said.

"We sent the ones who could to help with the first two places. The rest of us came back here."

"You did the right thing."

Debra came in and handled the worst of the injuries while Kaeden and Liz cleaned and bandaged milder ones. Liz's mind worked overtime. Their people held three of the six nodes. Bannig held two. That made five. And the diner sat on top of number six.

They got everyone patched up and sent them to the other building to rest. Their leaders sent reinforcements to the other nodes.

Liz went over to her seat at the head of the table—and found an envelope there. A heavy, lined envelope addressed to her in fancy calligraphy.

"Kaeden!" She picked the envelope up by the corner. He came around the counter and stared. "Jacob again?"

"Wait a minute. Look closely."

She did. "What?"

"The handwriting. That's not the same as what you had before. Don't do anything. Wait a minute."

She laid the envelope on the table and waited while he ran upstairs, then came back down with the other envelopes. When he placed them next to each other, Liz could see that the handwriting on this one did look different. But the paper was the same. "So maybe he had one of his guests do this one. Or maybe this is from Nick or the woman."

"Why now and never before? And why this one here when he handed you one earlier? There's something not right about this. Do you mind if I do some checking?" He'd always had good instincts—part of his elfin heritage she figured—so she let him have the envelope to see what he could do.

Liz watched as he clasped the envelope between his hands and closed his eyes. Two seconds later, he dropped the letter like he'd been burnt. "There's something wrong with this one. There's a darkness there. Oily. Heavy."

She picked up the envelope. He was right. This one was dark. Cold. Evil. Not at all like the others.

Kaeden stuck two fingers in his mouth and blew a whistle that pierced her ears. But he did get everyone's attention. He held the envelope up. "Anybody see who left this here?"

Negatives from all sides. Not surprising. Kaeden handed the envelope back to her. Liz slit the envelope, pulled out a sheet of paper, and read the letter inside. And nearly dropped the page in shock.

"Liz? What's wrong? What does that say?"

"This is an invitation."

"From whom? For what?"

"From Bannig. He wants to meet with me. Discuss terms."

"Terms? For what?"

"My surrender."

"Your what? Is he serious? We're in balance now. Nobody has the edge. How does he figure to force you to surrender?"

She pulled a second sheet out of the envelope and closed her eyes and sighed, then dropped the page on the table. Kaeden picked up the image with a sharp intake of breath.

The second sheet was a picture. Of Charly. Tied, gagged, and surrounded by watchers.

Chapter Twenty-Eight

Kaeden and Liz ran upstairs and checked Charly's room. Empty. They searched both buildings, top to bottom. Nothing. Kaeden pulled out his maps, and Liz grabbed one of Charly's crystals and tried finding her but was too upset to center herself. The others tried scrying, but nobody got anything.

"How the hell did they get in? And get her out without anyone noticing?" Kaeden asked. Nobody had an answer.

"Wait. Doesn't Chris have cameras on everything? Maybe he got some visuals." Her warning vibes were going off like crazy. "Where is Chris?"

Kaeden shrugged, and the others looked around. He usually sat either at the table or at the counter—anywhere close to the food. But not now.

"Do you remember seeing him anywhere when we did our search for Charly?"

"No." Kaeden went to where Chris had set up his bunk. The sleeping bag was there, as well as a suitcase and lots of candy and junk food wrappers, but nothing else. Kaeden grabbed one of Chris's T-shirts and held the cloth close to his chest. "He's gone."

"We know that."

"No. I mean really gone. As in I'm getting nothing." He and Liz both tried some other things, all with the same result.

"How well did you know him?" Liz asked.

Kaeden shrugged. "Not that well."

Debra joined them. "He moved here about a year ago from the Midwest, got a job with the local school district as their IT guy. Kept to himself."

"So how did he end up as part of Charly's circle?"

She shrugged. "I'm not sure. I know I didn't bring him in."

"He shows up, gets himself invited into the group so everyone trusts him. And he's the one who set up our surveillance."

"He'd know how to get around everything."

"And our schedules and where we slept. He knew everything. And because we trusted him, they now have Charly."

"What should we do?"

"We meet with the enemy and discuss our terms."

Kaeden's eyebrows shot up into his hairline. "We what?"

Liz shook her head. He really didn't know her as well as he thought. "Gather as many people as are around. We need to have a powwow."

"You have an idea?"

"Maybe. But first, we need to make sure Chris didn't leave any bugs behind. You know anybody with electronics expertise? Preferably someone you really trust?"

"Yes."

"Go tell him what to do. Then gather the others."

While Kaeden put his electronics friend on the case and called for a meeting, Liz sat and thought. First task—free Charly. Second—beat uber-evil. Third—kill Chris. Slowly. Painfully. And with no remorse.

But first, Charly.

Liz looked at the letter again. The kidnappers wanted her to meet them at noon out back in the parking lot. No problem there. But meeting with them wouldn't get Charly back. This wasn't an exchange. This was an ultimatum. They held all the cards. So where had they hidden Charly? And how could they get her back?

And just that fast, Liz knew exactly where they were holding Charly. And how to get to her. But in order to get her back, she'd need help. A lot of help. An idea formed in the back of her mind.

By the time she had a solid plan, Kaeden and the others had gathered. She rose to stand. "We have a problem."

Several chuckles and an outright laugh or two came from the ranks. She let them have their minute of joy. She knew she was going to tamp that down rather thoroughly in a minute.

Liz held up the picture of Charly. "You all know Charly and how good she is. She's been taken by our enemy, and I intend to get her back."

The chuckles turned to gasps of shock. Charly was well-known in the community—and well-liked and respected. The bad guys had picked on the wrong person. They'd have been better off taking Liz. Nobody cared what happened to her.

Liz glanced at Kaeden and amended her earlier thought. She might be wrong. The knowledge was warming, and chilling at the same time. She shook off her thoughts and turned back to the crowd. She had to concentrate on getting Charly back. The hardest decision she had to make was not going after Charly herself. But she needed to be here. She would have to trust others to get Charly. And that was even harder to do than to make the decision.

"I intend to get her back, but I need help."

"What can we do?" a voice from the back asked.

"Our enemy has demanded my surrender. I'm going to give him what he wants."

"What? No! You can't do that!" Those and other denials came from every side of the room. Liz finally held up her hand for quiet.

"No worries. I am only going to meet with them and make them think they are getting what they want. While I do that, a team of you is going to go after Charly."

"Thought we didn't know where she is," Kaeden said.

"I believe I do. And so do you if you think hard."

"The old Victorian. Downstairs. In the basement," Kaeden said.

"Yep."

"But we didn't see anything on our jaunt."

"We weren't meant to."

"What if you're wrong?"

"I don't think I am. Do you?"

"No."

"I need a group of the best of the best to go after Charly. You're going to need speed, strength, nerve, and numbers."

"We've got that," one of the vampires she knew as David said. "Tell us when and where."

"When is noon. Where is the address I'll give you. I don't know what you'll be up against beyond watchers, but you need to be prepared for anything.

And I do mean *thing*. I believe there will be electronic surveillance."

"That's not a problem," one of the elves said. "My brother and I have maskers and other items that can help us get past almost everything. Jon's taking care of this place now."

"What's your name?"

"Vince."

"Good to meet you, Vince. You and David are in charge. Gather anyone you think you'll need. If you need supplies, let me or Kaeden know. Does anyone need a weapon?"

Nobody answered. "Fine. Vince and David will take care of getting the team together. The rest of you, I'll need here. We are going to lay a trap."

They split into two groups. Vince and his group went into the second building, which was a good thing. Otherwise, Liz would have been trying to pay more attention to what they had planned than on what she needed to do. But she oh so wanted to be in that other room. And she could see from the look on Kaeden's face that he wanted to be there too. She pulled him aside.

"If you need to, you can be with them. I'll be fine here."

He was shaking his head before Liz finished. "I'll stay here with you."

His words filled her heart, but she knew how difficult the decision was for him. He'd known Liz for what? Three years? And Charly all his life.

Liz turned her back on the opening to the other room and got to work. She wanted as many elves as possible on the roofs. They were incredible marksmen.

Whether bows and arrows or guns, they rarely missed. If someone showed her an ace in shooting, she'd show you elf blood somewhere in their line.

"What kind of weapons do we have?" Liz asked. She bit back a grin as everything from crossbows to automatic weapons showed up shortly after she asked.

"Okay, I want you all on the rooftops. You decide where. The target will be the parking lot out back, a few feet past the hole in the middle." They nodded.

"Mandy, I want you with them. I know you've been practicing with throwing fireballs. I may need some of your firepower."

"Liz?" one of the elves said. "We can also use her to light arrows. They tend to disconcert people when they see fire coming at them. Plus, if we dip everything in holy water, that will also help."

"Good idea. Mandy, you work with the elves and take the holy water with you. The rest of you, I'll need your sharp senses. I want to set up a perimeter. They're coming here—I want them here on my terms."

They got down to business, setting up barriers and traps, blocking off all ways into the parking lot except one. The one on the direct route to the mansion.

"So how do we let them know we'll meet with them?" Kaeden asked.

"Like this." Liz pricked her thumb and let a drop of blood fall. As always, rather than stain the paper, the drop disappeared as did the note. Kaeden raised one eyebrow but said nothing. She hoped Chris had a will and good dental records. They'd need something to identify his remains once she finished with him.

The power in the node built faster and higher than before. She was having a harder and harder time concentrating when all she wanted to do was go downstairs and hug that wall where the node was.

By eleven, they were as ready as they could be. Liz paced the kitchen, checking the clock every couple of minutes.

"You're going to wear a hole in that floor." Kaeden watched her from where he leaned against the grill. Lunchtime and the ovens and grills were cold. Nobody had any appetite.

The buzz from the power node sang through her blood even a floor away. The itch got so strong, she wanted to scratch her skin off. "Can you feel the power?"

"Yes, but probably not as strongly as you. The others are getting something too."

She kept rubbing her arms. At a quarter till noon, Liz loosened the cane and palmed her knives, making sure the blank piece of paper Nick had given her was in an easily accessible pocket. She wasn't sure she could trust the cane. After all, Jacob had given that to her, and Liz wasn't sure she could trust him at this point, but she didn't have a lot of choice. And the cane was a good weapon. Kaeden and Uncle Ray would be at her back. Liz took a deep breath and blew out. "Let's do this."

Earlier, Kaeden and Ray had re-opened the ruined back door. They stepped through, Kaeden to her right, Ray on her left. She heard noise from the front but ignored the sound. That area wasn't her problem. This parking lot was. She had to trust the rest of her team to handle their parts.

The parking lot remained empty, but as they stepped up to the hole, a long, black limo appeared in the alley opposite them. The car rolled to a stop on the other side of the crater. Behind that came a stream of watchers, shades, and other nasties.

The rear passenger door opened, and out stepped Bannig. He did not look good. Oh, his body looked fine. She guessed the last node he'd taken in had helped him. But the look of pure evil on his face reinforced the fact her friend was really gone. She had no doubts about that now. Chris climbed from the driver's seat, and her blood boiled. Yes, Bannig was the uber-evil, but she wanted Chris's neck surrounded by her hands. She got a glimpse of the interior through the open doors. Though she'd hoped Charly might be there, the empty seats squashed that wish.

"Right on time," she said. "Guess being a demon has its advantages. You have a good concept of timing. And you've brought friends."

"As I'm sure you have people around us as well. We can avoid all this nastiness if you will come with me now, Ms. St. John." His voice did not belong to the Bannig she knew. The demon's emerged lower, raspier, with a wetness that did not sound human.

"Ah, well, you see, there's a slight problem with that. First of all where is Charly?"

"Safe."

"And you expect me to believe that? I want to see her. Now."

He waved his hand, and Chris came forward, laptop in one hand, tray table in the other. He came around the hole, stopping only when he saw Liz, guessing she didn't look favorably on him. Kaeden's hand on her arm was the only thing that kept her from taking Chris out right there and then.

He clutched the computer under one arm and set up

the table, then set up his machine. He stood there for a couple of minutes, a frown on his face, then a fearful glance at Bannig.

"Um, sir?"

"Show her."

"I can't, sir." Liz watched as Chris gulped and turned white.

Bannig spun toward him. "What do you mean you can't?"

"There's some kind of interference. I can't connect."

"Idiot!" He made a gesture with his hand, and two of the watchers bounded forward and attacked Chris. He screamed and backed away, and they all tumbled into the hole. The sounds that came from there were not pleasant to hear.

The hounds bounded out, and they heard nothing else. Liz wouldn't shed any tears over the man, but, damn, he'd gone too easily.

"My apologies, Ms. St. John, but I have no way to prove to you that she is safe, other than my word."

"And I'm supposed to believe you. Just like that."

Thunder rumbled around them.

"Enough already," Liz said. "If you think that scares me, think again." She let loose with some of her own emotions, producing a fairly good rumble herself. He stared at her with eyes narrowed to slits.

"You have been most irritating, Ms. St. John. You roll into our town and disrupt the natural order of life. As I see things, you are the problem here."

"Well, then, I guess my friends would have an issue with that." Her feet tingled. The power had almost reached the peak. She could almost see the lines coming together. Connecting. And Liz knew Bannig could sense the power too.

"We are past the time for you to leave. You can either leave peaceably, or my friends will encourage you."

She heard a noise from behind them. Liz didn't dare look around, but she knew. And she smiled. Bannig, on the other hand, didn't look so good.

"Charly?"

"I'm here. And I intend to take care of Chris and that piece of shit standing there." Her voice sounded weak, thready, not at all like Charly.

"Chris is dead." Liz glanced around and swore. Charly was far from fine. She had one arm in a sling, bandages on her head, bruises on her face. Debra stood in the shadows, tears streaming down her face. She shook her head once, and Liz knew. The knowledge almost did her in. Liz bit her cheek, using the pain to concentrate. She bottled her emotions up. She had no time for them. Not now. Not here.

"Oh. Fine. Then, I guess there's just this one." Charly coughed, a wet, heavy sound that hurt Liz's heart.

"He's nothing, Charly. Less than nothing."

A rumble came from underneath their feet, and the edges of the hole started to crumble.

"Get her!"

Bannig loosed his minions on them. As soon as he did, a rain of fireballs, fiery arrows, and bullets came from all around as the watchers and others rushed them. Lycans and vampires poured from the alleys, joining in.

Liz didn't remember much about what happened next. There was a lot of fighting, a lot of screaming.

She used her knives to good effect. At one point, she felt a tug on her sleeve and nearly stabbed Kaeden.

"The cane, Liz. Use the cane!"

She'd forgotten all about the damned thing. She grabbed the cane and twisted the top. Everything went still. Kaeden had been holding onto her, so he stayed mobile with her. Everything else looked like some sort of macabre wax museum.

"We need to get to Bannig. He's the key."

Kaeden and Liz worked their way around the crater. Pieces of pavement hung in mid-air. To her surprise, Bannig also remained mobile. He strode toward them, a cane with a red crystal in his left hand.

"You figured out part of the cane. But you can't know all the tricks." He covered the crystal with his right hand and muttered a spell. And everything came back to life.

And they were in the midst. Liz twirled the cane faster and faster until the rod spun away from her. She held out her hand to direct the cane, but didn't get far as the staff stopped, like running into a wall, and dropped to the ground. Kaeden tried his gun, but the same thing happened with his bullets. They hit a barrier and dropped. They didn't even carom, just dropped.

Fortunately, Liz had numbers on her side. Unfortunately, Bannig's minions had power. Also unfortunately, bad guys are often stronger than the good guys.

Kaeden and Liz kept heading for Bannig. They reached him, and a wall jumped up between the three of them and everyone else. None of the fighters got near them.

They had to keep moving away from the hole as

the perimeter kept growing.

"Seems like we're at an impasse," Bannig said. "For now. Though in a few moments, I shall have what I want anyway. Why not concede the point and go away?"

Liz glanced around and grinned. "Not so fast. If you take a good look, you'll see that our side seems to be winning the fight. You are the one who needs to leave."

He shrugged. "That's merely bodies. The true power will be mine. You have no clue how to use the energy." He raised the crystal above his head and chanted as the ground rumbled beneath them.

This time, Liz didn't hesitate. She threw one of her knives and hit him dead center of his chest, followed closely by another and another, but he merely glanced at them and kept chanting.

What happened next would be forever burned in her heart and memory.

In all the fighting, none of them had noticed Charly. Somehow, she'd found the strength to get through the fighting to the cane. She'd picked the staff up and headed directly for Bannig. Once there, she used the cane like a bat and knocked that red crystal from his hand into the pit.

His rage became almost a living thing. He yanked one of the knives from his chest and would have stabbed Charly except for Kaeden. Faster than Liz thought he could move, Kaeden jumped in front of Charly. The knife hit him, and he went down. Liz released her remaining knives into Bannig. He spun around and grabbed Charly as the ground gave way. Both of them disappeared into the hole. A moment later, there was a flash of brilliant white light that poured forth, covering them all. The bad guys screamed like they were one entity…and then…disappeared. And so did the hole.

And Liz knew Charly was gone.

But none of that mattered. She loved Charly, but she could do nothing for her. Her entire attention centered on one being. Nothing mattered to her now except Kaeden. She knelt next to him. Blood bubbled from his mouth and around the knife. Bannig hadn't hit his heart but had hit a lung. Kaeden would die if Liz didn't do something. She'd already lost Charly. She couldn't lose him too.

She heard Nick's voice in her mind. "Pull the knife and use the paper. Pull the knife and use the paper."

Paper? How could a piece of paper help Kaeden? But Liz did as the voice demanded. She grasped the knife and pulled. The blade came out with a sickening sound and a river of blood. Kaeden went beyond pale to dead white.

Liz grabbed the piece of paper and laid the sheet over the wound. As soon as the paper touched his blood, the page disappeared. And a minute later, so did the wound. Kaeden gasped, and his eyes opened. "Liz?"

"Shh. Be quiet. You've been hurt."

The others gathered around them. The silence broken only by moans of pain and sobs.

Kaeden struggled to sit up. "What happened? Where's Bannig?"

"Gone. Seems like he couldn't handle all that power after all."

"But—"

"Not now, Kaeden." She helped him stand. "How

do you feel?"

He rubbed his chest. "Like I've been hit in the chest by a sledgehammer. But I'm okay."

While Debra and her helpers went to work on the others, Liz went to where the hole had been. She could still feel a slight buzz, but so small as to be nearly gone. She knelt and absorbed what little power there remained, then rose and went to see what she could do to help.

To everyone's surprise, most of the wounds seemed minor. Unfortunately, there were a few deaths. She guessed the light couldn't bring back the dead, only care for those whose spirits were still intact.

"I don't understand this," Debra said. "I see scars, like they've been hurt, then healed."

"They were," Liz said. She could feel the tears coming and knew if she started crying she wouldn't be able to stop. "Healing them was the last thing Charly did. She took care of us all, like she always did."

Kaeden and Debra stared at her. "Last thing?"

"She's gone."

Shock. Gasps. Denials. Tears.

They'd won the war, but at what cost?

Chapter Twenty-Nine

Mother Nature showed all her glory on the day of the memorial service for Charly. The sun burst through the clouds, warming the air to almost balmy even though they were into November. How could everything be so pretty when Liz's heart hurt so badly? How could Heaven not weep with the rest of them? How could time not stop when Charly had?

Everyone in town came out for Charly. Everyone who knew Charly loved her. From the diner where they gathered to the funeral home, people lined the streets. The procession moved slowly like a parade. A horrible, tragic, shattering parade. They didn't have a body to bury, but that didn't matter.

The townspeople considered Kaeden and Liz as Charly's family, so they got the honor of riding in the first car. Liz just sat there—her hand gripped in his. She wore a long black skirt and a black shirt. Kaeden looked positively wonderful in his black suit. And Liz knew neither one of them would ever wear those clothes again. Except for maybe another funeral. They would have more than a few to attend over the next couple of days, but none so important as this one.

Today was for Charly.

They arrived at the funeral home much too soon. The car stopped, but Liz couldn't bring herself to get out. If she got out, she'd have to admit why she had come, and she couldn't do that yet. They sat there while the crowds gathered. Liz closed her eyes, willing the tears to stop.

"You have to get out, Liz."

"I know." Then Liz gasped. That voice. Kaeden had gone stiff, his hand clenching hers until her fingers went numb. Liz opened her eyes. Charly sat across from them.

"Charly?" Her voice emerged in a bare whisper. Charly sat there, wearing her favorite teal skirt with a creamy poet's shirt. A halo of light surrounded her.

"You have to get out, Liz. You too, Kaeden. You need to take care of things. I know you're tired, but you can do this."

"Charly?"

"Yes. Now stop that. Liz, you of all people, know there is more to life than, well, life. The reason for my earth-bound existence ended. I did what I was sent here for and moved on. And now is the time for you to move."

"What were you here for?" Liz was more than a little freaked out. She knew about spirits and ghosts and all that stuff, but this was Charly. She'd never met a spirit she knew before.

Charly smiled, that enigmatic smile that often made Liz so angry. "Not important any longer. Liz, you need to go out there. Everyone will look to you to set the tone. Please don't be sad."

"But Charly, you're…dead."

"Only in part. I'm still here. And I'll be around. By the way, you're right about the Santa look-a-like."

Liz couldn't help herself. She started to chuckle.

"Kaeden, Liz, I need you to go out there. You are

going to celebrate my earthly life. And celebrate my new life. I am happy. Possibly happier than I've ever been. Please don't mourn me."

"I love you, Charly," Liz said.

"And I love you, Liz. You are the sister of my heart. And I will continue to hound you. By the way, Liz, you need to answer Kaeden's question."

"Question? What question?"

"The one he asked you at the fire." Charly grinned at her, and Liz could feel the heat creep into her face.

"But…he didn't mean that. He was just trying to get my emotions going." She turned to Kaeden. "Weren't you? Did you mean what you said?" Could the situation get any weirder, Liz wondered. Sitting in a black limo, waiting to go into a memorial service, and talking about a wedding.

"I meant every word," Kaeden said. "And you never answered."

"But…" Liz gulped. Married? Her? She'd never even considered that an option in her life.

"No buts, Liz. The question is still out there. Will you marry me?" Kaeden gripped her hand tighter.

"I…"

"Come on, girl," Charly said. "You know you want to. Just say yes!"

Liz grinned as she shook her head. "You two! Yes! Okay? My answer is yes!"

Kaeden leaned over and kissed her on the cheek as Charly cheered.

"About time. And *now* my job is done. Go on out there and be happy." She leaned over and touched Liz's heart, and a warm glow surrounded Liz, healing her, comforting her. The sensation was everything Charly, and more.

And then she was gone. Kaeden and Liz took a collective deep breath and exhaled. "Shall we get this show on the road?" he asked.

For an answer, Liz pushed the door open and stepped out.

****

Later, back at the diner, they did a quick clean up, then Kaeden cooked, and Liz served. She thought the entire town stopped in over the rest of the day. More than a few of them stayed to help take down the plywood covering the windows or help clean up. Within a couple of days, Charly's Diner was not only back up to specs, but with the expanded dining area that several people with great carpentry skills put together, looked better than ever.

Kaeden and Liz found out a few days later that Charly had left the place to them. Liz was now part owner of a diner. Kaeden still tried to teach her to cook, but they finally decided to let him take care of that part of the business and Liz would handle serving and busing. To each his—or her—own strengths.

A month later, Kaeden and Liz got married. They wanted a small, simple ceremony, but somehow, word got out. The celebration turned into a party to rival all parties. At least they didn't have to do the cooking—or the cleanup.

That night, after the last guest left, they went upstairs to their room.

And found an envelope lying on their bed. Thick. White. With fancy writing.

Kaeden looked at Liz, and she stared back at him. "Should we open that?" he asked.

Liz chuckled. "We don't really have a choice."

They opened the envelope, and out fell a single puzzle piece—a picture of Charly surrounded by white light. Liz checked the envelope to make sure the packet was empty.

"I guess you finally finished the puzzle," Kaeden said.

"I hope I'm done for a while."

Kaeden took the envelope and frowned. "There's something else in here."

Liz shook her head. "Not possible. I looked."

Her nerves tingled. "Kaeden, don't you dare take that out. Please do not take that out. I don't want to see whatever is there. I don't want to know."

But he'd already upended the envelope and shook the contents out over her dresser. Inside were several thousand dollars and a letter. Kaeden opened the page and grinned.

"What's it say?" Liz's stomach clenched. She really didn't want to go back on the road. She had kind of been hoping to settle in here—with her husband.

"The letter says *Here's to a charmed future*. And is signed Jacob, Klaus, Marianna, and Charly."

Liz grinned. Seemed like Kaeden and she had some guardian angels watching over them. She could live with that.

He laid the letter on the dresser. "So, you done going out on jobs for a while?"

Liz tugged her shirt off, smiling as his eyes widened and that adorable, lopsided grin lit his face. "I hope so. But what shall I do with all my time?" She gave him a wicked smile as she continued to strip.

He came over to her and ran his hands over her

arms and down her back and drew her to him. "I think I can come up with something."

And he did.

Thank you for purchasing
this publication of The Wild Rose Press, Inc.

For questions or more information
contact us at
info@thewildrosepress.com.

The Wild Rose Press, Inc.
www.thewildrosepress.com